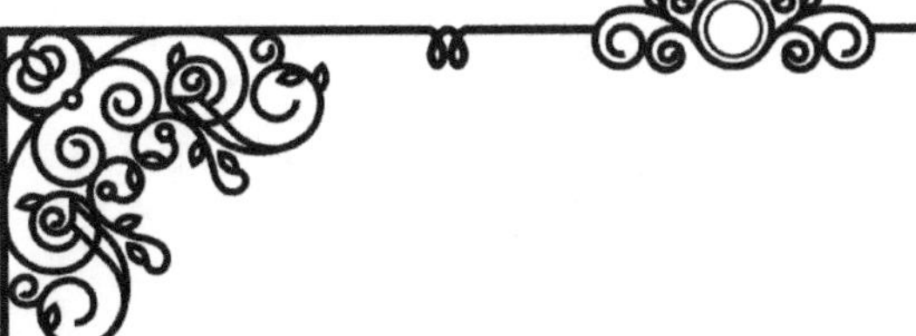

Madamn

J.S. Baehr

Paula Ferri Publishing
Lander, WY, USA
Editor: Maddison Race
Cover Designer: Taylor Douglas
Interior Print Design: Dayna Linton, Day Agency
e-Book Interior Design: Dayna Linton, Day Agency

Library of Congress Control Number: Pending

ISBN: 978-0-9997673-4-4 (Paperback)
ISBN: 978-0-9997673-5-1 (Hardcover)

First Edition: 2025

10 9 8 7 6 5 4 3 2 1

Printed in the USA

Table of Contents

Madamn

Prologue

June 1808, near Paris

A PAIR OF GIGGLES COULD be heard long before the source could be seen at the *Château* de Guermantes. The seven- and eight-year-old sisters raced into the large hall, brunette curls flying, and skirts flapping around their knees. They continued until they reached the far end of the room and instantly began bouncing up and down on the cushioned mahogany chairs, much to the dismay of their mother. The boom of her disapproval was dampened only slightly by the cacophony of the chair legs slapping the wood floor in thunderous thumps. It was a veritable symphony of laughter and flying furniture.

"*Mon coeur!* Why do you not sit still for your lessons?" their mother Eulalie, a regal and serious woman carrying a baby in her arms, scolded them. The pink linen brocade of her dress almost perfectly matched her flushed cheeks. She looked directly at the older girl–Albertine–who, despite all the activity, recovered quickly, stepping off the chair as eloquently as a duchess stepping off a coach. "You may play with your sister when you have finished. *Les enfants méchant!* No more giggles!" their mother reprimanded.

She then turned to the younger girl, Ernestine, Em for short, and simply sighed. Em knew exactly what that drawn out puff of air meant so she, too, stepped down from the chair, only to trip on her skirt and fall flat on her back. From her prostrate position on the ground, Em caught a glimpse of her mother's mouth drawn in a furious line, as well as Albertine's lips twitching–a sure sign she was trying not to laugh–and focused her attention on sitting upright.

"I need to feed your brother," her mother said, as she rocked baby Ernest. Em nodded, quite used to her mother's dark mood around her. She missed her father during times like this–or what she thought her father was like at any rate. He had been dead for years. Her mind went to an imaginary conversation she concocted that involved her mother and him sipping tea in the garden. She imagined his baritone voice, thick with whimsy, holding her mother's hand, cooing sweet nothings. Em couldn't decide if it was harder to accept her father was dead or that her mother ever had the capacity to make anyone smile.

Her thoughts were interrupted at the sight of Albie making a face behind their mother's back as her mother barked directions. "Albie, off to the music room to practice!" she ordered. "And you!" she said, her blue eyes searing into Em's brown ones, "Get your writing done."

Eulalie moved to the navy fainting couch while Albertine went through the heavy wooden door to Em's right, painted white with gilded accents. As it closed, it almost blended into the rest of the walls that were not covered in floor-to-ceiling windows or landscape paintings in their gilt frames.

Her mother now busy with Ernest, Em took a seat at the cream desk with the intricately carved legs. As usual, she had a hard time focusing on the writing lesson in front of her. She glanced out of the tall window nearest to her. She wanted to hide behind the thick, blue, velvety curtains that hung on either side of each window. Her mischievous grin faded and she decided today was not the day to test her mother's patience as she so often did. Besides, writing was fun for her, and she wanted to try some fancy embellishments when she wrote her name today. She dipped the quill in her ink and began to practice the flowing script expected from the daughter of a *comte*.

She loved the cursive loops and how grown up it made her feel to write her name in the scripted hand. It didn't look quite as beautiful as her mother's writing, but she was certainly improving. Em was finishing the final flourish of 'Ernestine' and starting on her middle name, when she felt an itch on the back of her wrist. Not wanting to upset her mother again, she continued to write. She made it through the "Émilie," trying hard to hold still as she looped the "P" in "Prondre," but the itch was so strong, her hand began to shake.

Ernestine had itched while writing before. Maman had told her that it simply meant she was destined to write many letters to her husband to bring him great joy, so keep writing. Pushing through the itch, her hand suddenly spasmed out of control. The quill flew through the air and across the room toward the door her sister had recently passed through, spilling black ink on the freshly scrubbed and polished wooden floor.

Em's mother gasped in surprise as she placed Ernest in his crib. "Are we really doing this again young lady?!" her mother shouted, shaking her finger in Em's face, eyes full of fire.

"I didn't mean to, it's just…"

"No more excuses! I am weary of it!" her mother exclaimed, now pacing and wringing her hands. "You are nobility! After the Reign of Terror, you should be thanking the good Lord for the privilege you have. So many lost their fortunes; their homes; their lives! You would not have been born if I had not lived. You are beyond fortunate that we held on to the *château* and our fortune against those awful mercenaries who called themselves revolutionaries. Despite everything, your father

and Imanaged to provide you with a safe and comfortable life that you may prosper. Instead, you insist on these…these outbursts!"

"I am not doing it on purpose—"

"Enough!" She was shouting so loud at this point Ernest began crying. Em caught glimpses of a few servants gawking at the scene from behind a door.

"Come now, Ernest," Eulalie said, picking him up. "Your sister is going to try this one more time, are you not?" It was less a question and more a demand.

"*Oui*, Maman," Em said, turning back to her writing lesson.

This time, however, the old sensation happened much sooner. Em was unable to hold still any longer. She was only to her middle name when the quill went straight up into the air. Em stared at the single drop of ink as it separated from the plume and landed on the corner of the writing desk as the quill fell gently to the floor next to her.

Her mouth opened, she glanced at her mother, and quickly clamped it shut again. Em could see the anger flashing in her mother's eyes as, once again, she set Ernest down in the nearby crib and quickly stood and made her way over to the desk. Em cowered a little lower with each step her mother took. Em had no words as her mother pulled out a spare bottle of ink and extra paper, then rang for the servant to clean up the mess.

"Ah, *mais non!* This *enfant méchant* shall have no tea today!"

"But *Maman…*"

"No, no, no. You are needing your writing lessons. Playtime is done, and these are not toys. You will now double your writing lesson. Write your name the usual one hundred times, then write 'I will not play silly games during my lessons' one hundred times. After that, you may begin your usual copying of a chapter from the Bible. ay you may write the 119th Psalm."

There was no fighting with her mother, and Em knew it. Hanging her head and mumbling another, *"Oui,* Maman," Em returned to her lessons. There was no more itching, and she was able to write in peace. The repetition was soothing and Em soon found a rhythm that seemed to calm her frayed nerves from the unusual experience. While her family had tea, she continued, finishing her work with no issues as Albertine was excused from the table. After she was excused as well, she met Albertine right outside the door. They walked silently to the back entrance of the massive home–a routine they knew well. They clasped hands and ran down the *château* stairs together toward one of the many back doors that led to the acres of beautifully combined gardens of cultivated and wild greenery.

Once they were safely outside, sitting on the grass beneath their favorite oak tree behind the *château*, Em started to tear up. The tree was safe from prying eyes, sitting just behind a line of trees and sur-rounded by several small bushes, yet the girls still had glimpses of the reflecting pond beyond.

Albertine's eyes widened at the sight of Em's tears and she leaned over to hug her sister. Em's hand started that itchy feeling again, and she didn't want her hand to fly so close to Albie. *What if I hit her?* she thought with alarm, rubbing her right hand with her left and grip-ping her wrist tightly as her sister embraced her.

"Does your wrist hurt from writing so much?" Albertine asked.

"No. It's…It's something else. Something strange happened. It's like I was pulled by a puppet string!" Em sighed as she related the events of the writing lesson.

Albertine giggled. "Oh, what fun!"

"How can you say that, Albie?" Em was shocked at her sister's levity.

"I feel terrible for you of course!" Albie reassured her. "It's just…I wish I could have seen the face on Maman! What did she look like?"

Em thought for a moment, then said, "Like a bull who had just been stung by a thousand bees." The two girls burst into laughter, only coming up for air to discuss some of Albie's concerns. "It didn't hurt, did it? It's gone now, right?"

"No, I'm okay, truly," Em said. "You're more like a motherly mother than Mother!" she said, this time hugging her sister despite her prior concerns of hurting her. She couldn't help herself. Albie was just so warm and soothing.

"I have something to cheer you up!" Albie said, breaking the embrace. "Close your eyes! Hold out your hands."

Distracted and obedient to her older sibling, Em closed her eyes and held out her palms. When she felt a slight weight in her hand, she opened her eyes to find a small collection of the sweets served during tea.

Albertine pulled out a small white linen bag, complete with little tassels and a large "A" embroidered in soft green thread. She pulled open the drawstring top and pulled out several more small pastries.

"Chef made such yummy snacks today. I had five of this one! I brought you some, too! And another for me, of course. I snuck them into my reticule when I showed Maman my lessons this morning. Then snuck it out of the *château* when she was directing the servants."

"I don't know what to say," Em said. At that moment her stomach made a sound, clearly from hunger, which launched them into a fit of laughter all over again.

"How about, 'I'm so glad to have a clever older sister to save me from starvation!'"

"I can't say that as my mouth will be too full of food!" Em said before diving into the delicious morsels. The pears in the custard tart–her favorite–were exceptionally sweet. There were also two *maccherones*, a madeleine, and a croissant. "These are the best I've ever had! If I went to heaven, I would eat these every day. You are truly the best sister!"

"No, *you* are truly the best sister," Albie responded. "You are smart, funny and so, so kind. Not to mention, well, misunderstood. You deserve better."

With those last words Em teared up.

"What's wrong, dearest sister?" Albie gasped, alarmed.

Em stared at Albie, taking a moment to catch her breath, then said simply, "It's just...I wish Maman were here when you said that. Just like you, I'd have liked to see her face."

This time it was Albertine that teared up. As only two bonded souls could, they instinctively reached for each other's hand and looked at one another, unspoken words of comfort emanating from their eyes. With no more food left to enjoy, they leaned against the tree, basking in the sounds of the birds and the sunlight dancing on their cheeks.

Chapter 1
SISTERLY BONDS

Em's Diary, June 1815

I CAN'T BELIEVE IT'S BEEN eight years since I was first plagued by this malady. The itching never stops no matter what they try. Rubbing still helps, but only for so long. It gets harder and harder to manage by the day. The movements get more and more out of control. They are starting to really hurt, and not just physically. It hurts to see this affecting the whole family.

Maybe I am some kind of monster. Is that what it feels like to be touched by the devil? Could I really be possessed as the servants say? I hear their whispers. I'm not deaf just because I can't stop when told directly to do so. I miss being a good girl, though it has been years since I was considered that. I was certainly able to get away with a lot more.

Every day it's the same thing. Maman yelling, Stepfather keeping his distance…I can't help the movements. I only hit him once and much softer than he hit me. I'm glad it was just the one time. He has avoided me since then. I confess I have done the same. I don't mean to hit. I want to keep my hands to myself. But it just itches so much and it's the only way to make it stop.

I can't help but wonder if things would be different with Papa. I wish I had known him or had any memory of him at all. I'd like to think he'd be as kind as Albertine. She is the only one who really understands me. She believes me when I say I cannot stop the movements. Albie certainly didn't get the kindness from Maman.

I wish so much that I could behave well enough to go out in public. But no matter how hard I try, I cannot keep my hands to myself for long. Not even when my hands were bound against my body as "practice." I long to be with the other girls my age. I want to dance with a young man. My feet are coordinated enough. I just can't slap my partner.

I'm so embarrassed by all of this. I'll have to talk to Albie about her birthday in a few days. I know she would love for me to attend her birthday celebration, but I just don't trust myself around anyone but her.

It will be yet another soirée *watched from behind closed doors. What a sad future lies before me. To be constantly hidden. But even the wild boy they found years ago near Aveyron was able to go out in public so he could be studied. And he was more animal than human, unable to speak and more comfortable out of doors—even in winter! I wonder if we are to share the same fate; to be studied, poked, and prodded like some kind of animal. I think I'd rather just be hidden away.*

I still wonder how alike I am to this wild boy. They call him Victor now. I heard that he moves a bit as I do—not graceful at all. At least I am able to speak, though. And I do have good days where I move like normal. So I'm not all bad, right? Do I have some redeeming qualities? If people are still willing to take in Victor, I must have some bit of value. I just don't know what it is.

HIGH PITCHED, EXCITED VOICES followed the sea of fabric woven with excitement that flowed through the halls for the festivities ahead. Of the pair of girls, Em was the most excited. "Mother and Stepfather finally agreed to let me attend a party!" she giggled. After so many years peeking at festivities from a cracked-open door, she would finally, finally be part of the celebrations.

Yet lingering in the back of her mind, pushing their way forward, was every single way the party could go wrong as a result of her malady. Em would have agreed with Maman and stayed in her room if not for Albie. It was Albertine who convinced Em, and Maman, that the party could not possibly be complete without her.

Albie argued with the skill of Talleyrand protecting his position. She needed her sister there. She wanted her best friend to celebrate with her. She vowed responsibility for Em and her actions. Albie even threatened to not have a party at all.

Maman didn't cave until Albie mentioned that she was turning sixteen. Soon, Albie would become a legal adult and heiress to her father's fortune. She would then be taking charge of the *château* and making all of the decisions. Maman conceded that it was time for her to slowly step down as Albie transitioned to being in charge.

Em was still shocked that Albie had that kind of power now. And even more shocked that it resulted in her finally being allowed in public after years of punishment and hiding. How liberating it felt to be among society! She really hoped she could keep herself under control. At the ballroom entrance Em lurched and gasped to see the room transformed and filled with people.

Finally, at fifteen years old, she stood at the edge of her dreams and it was already better than she had hoped. She used to sneak into this very room often, wishing she could be part of the grandeur, and here she was. Every gilded frame glittered more brightly. Even the white walls behind the numerous paintings and gold trimmings seemed to glow. Each candle seemed to dance with the music of the pianoforte, imitating the couples below as they waltzed.

Walking past the open drapes, Em ran a hand over the soft velvet that somehow felt more thick and luscious. The murmur of hundreds of conversations dulled the music that no longer echoed off the walls as it did when she was practicing her music lesson.

Such fine high-waisted dresses with the latest lace trim! Some even dared to wear brighter colors from the pastels that had dominated last season. Then there were the men! They all seemed so tall, with chiseled features, flouncing their cravats and smart dress coats with long tails. Albertine had already attended parties here for years and pushed past Em to enter the room before turning around to grab her hand.

"Come, come! You are not a wallflower. Do not just stand there! We are here to dance and make merry with the gentlemen! Who knows, but your future husband could be here! We did invite all of Guermantes and half of Paris, after all. But before he can sweep you off your feet, he must see your wit and charm."

Em smiled and rolled her eyes. She loved her sister's enthusiasm but feared her own lack of control from her illness. Pulling back, she whispered her concerns to her sister.

"What if it happens again? Would I not be the embarrassment Maman believes me to be all the time? Would you not be ashamed of me?"

Em tugged at her long sleeves, hoping to hide her hands. The taut fabric caused a kick in her shoulder, and her eyes widened in alarm as she pleaded for help from her sister.

"You're just nervous. It stops when you calm down, no? You'll be fine if you just relax! I would never be ashamed of you. I would be ashamed to know anyone who treated you ill."

Em nodded, let out her bated breath, and took a cautious step forward. Looking around the room, she saw her mother's eyes watching her, even as Maman leaned to give instructions to a nearby servant. Em's heart dropped, seeing the distrust in Maman's eyes. Em stopped, then pulled back. Shaking her head, she turned and ran from the room. Ducking her head from the faces that eyed her escape, Em's heart picked up speed to match the clack of her shoes on the freshly polished floor of the long hallway.

Her chest continued to tighten and she felt the tension rise in her chest to the knot forming in her throat. *No, I will not cry!* The tightness continued to climb into her jaw. She grimaced and her jaw shot to the right. In an attempt to put it back in its place, the muscles suddenly took over. As it straightened, the jaw dropped and Em found her voice leaping out gasping, "Ah! *Bon.*"

Em stopped in the middle of the empty hall and covered her mouth, eyes wide. A clacking pair of shoes behind her slowed to a stop.

Please, no. Please, mon Dieu, *don't let it be her.*

Em turned slowly to her left, shutting her eyes in an earnest chant.

Not Maman, not Maman, not Maman...

Peeking out her left eye, her hands dropped to her side as her body heaved a sigh of relief.

"Albie! Oh, Albie, what am I to do?! Could the malady now be taking over my voice as well?" Rushing to her sister, Em wound her arms tightly around Albertine as if her sister was the only anchor keeping her from slipping into some form of madness.

"My jaw did the thing again, I was just trying to fix it, I don't...I didn't...I don't know how..."

"Shhhhhh...I won't tell anyone of this progression if you don't. Stop that flood of words and tears. Come with me."

Em was limp as her sister took her arm, pulling her into the cool evening air and into the gardens. Once they were on the bench beneath their favorite tree, Albertine finally stopped and faced Em, grasping her by the shoulders.

"Deep breaths, Em…breathe in…breathe out…That's it, keep going."

Slowly, the tears subsided and Em's heart rate returned to normal. "Did you see it all?"

Albertine nodded. "Let us sit here a moment and enjoy the evening."

The girls sat in silence, watching the blue evening sky darken. Eventually, Em stretched her hands above her head as her shoulder kicked forward. Heaving a heavy sigh, Em broke the silence. "You never should have invited me to your party."

Albertine grabbed Ernestine's hand and gave it a quick squeeze. "But I need you there. You are my sister and I love you. You are my best friend just as you are. So does it really matter what happens at a silly party?"

Hanging her head, Em could only mumble a soft, "It matters to Maman…"

"We'll outlive her. She won't be around forever to treat you like this. Once I turn eighteen, I'm in charge; and you will have nothing to worry about, ever. Isn't it grand that we live somewhere civilized? Can you imagine living in an awful place like England? Those barbarians don't even let women inherit, even if they have only daughters! Simply dreadful, I tell you. We are far better off, and I will be sure to take care of you."

"What about at parties? People stare. I will be avoided as an outcast and become an old maid, I'm sure of it."

"Nonsense. Let's go prove you wrong. I'll be by your side the whole night. I'll cover for you; don't you think that will work well? I'll poke you to make it look like it's my fault you twitch and move the way you do."

Touched by her sister's words, Em's eyes moistened in the moonlight. It was so easy to separate herself, being the only person with such an odd happenstance in her life, but having Albie's support made her feel less alone. Giving her sister a tight squeeze, Em said, "I think you are the closest to perfect I've ever seen."

Albie laughed off the compliment, quickly getting lost in the soft rustle of leaves that surrounded them. The pair glanced back toward the house with its glittering lights, conversation, and lively music. Knowing they would be missed soon, Albie stood and dusted herself off before helping her sister stand. "Come, it's far too cold out for this time of year. Besides, we can't let them have all the fun! I'll race you back!"

In the branches of the tree, high above where the girls had just sat, a pair of eyes followed the girls toward the house. Jumping down from above, the shadow of a young man walked slowly toward the house.

Chapter 2
Touched by the Devil

The girls squinted at the bright lights as they entered the house and headed for the ballroom. True to her word, Albertine stuck to Ernestine throughout the night. Madame LaGrane might have had a cold, evident by her watery eyes and intricately embroidered rose handkerchief, but the sisters' smiles and giggles were far more contagious. The two made a perfect duo: Em and Albie could relax and be their true selves within each other's presence, and each hopeful suitor could take false satisfaction that their charms and easy-going affection were because of him. What a delightful ruse this party was turning out to be!

Is it really just as simple as being myself? Em found herself thinking. *Perhaps Albie's excitement about dancing wasn't so far-fetched after all.*

When she had almost convinced herself that her thoughts were true, Em felt a shoulder twitch coming on. Stiffness mixed with tingles radiated from her elbows up. Albie, who knew Em better than Em knew herself, gently placed her hand on Em's shoulder. This humane gesture immediately calmed Em down, but she felt the eyes of her mother's servant keeping a close watch from against the far wall. She pushed it to the back of her mind as Albertine gave her hand a light squeeze.

"You're doing just fine, dear sister," she whispered.

"Am I?" was Em's hoarse reply.

"Just proceed as normal," Albie responded, to which Em couldn't help but laugh.

"Normal!?" she guffawed, covering her mouth with her gloves to avoid stares. "Is that what this malady is?"

"It is for you. And so far, I've seen very little evidence of any such malady. I've seen a beautiful young woman with dancing eyes and exquisite brown ringlets catch more attention than a fly to honey this evening."

Em, who had been looking down, felt the soft nudge of her sister's hand lift her face up. "Enjoy yourself, Em. That's all you need to do, okay?"

With a silent nod, Em turned away from her sister to face a sea of guests in the finest couture. As she did so she could feel a tightness in her jaw. A grasp of her sister's hand indicated an impending twitch, but to her surprise, her jaw only dropped, with only a modest gasp. The young Marquis Sévigné, a chic gentleman barely out of his twenties, dark haired with a gold watch dangling from his breast coat, approached, an older Vicomtesse by his side.

"Lovely to see you sisters," he said. He turned to Em and continued, "I'm not sure what's more beautiful–those gowns or your eyes." Em and Albie curtseyed demurely as the young man continued. "I was just telling the Vicomtesse how highly inappropriate the scandal in Marne-la-Vallée was. And coming from such a fine family, too!" he scoffed, the Vicomtesse's curls and jowls bouncing as she nodded in agreement.

A blush crawled up Em's cheeks. The young man was not only handsome, he was all confidence, seemingly the complete opposite of Em. His blond hair shone under the candlelight, standing tall with

the ease and confidence that could only come with privilege. She had noticed him earlier—or rather the numerous petticoats that surrounded him like an ocean of silk all evening. He commanded the attention not just of the single ladies but the elder women as well who fawned on his every word and smile. He tossed a wink at Em and butterflies entered her stomach. While most young ladies could enjoy the privilege of such tickling pains, Em was only too aware of how this could trigger something far more dire.

"That sounds like a lovely story," she blurted out, adding a, "Thank you for sharing," before briskly turning on her heel, grateful to no longer be the center of attention.

"Em!"

She could hear her sister calling after her, followed by the Marquis' "*Mademoiselle*, Albertine, just because your sister is leaving you need not leave as well!"

Em turned and nodded an "I'm okay," to her sister.

"I'll just go to the ladies' retiring room to center myself," she thought, rushing through the crowd. Even before she was halfway there, however, she knew she was far from centered. Her mind was racing.

"This is the second time tonight I couldn't control not only my body but my voice. I must get this under control!" she scolded herself.

She glanced back at her sister who, despite being worried about her, had a huge smile on her face. Another young woman, a precocious redhead from a banking family, the Mallets, had happily stepped into Em's place. "Why do they get the privilege of enjoying the party, or if not enjoying, to have the choice to smile instead of scream. It's so unfair!"

On her way out of the ballroom, she had to pause to apologize for stepping on an old Earl's toe. Her thoughts then turned to her mother. Maman would never forgive her if she made a scene. She'd never forgive herself for that matter. If only her sister stood next to her instead of the chattering redhead who came up from behind and separated the two. She'd tell her how unjust it was. How she just wanted to relish her first real party and be carefree. For one night! Was that really too much to ask? Her answer came in the form of a neck twitch and light grunt which, thankfully, nobody could hear over the sound of the music. Moments before entering the retiring room she made a detour out of the *château*.

Once in the cold night air, she closed her eyes, taking a slow, deep breath against the same tree she had found herself under a mere hour before with Albie. Exhaling, she watched the swirls of breath dance in the cool night air. Finally, some peace and quiet…nobody to judge her movements and noises. Not unlike an itch that only gets relief by a good solid scratch, her body tensed, ready to release some new, fresh torture. Finally, she was alone!

"Pardon me, *Mademoiselle*."

No release after all. Instead, she gasped, not from her malady–but in shock. Em turned toward a young man, not much older than her own fifteen years. He was tall, emphasized by the fact that his pants were just a little too short, just reaching the top of his boots. His thick clothing was dirty. This was no party guest. He could have crawled out of the bushes for all she knew.

"What on earth–"

"I'm sorry to have alarmed you," he interrupted, his hands in the air. "I mean no harm."

"How long have you—"

"Just a few moments," he said. "Lovely dress."

"Thank you," Em responded, both flattered and irritated at the same time. "What are you doing here?"

"I was going to ask you the same thing," he said, leaning against the tree with an amused grin. "With all that food I saw the cook bringing in, you can bet I wouldn't be wasting my time out here with a mere gardener."

Em found herself about to smile but thought better of it. She had her dignity after all. She wasn't going to be appeased by some grounds worker whose name she didn't even know.

"I'm Théodore," he said, glancing down at his scuffed shoes for a moment before continuing to speak. "You...Um, it's late. Y-you should not be outside alone without an escort."

Em sighed in frustration, thinking Maman was keeping an eye on her, "*Bien sûr.* I *would* get in trouble for leaving and, well, of *course* Maman would send a servant after me. I never...oh." Suddenly realizing her mother would not have sent a gardener, she paused. "You... you weren't sent to fetch me inside?"

She saw hints of pink crawl up the young man's face before he bowed deeply to hide it. "I...I am a simple hired hand. I am at your service, *Mademoiselle.*"

He had crawled out of the bushes after all! Glancing toward the door, Em saw no other servants and more importantly, no scowling mother waiting for her return. She wasn't going back inside if she didn't have to. Shaking off the second look of shock in a matter of minutes, she stood just a little taller to show more confidence than she felt. "Ah-hem. I should really be with a female chaperone. This is not how it works, you know."

Turning away from him, she grimaced and stuck out her tongue before rolling her eyes in frustration at how often the movements were already starting to unleash.

Em noticed he was trying a little too hard not to look at her. "Actually, I do not know. I wasn't raised with so many rules. Besides, weren't most of those tossed out with the Revolution? I don't pay much attention to politics and rules, but we are living in a world with a lot of change."

Em gasped at his boldness. "Not that much change! If we were caught together, we would be pressed into marriage, I can assure you!"

Théodore chuckled, "Sounds like more of a problem for you than it would be for me! Marriage to a rich, beautiful woman? I accept."

Seeing Em take a few steps farther away, he continued quickly, "I promise that is not my design in making my presence known! I just don't believe women should be alone outdoors after dark like this. There have been wolf sightings, even on the grounds. I'll keep my distance, I assure you."

Em gave a small nod, allowing him to stay, but had no response to his comments. The awkward silence unnerved Em. She no longer felt free to wallow or unleash the beast that held her body captive, but she wasn't quite ready to go back to the party. Drumming her fingers on her arm stopped it from flying to the side, and it helped a little when suddenly her shoulders shimmied back and forth.

Instantly, Théodore turned toward her. With concern, he started to take a step toward her before backing away, keeping his place as a servant from the young noble. "*Mademoiselle*, you must get back inside. You must be cold, shaking like that."

"I do not feel cold. If you are so worried about it, you may seek shelter wherever you wish."

"You sure act like you are. And it is unreasonably cold for this time of year. I don't want to get in trouble if you were to get sick."

Em's convulsing body needed a place for the energy to go, so she didn't even try to hide the eye roll that came. She turned to face the boy, watching as he kicked the toe of his opposite boot. She squared her shoulders, let her arm fly to the side, stuck out her tongue, and shimmied again before announcing, "If you really were a gardener here, you would know the whispers. I am possessed by the devil, you know. I do not need an escort, for the devil himself already has laid claim to me. It would be in your best interest to leave me alone and let me release his energy in peace before you are likewise cursed."

Théodore suppressed a laugh and seemed to relax a little. "If that were true, Miss Albertine would also be cursed. You two spend so much time together. I didn't realize that was one of your…things you do. And I know you feel ashamed to spend time around the others in your class with it, but I'm no noble. I'm lucky to spend any time with you, considering our different lots in life. I do plenty of things your kind would be ashamed of. Shaking your shoulders is the least of your worries, miss."

Em squinted her eyes at the young man. "How long have you worked here?"

"I came to work here when I was about thirteen, so I would say, oh, three or four years now."

"Yet you don't think I am possessed?"

"That's just those uppity house servants. They think they are more righteous than the outdoor folk. Me, I don't believe in no devil, except maybe those bloodthirsty, power-hungry men trying to run the country."

"Which ones? Napoleon's men clinging to what power they have, or the Bourbons' reclaiming the throne?"

"Any of 'em. Politics, current events, and even religion do not hold my interest. I may attend mass with my family, but I serve my God here in the gardens. Nature makes so many different things, but none of them wrong. Including you, *Mademoiselle*."

Em turned away from Théodore and allowed the release of a few more spasms. Her left arm bent at the elbow as her fist came up to her rib cage. While her right shoulder came up to reach her ear, her head tilted down to meet it. Her mind was too busy to even consider what her body was doing.

What a strange and unusual thought. Albie loved her as she was, but she had never said it quite like that. No, it couldn't be possible. Trees and flowers were at least consistent. Em wasn't even sure how much to trust such a foreign idea. After all, he was just an uneducated gardener. Rules were different for him. He didn't have society watching his every move, as long as the flowers looked nice.

As the thoughts circled in her head, she started to get dizzy. The same thoughts repeated enough that she wasn't sure she could ever believe the things the young gardener had just said, though she desperately wanted to. Eventually, Em simply couldn't spend another moment on such thoughts.

Needing a change, Em's thoughts shifted to those of the young man before her. "What are you doing outside the party, pray tell? Shouldn't you be in your own quarters, or at the very least, with your own family?"

Théodore turned red all the way to the tips of his ears. Reaching his hand out, he played with some low hanging branches as he stumbled to find any words to say. "I…was just finishing work and headed back to the servant's quarters. I noticed you here by yourself and thought to offer my services since you were out here all alone."

"This late at night? I suppose the sun has just recently set…" Em began fidgeting with the lace trim at the end of her sleeves, unsure of what to say next. She realized this much time alone with a young man was bordering on improper, but she wasn't quite ready to leave.

Em's head swam with new ideas. She didn't quite know what to think of this gardener who was so bold, yet so unburdened by anything. He seemed so at peace with himself, something she had not experienced since she was a child. Were his odd ideas to be trusted? It had been made very clear to her by her mother that she was not natural.

How could someone like her dare return to society? She didn't really want to risk a return to the party and make a spectacle of herself. It was really only a matter of time, after all. With no control over her own person, how could she not make a scene? The evening air had a chill that would push most indoors, but Em's desire for solitude felt like a physical weight, almost a burden that she was not permitted to carry.

With a sigh, she turned to face the house, watching the flickering lights. She saw her mother through the windows, chatting with the young Marquis. She wondered if Albie was starting to wonder where she was. That thought was quickly replaced by what Maman might be saying to the Marquis.

"You really should consider Albie over Em. My Em might have a certain physical beauty, but her behavior would not make a regal wife!" Oh, how she wished she could make her mother proud. Maman was her only surviving parent and she desired a relationship far closer than they now shared.

"Are you well, *Mademoiselle*? You look troubled." The kind gardener's words broke her musings.

As she faced the young man again, she noticed his eyes, wide as saucers. His head was cocked to the side and he was staring at her intently. She could see the concern on his face.

He pities me, she surmised. *Why should I be surprised?* She turned back toward the house. "I must return to the party." And with that she spun on her heel and headed back toward the *château*.

"I don't understand. Did I do something wrong?" she heard him call out to her.

Stopping in the frame of the door, she paused, her mind a jumble. Could it be that it wasn't pity after all but genuine concern for her wellbeing? That he didn't feel sorry for her because of her tics but he felt compassion in spite of them? This boy—this, dare she think it, *handsome* boy—had given her a gift. It was only a small glimmer of a possibility of hope, but a gift, nonetheless. Turning her head slightly, but not enough to see the young man's face lest the defensive fortress she'd built around her feelings crumble like Jericho's walls, she whispered softly, "No. Not at all. Thank you," before rushing through the wooden doors and back into the noise of the party.

Chapter 3
The Episode

ALBIE BOUNCED WITH JOY, curls following suit, when she saw Em enter the room. With a grin that could be seen across the English Channel, Albie rushed to her sister's side. "Em! Wait til you hear what Baroness Cuvier just shared! But where have you been?"

"Was it another awful story about that poodle she never lets out of her sight?"

"At least the dog didn't drag in any mud. Where *have* you been, darling?"

Em glanced down at her dancing shoes. The silk ribbon and embroidery were hardly visible from the mud. Em couldn't help but think how she had committed yet another *faux pas* her mother would use against her later.

Shuffling her feet to remove the evidence as best she could, Em could only respond with a sigh.

"Oh no, Em, you had another episode. Twice in one night, too!" Her eyes were almost identical to Théodore's in energy: kind, soft, questioning.

Maybe it was concern Théodore was showing, she thought. The realization was enough to start the floodgate of tears she had managed to suppress with the gardener. It was both a relief to feel free from the judgment so prevalent in society while also a horrid frustration that such kindness was a rarity.

"Em, darling, are you okay?" Em could only nod as a few drops of anguish squeaked past, dropping down her cheeks.

"Your shoes!" Albie gasped, not in remonstration but in shock.

Pulling out her handkerchief, Albie gently wiped the tears away. "Here, let's put this moisture to good use and wipe off some of this mess before Maman sees it, shall we?" At that very instant a housemaid walked by. "Perfect! Anne, please take my sister's shoes up to her room and bring down her spare set of dancing shoes."

"But then she'll be in her bare feet–" the servant balked.

"The skirt is long. As long as my sister doesn't sit, and you say not a word of this to the household staff–especially my mother–we shall not have a problem, isn't that right, ladies?" Em and the housemaid nodded in unison before the housemaid scurried away, the shoes delicately covered with a napkin she quickly grabbed from a side table.

"So now on top of suppressing my noises and movements, I can't sit down? This is getting so complicated," Em smiled for the first time in a while.

"Perhaps you should have considered that before staying so long in the garden!" Albie retorted. "Besides, I've seen the way you practice your sums. You're quite intelligent. I think you'll survive for a few minutes."

"If only that were true."

Albie sighed in solidarity for her sister. "Sounds like a bad one."

"Well, yes and no. I thought I was going to, but I never actually got them out. A gardener stopped me and we spoke for a few moments."

"You spoke with the gardener? What could he have to say?"

"Not much at first, but he shared some rather unusual ideas. Certainly more entertaining than the Baroness and far cuter than her dog."

"Ernestine Émilie Prondre! How scandalous, I'm sure he *did* have some unusual ideas!"

"As if Marquis Sévigné didn't?" Em shot back.

"I won't bother with a response to that insinuation of a man you just met—"

"I could say the same about your ideas about Théodore."

"Théodore? The gardener? You're on a first name basis with the hired help?"

"I am simply stating that it's not a good idea to judge someone before you know them. If you are going to make a statement about Théodore it's only fair play I make the same one about the Marquis. Perhaps they are both scoundrels!"

"Well, even if you are correct, my sister, at least the Marquis would be a rich one!"

Em threw her head back and laughed uproariously.

"It's not funny," Albie said, her eyes brooding and flat.

"Oh, sister," Em said, composing herself, "You are starting to look like Maman now. It scares me."

"Em, love, I'm just worried about you. I want what is best. I don't want to encourage such a scheme between our people and…" she pointed to a nebulous place in the air, "…theirs."

"It wasn't like that at all! I would think you of all people would know how I hate to be judged. Doesn't he deserve the same kindness?"

Albie didn't respond. A pause hung in the air, broken only by Albie gazing over at their mother who was grabbing another glass of champagne from a passing tray.

"Please don't tell Maman!" Em said, her concern finally matching Albie's. "She would never let me out of my room if she knew I was talking like that."

Before Albie could respond, Anne approached with a new pair of shoes. Without a word exchanged, she surreptitiously placed them on the floor and walked off as Em stepped into them.

With a sigh of relief, Albie grabbed Em's hand. "Enough of such talk for now. Let's return to the guests and discuss it later. This evening is for nonsense and fun and joviality, not inappropriate scandal or intellectual discourse."

Em wanted to reply, "Not if you're Théodore. Théodore is full of such intellectual discourse. It was the only highlight of the evening!" but instead she allowed her sister to pull her back toward the ballroom. Plastering a smile on her face, Em took a few steps inside before catching her mother's eye. Maman did not look pleased. *Could she have noticed my multiple absences?* she ruminated. At the thought, her stomach began turning in knots. She found herself biting her lip in an all too familiar sense of dread and dismay.

Pausing to turn back, Albie saw the distress on her sister's face. "Em, are you alright, darling?"

Shaking her head clear of her mother's influence, Em turned to Albie. The knots in her stomach stayed firmly put, but Em was determined not to ruin her sister's evening. "Yes, of course. I guess I'm still just a bit nervous is all."

"You and your nerves," laughed Albie. "You are doing splendidly. Come! The night awaits!"

Plastering a smile on her face, Em followed her sister into the crowd, rubbing the back of her right hand. The pair weaved through the crowd and the stories, yet the knots continued to tighten rather than unravel. The deeper they went into the room, the deeper Em's despair became and the more her stomach hurt. Her mind flashed back to Théodore and how he had distracted her. *I should have known better than to come back here without releasing my movements*, she rued. *I can't do it now—not in the public eye!*

Now she was unlikely to escape the party for a few more hours. As Albie gushed with exciting stories and conversed with the guests, Em plotted a way to be able to leave the party for good. The kitchen. The retiring room. "I don't feel well," she could possibly say to Maman, then rush to her bedroom. The longer she stayed, the worse she knew it would be if an episode began before she quit the room.

She felt like she was about to entirely leap outside of her skin.

The lights of the chandelier and sconces suddenly seemed brighter. Every conversation in the room leaped into her ears at the same volume, demanding to be heard, and suddenly her dress felt much tighter than when she first put it on. Her breathing became shallow and harder to control. Her stomach twisted in knots as her mind grew foggier.

For a moment, Em was able to glance into Albie's eyes with a look of sorrow and regret. There was simply too much going on. She felt her control slipping away.

Em watched as couples danced, weaving in and out while the walls were filled with crowds of conversation, climbing to the ceiling like ivy. "Such a lovely family", "Little Albertine has grown so much", "I simply adore Schubert", "They say Napoleon is gathering an army to head to Waterloo", and much laughter forced their way into Em's ears. Each candle around the room and those hanging from chandeliers danced to the bouncing music of the violins as they played Schubert's Presto Quartet No. 2 in C Major.

Every conversation, musical note, and flicker of light teased at her senses. Every muscle in Em's body began to tighten from the onslaught of so much coming into her head at the same time. Her dress felt two sizes too small and itched terribly against her arms. She needed to move but felt so constrained. What could she do without upsetting Maman? Her chest tightened with the pressure. She had to go. Now.

Without making her excuses to the guests nearby, she turned for the door. How had they managed to go so far into the room so quickly? She began to push her way through the throngs of people. Halfway to the door, like a puppet, both hands flung themselves high into the air, hands limp, then dropped quickly to her sides. Em's head slowly tilted back as she sucked in air with a high-pitched shriek. Her shoulders tightened around her ears. Suddenly, her shoulders dropped as she shouted, "*Enculer!*" with all the breath sucked in with her shriek.

The entire room went silent as a tomb. Musicians stopped playing, all conversation halted so that each person could turn and find the source of such obscenity. Em's eyes went wide as she covered her mouth with both hands. The very air was as still as the statued crowd. Only Eulalie moved in brisk steps toward her daughter. Once in front of Em, no one even saw her hand fly across the embarrassed girl's cheek, though it sounded like a gunshot had echoed across the room. Several guests flinched at the sound.

Eulalie then grabbed Em's arm, her perfectly manicured fingernails digging into Em's flesh through her sleeve. Em's knees seemed to completely give out as she took each step behind her mother. They moved in silence until they reached Ernestine's quarters. Throwing her daughter onto her bed, Eulalie simply fumed. Her mother was never short on words, so the silent glare tore Em's heart to pieces as the blood rushed to her face.

"I didn't mean to..." was all Em could quietly muster. She couldn't quite manage to keep her hands still, despite the desire to freeze. Em knew additional movements would not be looked upon kindly.

This released the floodgates from Eulalie. "DIDN'T MEAN TO?!? How is that a possibility? Where did you even hear that word? What kind of company are you keeping, child? A woman's role is to be demure and agreeable, have I not taught you this? Have you not listened to a single thing I have ever said to you? You rebellious and disobedient child. And would you PLEASE sit still?"

Try as she might, her fingers rubbed the length of her thumbs down to the heel of her hands. As she tried to sit still, she could feel her right shoulder creeping up into her ear as her mother continued her lecture.

"A century ago I could have simply shipped you off to the Americas to run with the other savages. This is completely unacceptable. You will not leave this room without express permission from me. You will take your meals here since you are not to be trusted around your younger siblings. I will not have you corrupting them with your wild ways."

With that she spun, graceful as a dancer, to make her apologies to the crowd, slamming the door behind her. Tears fell from Ernestine's eyes as she heard her mother demand a servant outside the door at all times. Her body shook from her sobs. Or maybe the stress. She couldn't tell if it was the malady or the emotion. Either way, her body seemed to spasm as she cried uncontrollably.

What a night this had turned out to be. It had begun with so much excitement and possibility. It ended as a nightmare. If only she could wake from such an experience. She could never trust herself again in public, she knew it. Her life was simply over. She would be hidden away for the rest of her life. Likely only Albie would be her companion. She really would become like the wild boy, deemed unacceptable for society and seen as an idiot.

Tears continued to flow until Em was thoroughly exhausted from the events of the night. She fell into a fitful sleep, filled with nightmares of large crowds gathered outside her room, staring eyes through large open windows, whispers penetrating through walls, and the future of a life spent in isolation.

Chapter 4
PUNISHMENT

I'VE REALLY DONE IT this time. I can't believe things actually managed to get worse. Maman has put me into isolation. I am not allowed to see anyone, not even my siblings. I only know this because dear Albie has a mind of her own and a very strong will. She has come a few times to see me. Even if Maman had placed a guard at the door, I don't think it would have kept Albie out. She's so clever, she would have found a way in. I don't know what I would do without her. I wish I could be even half as strong. I don't dare set a single toe outside of this door.

Maybe if I was stronger, I could control whatever is happening in my body. Maybe then I wouldn't be so afraid. Even just a few days like this have been completely miserable. I want to be with my sister. I want to be outside in the garden. I would love to talk to the gardener again. I can't stop thinking about his words. I am so different, it's hard to believe there is nothing "wrong" with me. I want to see more of nature and pay attention to how different things really are.

Since I'm not allowed to exit my room, I asked Albie to bring me a book from the library about flowers. There was a picture of one called the Kalanchoe daigremontiana in Madagascar. I have never seen anything like it! The flowers sprout off the edges of the long, thin leaves. They form a line along the edge of the plant! It almost looks like a chandelier and it fascinates me.

They are still beautiful at least. Who could find beauty in an illness? Sometimes things just break and I am broken. It's really a wonder how Maman has kept me around so long. She could have sent me to an orphanage at any time. I wonder if she would ever disown me. What would I do? I do not have the skills of the laborer. I am mostly healthy and strong, aside from this curse of mine. I suppose I could learn if needed.

Fifteen years' worth of lessons must prove good for something if she turns me out of the house. There must be something I could do to earn a living if she will no longer have me. Oh, I can't bear to think about it. I wouldn't survive on my own. I would end up begging on the streets of Paris. Cursed by the devil as I am, no one would come near me.

So maybe it's for the best that I sit in this gilded prison. As long as I have Albie visiting me on occasion, maybe I could do fine. Could one adjust to living in isolation and find any kind of joy? Neither life really seems worth living. What is the point? A long life of seclusion versus a short life of desperation and lack.

I just really wish there was a cure. I wish there was a doctor even willing to try something new. I feel like I must have seen every doctor in Paris by now. It's hopeless. I'M hopeless.

THE NEXT TIME ERNESTINE saw her mother was a week after the celebration. One week since the worst night of Em's short life. One week of solitary confinement, not knowing her future. One week of excessive tension and uncontrolled movements. One week of vulgarities echoed against the decorated walls. Things had never been this bad with her malady and life had never looked so grim.

Albie had provided updates on Maman's moods every time she snuck in. It seemed her mother's temper had not cooled at all and had the entire family and staff treading lightly so as not to disturb her. Em didn't dare leave and no one except Albie dared enter. Even the kitchen maids left food outside the door, knocking before dashing off to avoid contact with the demon contained therein.

When Eulalie finally appeared, her face was hard as stone, ready to crack anyone or anything that dared to contradict it. She stood just inside the doorway for far longer than Em would have liked, not saying a single word. She fidgeted, massaging the tickling sensation in her arm and blinking a little more than normal. Finally, taking a deep breath and with authority in her voice, Eulalie spoke.

"Help Anne pack your trunks. The two of you leave in the morning."

"*Du matin?* Where? For how long? Will…will I get to come home?" Em's worst fears seemed to be materializing before her eyes. She was being sent away in shame. Disowned. How would she survive? Would she at least receive an allowance? At least she was allowed a few possessions that she could sell off to survive. Tears formed in her eyes and she found herself unable to stand. Falling to her bed, she buried her face in her hands as if she could cover her shame and to hide her tears from Maman.

For the first time in a week, her mother's face softened. She quickly found her way to Em's side and joined her sitting on the four-poster bed. It was like the Maman she knew as a child had returned. She felt small, yet oddly normal, as she was before the malady began. Placing a hand on Em's cheek she said, "Oh, *mon coeur*, that is not what I meant at all. Of course you will return. You can return home when these…impulses are under control. I have found a place that will help. But it is all up to you when you return home.

"I just want this under control for your safety. I only survived the Revolution due to my ability to hide when needed. Blending in can be an extremely useful talent. If we have to hide again, I want to know you will live. We are safe now, but will we always be so?"

Reassuming her authoritarian demeanor, she stood, "That does mean, however, that you must pack for a long journey. I'm sure you will love the Swiss Confederation, the mountains there are simply stunning. You will be staying with a cousin in her *château* and will be properly looked after. Anne will be with you during the journey to dress and chaperone you. Be sure to write and keep us updated on your progress."

Eulalie glided out the door and the visit was over. So, it was to be the Swiss Confederation. Her mother had not provided many details and Em's head was simply swimming with questions. What kind of place was she going to? An asylum? She may as well be disowned. Em sat, overwhelmed with questions, unable to move, and wondering what to pack.

Not long after, Anne entered the room with several trunks and went straight for the closet. Sweet Anne was unusually quiet. Em was unsure if it was due to the large task of packing, the thoughts of a long journey to a foreign country, or even worse, if Anne had also begun to think of her as some kind of monster, possessed and ripping her away from her family and home.

Em was reminded of Théodore and his impression of the house help. *He* didn't think she was possessed or some kind of monster, even if Anne might. She had missed her time in the gardens under her tree and wondered if she would have run into him on her walks, had she been permitted to take any.

The boy seemed nice enough. She didn't fully trust his words, but she wondered if there was something to his nature theory. Maybe she should leave a message for him. It would be rude to leave without some kind of notice, wouldn't it?

"Anne?"

"*Oui, Mademoiselle?*"

"Do you know…"

Then again, maybe asking about the boy that called house servants "uppity" might not do her much good. Besides, he would hear the gossip that she had been sent away. He probably wouldn't care anyway. Not to mention the repercussions if her mother found out. It would be unseemly.

"Do you know if I should take any evening gowns to this place? Please ask Maman for her advice on any events that might take place."

"*Oui, Mademoiselle.*" Anne left the room with haste, seemingly grateful for a reprieve from Em's presence. Em couldn't help but feel sorry for the poor girl, who seemed to be suddenly afraid of her mistress. Who could find blame in poor Anne? Em knew the whispers that followed her in society. No young woman, no matter her station, would want to be attached to such disgrace.

Em was left to the task at hand. As she found herself swimming in gowns, underthings, shoes, and stockings, she couldn't shake the thoughts in her head of nature and a certain young man.

The day passed quickly, and suddenly Em was on her way out the door to stay with a cousin in a *château* called Oberhofen. She was not surprised to see her younger half-siblings absent from the farewell party in front of their home. Little Eulalie (named after her mother) and Ernest weren't really close to her on the best of days. It seemed only the servants were present to witness her shame as they loaded her luggage onto the carriage, Anne climbing up top to settle in for the ride.

Maman exited the *château*, delicately descending the steps to oversee Em's exile. Albie had managed to sneak out behind their mother, darting around her to reach Em first, nearly tripping from the loose gravel. When Albie reached her sister, the impact knocked them both off balance and Em squeezed her sister tightly.

She had no idea how she would survive without Albie. Albie was the one person who was always by her side, always loved her, and could help calm her down when she got out of control. And she was expected to control herself without such a calming influence? Tears threatened to fall as the pair faced separation.

Albie broke away from the hug and pulled a small box tied with a ribbon. "Don't open it until you are outside of France. I'm so jealous you get to be the first to travel abroad! I do wish I could go with you."

"I, too, wish more than anything that you were coming along. How shall I ever survive without you?"

The pair embraced once more with tears running down their cheeks. It wasn't until Maman cleared her throat that the pair separated but continued to hold hands. Em squeezed Albie's hand and dropped her head as Maman stepped closer.

Em looked around as if seeing the *château* for the first time. The color of the red brick was soft, almost a rosy color, yet still contrasted with the white columns and rows surrounding each of the many windows generously placed along each wall. The white clock face sat front and center above the double front doors. The doors sat atop the grey–almost silver in the sunlight, Em noticed–staircase that descended from either side of the door. Em turned to face the large grassy expanse just beyond the tan gravel rocks that made up the entryway. The intricate iron fence seemed so far away, yet the thought of knowing she would soon cross the threshold, not knowing when she would return, hovered over her.

Em let out a soft sigh and hung her head as her mother approached. Lifting Em's face until their eyes met, Maman broke the silence. "*Voyage sécurisé, ma biquette.* I cannot wait to hear about your progress. You shall return quite the dignified young lady! We shall hold a party upon your return. I shall miss you."

As Maman leaned in to hug her daughter, Ernestine's entire body went stiff and she still wouldn't release Albie's hand. Maman embraced her quickly before jumping back when Em's shoulder tightened. After all, no one wanted to risk physical injury when Em's hands started to move as they did. The truth was that Em was still embarrassed and upset with her mother. The last thing Em wanted right now was a hug from the woman who was sending her away from the only home she had ever known and loved with all her heart. "Well then, off you go! Into the carriage, *mon coeur.*"

Albie didn't release Em's hand until the carriage door was about to close. Then, Albie ran alongside the carriage for as long as her legs could keep up with the horses. In the background, Em could hear Maman scolding Albie for the undignified act. Em stared out the window until her sister became a mere speck on the horizon. The pair had officially been separated. It hardly seemed real.

As the carriage crept farther away from the *château*, Em passed various places on the grounds where she and Albie had played hide-and-seek, or had a tea party, or where they brought their new dolls after their mother remarried. The new doll from their new stepfather was still in Em's room, but now used more as decor. Maman insisted she was too old to play with dolls the moment she turned twelve.

Em began her journey, bumping and rattling her way to the Swiss Confederation; her new home until further notice. Em held Albie's gift in her hands for only a few minutes until her curiosity got the better of her. With fresh tears on her face, Em pulled at the lovely ribbon. As the paper fell away, Em found a beautifully decorated wooden box. Upon opening the box, she discovered a magnificent goose quill set, complete with ink, sand, letter paper, and a small knife to sharpen the quill.

Tucked inside the box, Em found a letter.

I knew you couldn't wait until the border of France! I miss you so much already, my darling sister. I do not know how I will survive so long without you. Know that I am already in negotiations with Maman to arrange a visit. Once it is decided, I shall not tell you. I will simply arrive one day and surprise you!

I know you will likely have access to quill and paper upon arrival, but I wanted you to have this for many reasons. First of all, you had better write to me the moment you arrive! Secondly, this set was simply stunning and I couldn't pass it by! It is as beautiful as you are, it simply has to belong to you. Thirdly, as a reminder that you had better be home before the paper runs out! I couldn't bear to have you gone much longer.

Does this sound like an agreeable deal? I thought it was quite reasonable and dare I say clever! With these joyful things in mind, it is time to dry your tears, for we won't be apart long. I hope thoroughly that you enjoy your stay at Oberhofen.

As always, your favorite sister,
Albertine

Despite the giggles that came from reading Albie's letter, the tears continued to fall. She was certain she left her entire soul back at the *château* and it was simply her body riding in the bumpy carriage. Looking up from the letter and glancing out the window, she saw a tall boy with pants just a little too short pushing a wheelbarrow to clean out the underbrush of the hedge lining the *château* grounds.

She leaned back into her seat, a flush rising in her cheeks. She didn't want him to see her all red and puffy from her tears. Though she wasn't sure why that mattered.

Clutching the box from her sister tighter to her chest, Em stared straight ahead, willing her mind to turn off until they stopped for the night in Maisoncelle-en-Brie. She might not survive the trip if she allowed herself to think too much. With no other passengers with whom she could talk, she resolved to pick up a new book or two to read along the journey.

When she arrived at the inn, she alighted from the carriage, hung her head as she followed Anne up to her room. Still clutching her sister's gift, she gently rested it on the simple wooden table by her bed. Her sister's thoughtfulness never ceased to amaze her and it made her feel close to Albie to keep the box and letter nearby, almost as if she were clutching her sister instead of a writing set.

The room was much simpler than she was accustomed to. Compared to her *château*, the room was simply dull. There was no decoration on the walls, only solid brown blankets on top of white sheets, and a darkness that seemed to pervade the room. It seemed to match her mood perfectly, if anything. She fell asleep homesick for her sister and her own bed.

The next morning, Anne woke her before dawn. Em crawled into her carriage before most hotel guests awoke and sat in her bumpy carriage with the curtains drawn. Maman's rules. They rode until well after dark, timed precisely to avoid other guests as often as possible.

She saw almost no one except her servants who kept her on schedule and hidden like some shameful secret. At least they were getting in a few extra kilometers each day. One or two fewer days in the carriage was a blessing. This pattern continued day after day for a month until she arrived at the *château* Oberhofen.

Chapter 5
ARRIVING IN OBERHOFEN

I'M SO TIRED OF carriages. Anymore, they mean that I am only on my way to being poked and examined yet again. Nothing even helps, so why do I have to continue such useless travels? I don't even know the people I will be staying with. Maman claims they are family, but how exactly? I would love to meet Papa's family. Maybe they could tell me stories of his childhood and if he was like me at all.

Wouldn't that be lovely? I would love to have things in common with Papa. I feel so distant from the rest of my family. Could he maybe have done things like this when he was younger? Is there a chance I have a bit of him always with me when these episodes happen? Maybe he grew out of them, since I've never heard Maman mention that he did anything out of the ordinary…If he did, maybe there is a chance that I could grow out of them as well.

Is this my last chance to become a proper young lady, as Maman states? I simply wish to be good. I don't know why it's such a challenge for me to control such basic functions of my body. I wonder what it would be like to have full control of myself. Would I still be home with my dear sister? Could there be gentlemen interested in spending time with me? I want to go to parties and flirt and dance the night away, watch the shows in the theatre, go to concerts, like a normal person would.

Ugh, why do I even do this to myself? What torture to consider the life I wish I could have but never will. I am so nervous as to what will happen in the Swiss Confederation. Albie is right, my nerves tend to make things worse. I'm grateful to be shut away in a private room in each hotel we stay at along the way.

Will my distant relatives be kind and understanding? Will they be more like Maman? Will I be able to make any friends there? Not likely. Maman has instructions for me not to leave the château *there unless necessary. My friends will be the doctors rotating in and out.*

At least I will be away from all the rubbish of Napoleon trying to gather his army again. I'm so sick of that name already, and I don't know what I'll do if I am ever faced with him. Maman is right; I must control this so I can be out of harm's way.

I should probably be using this time to write a letter to Albie. I don't have much longer before this condition takes over and I'll not be able to write. Right now, my neck keeps twisting every which way which makes it difficult. My hands aren't likely far behind. I just don't know what I would say to her and it seems foolish to waste a perfectly good piece of paper simply to tell her I have arrived. What if I stay longer than the paper supply lasts? She would be furious with me, I'm sure.

I have spent more time than I care to admit simply thinking about the gardener. I know it was only one conversation that we shared, but I confess, the thoughts of "what if" have kept my mind occupied through-out most of the journey. What if I'm not broken? What if I'm not cursed? What if more people thought like Théodore? The words have begun to haunt me. What if?

What if life didn't have to be so dreary?

OBERHOFEN WAS A MUCH more traditional castle than Guermantes. Smaller, but certainly far older. The outside wall was built in the style of medieval battlements and the tall center tower was certainly the prison of some real life Persinette. If it wasn't, it was about to be hers, though Em didn't have the thirty-four-meter golden locks or any hope of a prince to rescue her.

"Ernestine! My goodness, what a lovely young woman you are! The letters we have received from your Maman make it seem you are still a child at play!"

Em's relative seemed to be just a few years older than her, skipping out of the *château* to meet the carriage as it arrived. Her blonde hair was pulled up, as a proper wife's hair should be, but the ringlets framing her round face bounced with each step she took, making her seem more like a child. Her pale green taffeta gown was cutting edge, with more fabric around the shoulders and a fuller skirt despite her trim figure. She seemed so much more free and unrestrained than anyone she had seen at Albie's party, despite the imposing structure of the castle.

After so long on the road, Em could only manage to smile politely and curtsey at her hostess, for words completely failed her. She was too exhausted to be nervous. She wanted to make a good first impression, at least.

"It's nice to meet you."

Em had so many questions, but none of them seemed polite. She could at least ask the name of her hostess, surely? Before she had a chance to ask, she was enveloped in a hug from this spritely woman who quickly filled the silence.

"Let us quickly drop the formalities, you may call me Marie. I am thrilled to have you here! It has been far too long since I've seen or heard much of you, until I received the recent request from your

mother. You simply MUST tell me all about you and sweet Albie. Your father last wrote to me when you were first born and I simply must know how he is. He used to be so good about writing letters, then again, children do tend to take up so much time and I'm sure there are several of you running around Guermantes by now!"

Em stopped listening at this point as Marie continued her joyful chatter. Em turned to watch Anne climb down from the top of the carriage and begin to unload, handing trunks off to Marie's staff.

"Are you all right, my dear? You look a thousand miles away."

"I...I guess I'm just surprised you didn't know. My father had only two children, me and Albertine, he...he died when I was three months old. Maman remarried when I was seven and has had children with him. My younger brother Ernest and younger sister Eulalie. Um, I go by Em, by the way."

The shock was apparent on Marie's face and Em wondered if she shouldn't have waited to tell her until they were inside with chairs to collapse into. While Marie's speech slowed considerably from her initial bubbliness, there seemed to be an inner fortitude that kept her on her feet.

"Oh goodness, you poor thing! So...you never really knew your sweet father? That is simply tragic. He was such a gem. I haven't seen him since we were children, he was like an older brother to me. My mother was actually his sister, so we were frequent visitors to Guermantes when I was young, before we moved to the Swiss Confederation during the Revolution."

Em just stared at her, both intrigued by this new information about her father but also absolutely exhausted from the journey.

"Look at me going on and on!" Marie cried, once again grasping Em's hands. "Let's get you some refreshment. You must be spent."

She walked Em toward the double doors, her chattering silenced. It wasn't until Em saw Marie kindly smiling at the servants, using words like "Please" and "Thank you" that she let her guard down.

"May I dare to ask a question, cousin?"

Marie stopped walking, having almost arrived at the massive oak door.

"Anything! What is it?"

"Are you…" Em stammered, and not from her tics but from shyness. She was not used to a woman being so jovial. "Are you happy here?"

She stared up at the massive house, craning her neck until she was practically dizzy.

"Oh, yes, dear!" Marie laughed "I was so young when I got married, and this place appeared more like a dungeon than a cozy home at first, but Daniel—my husband—is a dear and we have been very happy here. And wait until you meet little Albert, you'll love him. I always wished your sweet father could meet them, but I'm glad his legacy continues with you."

"I'd love to learn more about my father," Em said, earnestness in her eyes.

"In time!" Marie answered, once again moving them toward the entrance. Upon a nod of her head, two servants dressed in cream suits on either side of it bowed and opened the large wooden doors for them, showing peaks of a great hall with a massive chandelier on the other side. "Daniel is away far more than we would like, so that will give us plenty of time to talk. Oh, did I mention what a sweet man Daniel is? You'll love him!"

"You did," said Em, letting Marie's sweetness descend over her like bubbles. "I am truly delighted to be here."

And for the first time since her travels began, she breathed a sigh of relief.

Left alone, Em wandered the room that she was to occupy for the time being. She was instantly drawn to the window that provided the most magnificent vision. At least, it seemed to be such. She had an unobstructed view of the crystal blue waters of Lake Thun with the grand snowcapped Alps standing proudly behind. They were separated by a line of solid green on the other side of the lake and the clouds almost seemed to blend in with the snow on the mountains. She wasn't sure, but it almost looked like she could see the famous Matterhorn, right from her window. Em instantly knew she could never tire of such a view. The rest of the room, and the request to change for dinner, were promptly forgotten in favor of the stunning view.

The knock on the door snapped her out of her reverie to be reminded by the growling of her stomach. She was expected at supper. With a quick change, she was only a touch late and promptly made her excuses.

"I have never seen such a stunning view! How do you manage to get anything done during the day? I could easily get lost simply staring out my window!"

Marie laughed. "Yes, indeed, it is quite lovely. But my young Albert demands so much of my attention these days, and I am…"

Marie had to stop as her young toddler had wandered up to the table and grabbed the tablecloth (though he seemed to be aiming for his mother's skirts). With a smile, he glanced at his mother and demanded, "UP!"

"Forgive me, this child is a bit rambunctious. I love him dearly, but what a troublemaker! I hope you do not mind having a little one chasing after you. He is a very affectionate child."

Giggling, Em could only be reminded of the trouble she and Albie still managed to get into. She loved to laugh and had the heart of a child, despite expectations placed on her day and night. "I'm sure we will get along quite well."

Em loved watching Marie with her son. Marie seemed to be part child herself, quick to laugh, even when things didn't go as planned. This was eye-opening for Ernestine. Quite the opposite of her mother, Marie was loving and doting, instantly putting Em at ease anytime she was around her.

As dinner progressed, Em became more and more anxious about what would happen if her hands suddenly started flinging food all over her hostess, or what atrocities would fly out of her mouth instead of polite conversation. Had her mother written to warn her hostess? How much did she know?

"Are you alright my dear? You are grasping that fork so tightly it could easily snap in half!"

"Oh, my apologies. Yes, I'm quite well. Nothing is the matter here." Em plastered a wide grin on her face, unconsciously gripping the fork even tighter.

"You are certain? I like to think I'm quite adept at reading people. Maybe I have been away from France for too long, but I do not believe that to be the case."

Forcing her fingers to relax, Em smiled at her hostess but was unable to hide the flush of red rising in her cheeks. In a state of embarrassment, she forgot to focus on keeping her hands still. Her left hand tightened sharply and rotated away from her. Her fork, which had just begun picking up a slice of potato, flung the food across the table.

Luckily, the seat was vacant, but yet again, Em was caught off guard. Suddenly, a high-pitched squeal, followed by a deep growl of "*merde*" flew from her lips. Em covered her face with her hands, afraid of the reaction sure to follow.

There were no shouts or indignant sighs as would be expected from her mother. Em peeked one eye from her right hand to glance at her hostess. Marie seemed not to have noticed that anything had even happened. Peeking out her left hand, Em saw that a servant had already cleared up the food, and Marie was simply feeding young Albert another bite of his meal.

Em's exposed eye watched Marie, still hiding the rest of her face. "You don't have to talk about it now, my dear. Whenever you are ready, know that I have a listening ear." With that, the conversation turned back to the daily routine, rules, and cultural norms that Em needed to be aware of during her stay. Marie did most of the talking, allowing Em to gather her wits and continue her meal, grateful that a crisis had been so smoothly averted by Marie.

After dinner, they retired to the drawing room. As Em detailed the events of her journey, she felt the familiar itch building up. It was small enough; the rubbing was sufficient to keep her odd actions at bay. Yet as the conversation continued, it became more difficult. It must have been exhaustion. However, if it wasn't, she could still use the excuse to remove herself before she made an embarrassment of herself in front of her considerate host.

As she began to make her excuses to retire to her chamber, Em grew nervous about a sudden explosion. Her jaw tightened, making it difficult to speak. Before she could finish her sentence, a blast of "*merde*" escaped her lips yet again. Em reactively hung her head and covered it with her hands while offering every apology she knew. When she heard no response, Em peeked at Marie to see her reaction.

Marie looked at Em with concern, while still bouncing Albert on her lap. "Are you alright, my dear? Did you forget something? This must be a really harrowing day, not just from the journey, but a new home and new people must really have you on edge. Is there anything I can do for you?"

Speechless, Em began to tear up. Such a reaction would never have crossed her mind. The two women looked at each other for a few moments while each tried to process exactly what was happening.

When Em shook her head, she began fumbling for the words to explain the curse that had been plaguing her for years. "I'm sorry...I have...I don't..."

"Oh, don't fret so much, my dear. Your mother had written about some of these episodes and the reason you were sent here. I was hoping you were comfortable enough to tell me on your own. Now that they have come up, there is no need to be so nervous about them. Your mother actually seems to have exaggerated your condition. This doesn't seem so terrible thus far. Judging by your reaction, this might be as bad as it gets, don't you agree?"

Em was lost for words. Only Albertine had such an attitude regarding her curiosities. Not even Em herself was so optimistic, though Marie did seem to be correct; it usually didn't get to be much more than what she had shown. Flinging food had seemed to be among the worst of her transgressions, aside from her unladylike mouth.

"Um, well, yes. That is, I have not seen many episodes worse than that."

"Lovely, then you shall be quite at home. Albert makes much more of a mess and a fuss than you do, so do not fret in the slightest."

Blushing yet again, Em responded with her gratitude and a small smile. Marie seemed to be an angel. In contrast, Em's mother had never had such patience with her and Albie, even when they were small like

Albert. Now that Em was an adult, her mother's patience grew ever thinner. Her outbursts were absolutely unacceptable in an adult. Yet, Marie took it all in stride. It almost seemed too good to be true. Em was wary. Not that she didn't trust Marie, but habits don't change overnight simply because Em was more comfortable. Marie would soon tire of her antics. But she was grateful for even a short reprieve.

Chapter 6
SWITZERLAND

THE FIRST WEEK SHE was in Oberhofen was spent familiarizing herself with her new home. She was finally able to meet Marie's husband, the elusive Daniel. A servant announced the approaching carriage, so Marie, carrying little Albert, and Em made their way outside to greet him.

He was shorter than Em would have thought. Marie spoke of him as if he were larger than life itself, though he was still taller than either of the women. His blond hair was worn in fashionably wild curls brushed forward.

His wide, easy grin as he approached informed her that it was Daniel long before he reached her. Not to mention the way Marie's face lit up when she saw him. Gently setting down young Albert, Marie moved her skirts just enough out of the way to allow her to run to his embrace. As they met, Daniel spun Marie around, holding her close. After a few rounds, he pried Marie off and set her down to give her a gentle kiss on the cheek, which Em was certain was only for propriety's sake.

In the meantime, Albert finally wandered close enough to cling to his father's leg in this adorable family reunion. After bending over to place a kiss on his son's head, Daniel took exaggerated steps as he carried the boy on his foot while making his way over to Em.

"And this must be the young maiden who was brave enough to run away from home at such a tender age!" his rich baritone voice contagiously chuckled.

Em shyly stepped forward, a blush on her cheeks as she held out her hand. He took it, placing a brotherly kiss on the back of her hand.

"It's nice to finally meet you," he continued. "From the way your mother spoke, I would have thought you to be a heathen, but I don't blame you for trying to get away from her grasp. I only met her once, but that was plenty for me, I assure you!"

"Darling, behave! Eulalie is a tortured soul with a good heart and you know it," Marie chided. Turning to Em, she continued, "Don't take a thing he says seriously, he doesn't know the meaning of the word!"

Picking up his petite wife, he bellowed, "I should say not! Not if I am to keep such an irrepressible wife!"

Marie giggled and squirmed to be set down, sneaking in one more kiss before turning to throw a wink at Em. Turning back to face her husband, Marie's blush deepened, highlighting her porcelain skin and she seemed to simply glow in her husband's presence. Em shifted her weight from one foot to the other as she waited for some kind of signal for…something. Anything else to do would have been helpful. The couple seemed to want a bit more privacy.

As if granting her wish, a bell rang, announcing it was time to change for supper. As Em watched the couple turn and walk hand in hand into the castle; Daniel continued to drag Albert on his leg. Em couldn't help but smile as she followed them inside. How fortunate that what had initially seemed an exile would end up in such a happy home.

EM SOON FOUND HERSELF comfortable in her new home. She had very little time to write to her mother, nor did she care to, but she made it a point to write to Albertine. If her sister couldn't be by her side physically, her letters would have to suffice. She wrote with glee about all the adventures she was having in the magnificent gardens and playing with Marie, occasionally Daniel when he was home, and baby Albert. On the occasion that Em did write to Eulalie, it was to report on the various therapies she was attempting with local doctors: the demands for her to showcase on command something she had no command over before declaring they cannot help if they do not know what was happening, the poking her for "observation," and the endless questions that Em didn't know the answers to. While Em did enjoy the recommendation for weekly massages, most doctors were not helpful.

Around mid-August, Em was writing her weekly letter to Albie in the gardens of the castle when she had a realization.

Has it really been a month since I arrived in Oberhofen? Albie, I simply love being here. Aside from not having you here with me, it is next to perfection. The gardens are among the best I have ever seen. I enjoy weekly massages—a recommendation from one of the doctors. Marie and little Albert have been such fun, and the stunning view of the lake and the Alps takes my breath away.

We had a bit of rain earlier this week, but when the clouds parted and the sun's rays shone through, oh, it seemed like I had landed in heaven. There seems to always be snow on top of the mountains, even in such warm weather. The blue lake water is surrounded by green meadows and darker green trees that rise up into fantastic mountains. Occasionally the trees break and you can see the grey rock underneath. The colors are simply divine, especially with the sun's rays shining down like the hand of God on the whole of it. The gardeners here make designs using the colors of various flowers to make images. It's very picturesque.

With all of this in mind, it is not perfect. I still have appearances of this malady that Mother hates so much. It certainly puts a damper on my day when I have to write and report that things are still happening. Although, now that I think of it, it has been significantly less than when I was at home.

Maybe there is something to this idea you mentioned of doing it less when I am not so nervous. While the malady is still unpredictable and different every day, I think the interruptions are once or twice per day, rather than the frequent occurrences back in France.

The change doesn't seem to be from any of the treatments by local doctors, at least not in my mind. I end up doing things more often before or after appointments than when I am simply enjoying my time around the castle grounds. The place itself seems to be the very therapy I needed. Could you not just move here with me? I would never want for anything again if such perfection existed.

I beg you not to tell mother. I'm not sure if such is really the case, and I would not want her hopes up should I be wrong or if it is a temporary state. I would hate to disappoint her. Again.

As Em's birthday neared, she wasn't sure if Marie knew about it and hesitated to bring it up. Unsure if she even wanted a *soirée*, she also did not want to appear a burden by demanding a celebration in her honor. Not to mention Maman's rules about keeping her hidden. Em tried not getting her hopes up knowing Daniel was away on business. A *soirée* must have a proper host, after all, so of course nothing would be planned. However, dear, sweet Marie had other plans.

Early one morning, the 22nd of August–Em's birthday to be exact–Marie shoved her way into Em's room, her arms carrying a small bundle close to her stomach. Tossing it at Em, she announced, "Em, darling, put these on."

"What…What are these? Is…is this men's clothing?"

"Indeed, we have a gardener about your size. Hurry, we have no time to waste!"

At the mention of the word "gardener" Em had a sudden flashback to the gardener of a certain size and age from what seemed like ages ago, but she quickly snapped back to reality.

"But…but why? What is all of this, Marie?"

"Oh, you and your questions! Just put them on! I have a surprise for you!" Marie chirped. Marie slipped out the door to allow Em some privacy.

Pulling out the britches of brown linen, Em was confused. Pants? What would Maman say? Is this a cruel joke? Yet, she trusted Marie. With confused excitement, she slipped off her dress and put on the britches. Em's first thought was how soft and well-worn the cloth was. How different it felt from wearing a skirt! Her second thought was that it didn't matter how soft it was, it was a bit too constricting for her taste. Stronger than her dislike, however, was her curiosity at Marie's odd behavior, so she pulled up the trousers and picked up the shirt to slip over her head.

As she continued to dress, pulling on the cream top, Em started in again loud enough to be heard through the door. "Am I now to become a servant to your every whim?" she shouted to her cousin. Marie's raucous laugh reverberated against the door.

"Something like that!" She tossed back.

A few moments later, Em emerged in the gardener's clothes with her hair tucked under a cap. To her gleeful surprise, Marie–beautiful, well-heeled, respectful Marie–had already donned a similar costume.

"You know, had you dressed like this first, there might have been fewer questions, Marie," Em remarked, still in shock at her high society cousin dressed like a groundskeeper.

"Nonsense, there would have been at least half a dozen more! I've never seen someone question every move as you do. You seem to have no trust for people, my dear. But don't you fret, you will understand soon enough."

Em couldn't help but smile. Her mother could not have known her hostess would be quite like this. If she had, she would never have permitted her to come, much less to spend so much time around this bold and daring woman.

"Marie, are you very good at keeping secrets?"

"Do you think I would be running around in gardener's clothing out in the open if I wasn't? Of course I am!"

"After our little adventure, whatever we are doing, may I sit with you and ask your thoughts on…about something?" Em asked.

"It is always an option for you to ask me anything, my dear, but for now, hush."

With that, the two ladies darted into the gardens. Marie was insistent on quiet as they walked to the edge of the castle's vineyard. Which of course meant that Em had to basically wring her hands off and bite her lip until it bled just to be sure there were no accidents.

At the far end of the vineyard, there was a gap in the stone wall, just wide enough that a small woman would be able to push through. The wall was thinner here, less than half what it usually was. Marie wiggled through first, followed by Em. First, her right leg, followed by her left, leaving her facing the stone wall she had stayed behind for the past months.

Funny how the wall looked just the same as from the inside, but it felt so different. Her nervousness melted into excitement and the need for an outburst melted away into a soft hiccup followed by a gasp. Letting go of her breath brought butterflies into her stomach, knowing she was finally outside the castle walls.

Turning around, Em gasped again out of surprise. A large head covered in reddish brown fur was just inches from her face. She threw herself back against the wall, just right of the crack she had come through. Marie giggled while the cow in front of Em slowly chewed her cud. "Do not mind her, she is always here along this wall. Come, let us be off on our adventure!"

Marie turned toward the town, but Em glanced at the castle one more time to be sure that escaping its walls–if only for a bit and dressed in a mad costume–was not a dream. The first rays of the morning came peeking over the horizon, bathing the castle in gold light. She marveled at how the light made everything a bit… more. The stone tower stood a bit brighter, the contrast with the dark brown roof was more striking, and the colorful accents stood out with a golden shine.

"Are you going to stand there all day, young man, or are you going to follow me?" Marie chuckled, breaking Em's reverie. Nervous but excited, Em didn't dare offend her gracious cousin. She turned on her heel and darted after Marie who had slowly begun walking away from the wall. After darting through trees and bushes of every size and shape, the glimpse of a village soon appeared.

"You've done this before?!" Em said. It was less a question and more of a statement.

"Perhaps," said Marie, forging her way over a giant rock. "But never with such good company. Look, we're here!"

Chapter 7
BIRTHDAY SURPRISE

OGETHER, THE TWO WOMEN walked until they arrived on what was obviously a main street. The town was just beginning to bustle around the square. Em could feel the life breathing into the very cobblestones beneath her feet. The warmth of the sun chased away the still night air. It was quiet, though there was movement all around. The only sounds were the gentle footsteps of people starting their day and the swishing of a few skirts. As more people joined the throng, the stillness was replaced with the daily in and out of hundreds of locals.

Em had never really been out in a public square before, she was considered too much of an embarrassment to the family name, so every movement seemed to catch her eye. Each man, woman, and child on the street in their everyday linens were moving in different directions. Every conversation from locals on the street at the same volume demanded to be heard. Smells of fresh baked bread, stale straw, flowers, grass, and something from the butcher shop nearby all entered her nose and she could barely tell them apart. Em stood frozen in place trying to take it all in at the exact same moment.

Marie slapped Em on her back, waking her from her reverie. In a booming voice, she exclaimed, "Come, lad! We have errands to run and chores to complete. Can't just laze around all day gawking like a child!"

Remembering her disguise, Em closed her mouth and simply nodded at her companion. Taking long steps, Marie strode confidently toward the bakery. "Half dozen of your finest tarts!" Marie called out the second she was inside the door.

Quietly, she turned to Em, "You will adore these! I have never seen the likes of them in all of France. No one quite makes them as Frederich here does, you'll see. They are called tarts, just like in France, but they are not so complex. The simplicity of the jam is divine!"

Turning back to the proprietor, Marie boomed that it was for "the missus at the castle" and that payment would be delivered in the usual manner. When Em asked what the usual manner was, Marie simply winked, replying, "Perks of titles and servants. I get to do the fun part, while they take care of the details for me."

The baker simply shook his head. "My wife will send up our apprentice tomorrow to collect, ma'am. I mean, sir." Throwing in a wink of his own, he turned back to a young couple admiring his pies. Em gawked until Marie pulled on her arm to drag her to the next shop.

Once free from the shop but before Marie could start chattering about their next stops, Em blurted, "He recognized us! What will we do? Will he tell?"

Marie simply chuckled. "Of course he did. I see Frederich at least once per week. He knows my little game. It's much more fun to go about this way than with an entourage, don't you think? Don't you fret; he will keep our secret. He'd lose his best customer if he told a soul."

Em felt the now familiar tug on her arm as they wandered into a shop with tiny boxes in the window. Marie pulled Em close enough to whisper, "This shop owner does not know me, this is a special treat, just for your birthday. Just remember that you are a young man, understood? Don't blow our disguise. We are looking for a gift for the young miss visiting the castle. Wait until you see what a delight these are!"

Boldly, Marie went directly to the owner of the shop and asked for his recommendations. Holding up one finger and with a knowing smile, he pulled out a small wooden box. It was about the width of a piece of paper, though not so long or very tall. The top was painted with an oval of vines and small white chamomile flowers. Other than that, the design was fairly simple with just a small clasp on the front.

Em was unsure if it was a folding writing box for traveling or a small jewelry box. She didn't dare voice her question. Her voice was much more decidedly feminine, and she lacked Marie's practice to change it. Instead, her eyes almost bulged out of her head as the gentleman behind the counter gently lifted the lid.

Before she could see inside, she heard a simple, beautiful tune. Em let out a small gasp of surprise when she saw the small metal tube rotating as the source of the music. She instantly fell in love with it. What a treasure! To have something like this would certainly help calm her nerves. To have music anytime one wished!

In the background, Em could hear Marie ask the shopkeeper, "This is Mozart, correct? Such a gifted composer! The lady of Oberhofen will pay the bill for this one." Her entire focus remained on the spinning cylinder and the sonata that emerged from the tiny box.

Arrangements were made for it to be wrapped and sent to the castle and payment to be received there. Em's heart dropped a little when the box was shut, yet she was in awe that she was to be the recipient of such a gift! Now her inability to speak was due to shock and gratitude more than from fear. This might just be the best birthday gift she had ever received.

Thus went the entire morning. Marie bursting into places demanding goods from various eateries and shops, claiming to be on an errand "for the missus at the castle" anytime she was questioned. Most didn't mind as long as she was able to pay.

It wasn't until about midday when Em noticed the itch starting in the back of her throat. There was no water handy to try to quelch the itch. It was one of her favorite tricks at home to avoid her obscene tongue. Stopping in her tracks, Em grabbed Marie by the hand, while covering her mouth with the other.

"Are you ill?" Marie inquired with concern.

How Marie still managed to stay in character was beyond comprehension. Shaking her head, Em begged with wide eyes to find someplace away from the bustle of the streets. However, Marie seemed oblivious to her request and pulled her forward. After a few steps, Em had to stop again, this time dropping Marie's hand in favor of clutching her stomach which was quickly tying itself into knots.

Moving in close, Marie whispered, "Really darling, are you ok? We have to keep moving, we are attracting unwanted attention like this."

Em wanted to explain, but was afraid of uncovering her mouth for what might emerge. Yet she was also unable to move, completely paralyzed by her fear. She doubled over to increase the pressure on her stomach to keep her body in place.

Suddenly, her neck tensed and her head rolled to the right, moving her hand away from her mouth and resting the hand on her cheek. She felt a sudden release, which then forced out an even stronger, "*poutain!*"

Out of sheer horror, Em jumped up and began running, buildings and trees on both sides of the street becoming a blur through her tears. "Wait! Come back! Turn around!" Marie called as she gave chase. This only made Em run faster, losing Marie as she rounded an inn several feet ahead of her. She didn't care where she was running, she just had to get away. Em blinked away more tears as she made another turn. Then another. She only slowed when she began gasping for air to fill her burning lungs. As she came to a stop, her shoulder began jerking forward as her malady began to take control of her body.

Slowing to accommodate the beast inside of her, Em allowed her body to convulse as she finally began to take in her surroundings. It looked exactly the same as the square, but the buildings were homes instead of shops. The busy streets were full of people now, and Em could find no distinguishing landmarks. Her embarrassment quickly turned to fraught nerves when she realized she had just run away from the only person she knew in the entire country. A country which she had never been to.

Em plopped to the ground, unsure what to do next. She recognized mostly German spoken by those around her, but nothing was familiar to her. Surely, someone must speak French? The border of France wasn't too far away. Though they were closer to Germany, so it did make sense.

The idea of speaking to anyone quickly disappeared when her shoulders began their usual dance. She felt her right side slowly creep up to her ear until her head rested on her own shoulder. *My own shoulder isn't near as comforting as another's.* Rolling her eyes, Em stretched the muscles that continuously wanted to tighten. As Em tried to focus on her next course of action, her mind kept returning to Mozart's Piano Sonata No. 11 in A. She didn't even notice her leg bouncing, keeping time with the music as she continued to stretch.

It wasn't long before the stares began. A glance over the shoulder as they passed. A craned neck around a mother's skirt. Em was so focused on finding her way back to Oberhafen or to Marie, she didn't notice. A little girl around six years of age stopped as her mother continued walking. She stared blatantly at Em's movements.

The little girl took a cautious step closer to Em. *"Geht es dir gut?"* (Are you ok?) Her mother returned and grabbed her hand, but the little girl wouldn't budge. "Ach! Come, we are late!"

"But mama, what's wrong with him?"

Throwing down a few spare coins, the mother tried once again to pull her daughter away to their destination. "We do not have time for this, let's go!"

Em stopped moving, suddenly aware of her surroundings. The Sonata in her mind continued, but Em attempted to listen to the conversation happening in front of her. She was unsure what to do. They were speaking German, and hers wasn't the best. Her studies leaned toward the Russian language, and she doubted that was spoken here.

She obviously already had their attention. This could be a lifeline for her. She could at least try. *"Parlez-vous français?"*

The mother and daughter turned to face Em as she tried to control her face. She began to itch, but she refused to let it show. She figured her best chance was to appear normal. Otherwise, all she would receive was the few coins tossed at her feet and they would be off.

The turning was a good sign. Maybe they could help. "Oberhofen? *Quel chemin pour le château d'Oberhofen?"*

Tugging on her mother's skirts, the little girl exclaimed, *"Château! Schloss!* I know this word! He wants to see the castle!"

Though she didn't understand much of the child's exclamations, she heard her repeat *château.* And of course, anyone would have recognized it when she said "Oberhofen." Relieved, Em could only nod. With a quizzical look, the mother pointed to her left. Turning, Em could see the lake. Of course! The castle was on the shores of the lake. Embarrassed, Em turned to nod her thanks. She sheepishly headed back toward the castle. She knew the castle was on the lake. She kicked and scolded herself the entire walk.

As she grew closer, her frustration with herself took a back seat to try and remember how Marie had snuck off the grounds to begin with. She couldn't just waltz back in the front entrance. Marie was supposed to guide her back, so she had no recollection of where the gap in the fence was, either. Foolish, irresponsible girl.

Deep in her own thoughts, Em didn't notice the lady dressed as a servant approaching from the side. Marie was cautious in her approach, wanting to ensure it was really Em before revealing herself. When Marie was sure, she quickly closed the gap between them, clutching Em's arm and waking her from her dream walk.

Shocked by the sudden leap into reality, Em saw only the servant's clothing and gave a shout of surprise. Several heads popped out of shop windows, and a baker even stepped outside to make sure Em was ok. He was placated upon seeing the two embrace and returned to his wares.

"Where have you been, Em?" Marie's voice whispered. "I have been looking everywhere for you! Also, how are you so fast?"

"Oh, I didn't recognize you! I am so sorry, I was not thinking at all! I can't believe I acted so foolishly. I completely ruined the adventure. I apologize for spoiling all the fun you had planned..."

"Em darling, hush! First of all, I'm just glad you are safe and that we were reunited! Secondly, we really must come up with a plan for a meeting spot should we be separated again."

"Again? You mean, you are willing to risk another outing with me? But…"

Em couldn't seem to find the words to gain any kind of understanding of the situation. Surely, there must be some kind of punishment for her actions? Maman would be furious when she found out Em had not only left the castle but gotten herself lost. What a catastrophe.

Surely, she would no longer be permitted such freedoms as this. Em was used to this scenario. Having such freedoms was unnerving in a way. She was always so nervous, wondering when an episode would occur. Not going out meant she couldn't stress over it. Em hung her head as she responded, "No. Maman wouldn't approve. There should be no more outings."

"What on earth do you mean, child? Next time we shall just have a better plan. Or avoid running away altogether? Really, darling, the language among the common folk is much more casual than that of nobility. Such a word here or there doesn't matter. You would have been fine. No need to run off. But just in case, let's set a plan of where to meet, or at least teach you a few basic German phrases. Goodness, you had me so worried!"

"I think I'd like to lie down for a bit. May we head back to the *château*?"

"But of course! You poor thing! There will be a meal prepared for you when you awake. Let's get you home."

Em paid no attention to the scenery, making no attempts to memorize the area, as Marie had suggested. Rather, she composed several drafts of a letter to Maman in her head. None of them seemed to show any type of progress, and all Em could do was miss her Albie, their tree, and the lush gardens surrounding her home. She had started to forget that the Swiss Republic, as lovely as it was, was not home. Life may have been better at Oberhofen, but she wondered if she was even deserving of anything better than a life hidden in shadow. She was a hopeless case. Marie spoke of getting her home, and Em planned on doing just that.

Chapter 8
MEETING DR. ITARD

HOW IS IT POSSIBLE? After all those letters I've sent to Maman complaining about my time here, the letters I receive back sound like I had not mentioned anything at all! In fact, Maman actually sounds loving and doting! Why? Why isn't even Albie coming to my rescue? To my dear sister's credit, she does sympathize, but that makes me only miss her more. The talks of the gardens and her shopping trips, as well as what the servants are cooking up both at dinner and in their busy lives makes me long for France so much I can barely stand it. And yet, to give my cousin credit, she has not turned her back on me. When I cursed in front of the fire she acted as if she hadn't heard anything. When I spit on the piano keys, she took a rag and wiped them. Herself no less! At dinner, when I threw a spoon, she threw a fork and even laughed, yelling to the confused servants, "At least no one threw a knife!"

Yesterday I awoke to a new set of gardening clothes on my bed, but I declined. I just couldn't take a chance. Marie understood, and instead spent the morning teaching me a few basic German phrases in case I get lost again, but German is far more complicated than French and so much more rough sounding.

Marie does, indeed, share so many of Albie's qualities, I sometimes feel like she's my sister. But of course, no one could replace Albie. Dear, darling, precious Albie. Come to think of it, I have not heard from her lately! I pray it's just because she's busy prepping for the upcoming social season.

I wonder if she'll take advantage of the light lavender she so admired on Countess Angelique? I hope she won't pick up with Marquis Sévigné. He is handsome as a stallion, indeed, but my sister has the unconquerable spirit of a wild filly, and I hate to see her tamed, even if she does have to carry on the family name. Heaven forbid I produce an heir!

Oh, this wretched curse. If my life were, truly, a fairy tale, the curse might be broken. But until then, I shall carry on. After all, my many doctors need employment! While Albie has dances to perform, I have remedies to perform. Both are challenging, and both promise no positive results, but sincere effort is required.

WITH NO SUPPORT FROM anyone about returning to France, despite her pleas, Em turned all her focus into finding a cure. "It's the only way I even have a chance," she'd remind herself first thing every morning. Sadly, none of the visits from the various doctors had been very productive.

One doctor, a stout man with a gray mustache that reminded her of a walrus in spectacles, demanded she perform her outbursts. "Flail your arms!" he shouted. "Make a noise! Throw something across the room!!" He spoke–more like barked–so quickly Em couldn't keep up. Luckily, Marie was there to translate. At the last command she felt her cheeks turn red. "Curse if you must!" Never had Em wanted to curse simply to be rude, but she declined. "I cannot perform on command, Doctor," she said in fledgling German.

"*Dieses Mädchen ist ein Idiot!*" the doctor sputtered. It translated to "This girl is an idiot."

"What did he say?" Em inquired of Marie.

Marie smiled and responded, "He said, 'This girl is trying.'"

Em smiled also as the bumbling doctor packed his bags and

wiped his brow with Em's handkerchief. When all of the shiny, metal poking sticks were safely placed in his leather physician's bag, Em drew a breath of relief.

Later that week a young doctor, thin with feminine mannerisms, looked at her flatly and said, "It must be some kind of muscle spasm if there was no control." He prescribed a new type of medicine called morphine, but either the dosage was too high and she slept for several days, or the dosage was too low and had no effect. There was no happy medium to be found.

On the other side of the spectrum were the truly enjoyable visits. Some doctors believed that relaxation was the way to cure her ailment. Deep breathing exercises, wine with every meal, long walks around the property, extra sleep. The massages were by far her favorite. However, even if she wasn't particularly anxious, movements and words burst forth with reckless abandon and shame for Em.

Em's next letter to Albie was less hopeful. "I fear nothing is working," she wrote, her handwriting shaking with frustration. "I am beginning to wonder if Maman is wasting her money. What is the point of me being here at all if there's no cure?"

Em put down the quill with a start. What she had hoped wasn't true appeared to be as clear as day. Maman had, indeed, exiled her. Maman's happy attitude in previous letters was because she did not expect Em to return. Em would simply no longer be her problem and shifted the shame to Marie. She was never going to make it home. Em wasn't sure if she was sadder because there was no hope for her movements or because her mother didn't want her.

The next morning at breakfast, Marie found Em with her face in her hands, her tea cold. "Chin up, Cousin!" she trilled. "Have you ever heard of the wild boy that was found? He was this—"

"Yes, Marie. I have heard of him. Just like me, he was an outcast from society."

"I see, you know of him!" Marie smiled, refusing to acknowledge Em's mood. "Then you must have heard of the doctor that took him under his wing? How much he helped him?"

Em looked up. Her cousin never failed to rouse her spirits.

"His name is Dr. Itard. My brother served with him during the revolution," Marie continued. "Your mother and I have discussed him in our letters. She has sent him here to see you and should be here in the next few days."

"My mother doesn't care about me—"

"Nonsense!" Marie interjected. "Now, I know you aren't a fan of all of these visits; I don't blame you. However, it surely must give you some kind of hope to know that they haven't given up on you. I'm certain one of them will discover what ails you. Maybe he will be the one."

Em's shoulder began to twitch, causing pain up and down her right side. "Or maybe not!" Em cried, "Things seem to get so much worse, not better."

"We just haven't found the right doctor yet—"

"—NO!" Em shouted louder than she meant to. Baby Albert started to cry. "I'm sorry…I didn't mean to startle him. I just…I feel like everything gets so much worse when I see them, not better!"

"I can only imagine your frustration, but your mother has already sent him–and he's coming from so far away."

"These doctors–most are so rude and intrusive. If they aren't poking me with instruments, they are touching me as I lie there at their every whim, as if I am an object to be toyed with and—"

"Then you must develop more patience!" Marie forcefully interjected. Normally so gentle spoken, this surprised Em. She sat back in her chair, arms folded, but listened.

"Truth be told, I have never interacted with him personally. I've heard stories of him from the war, but those situations never really bring out the best from men, do they? So, I can't promise much…"

Em shook her head and let out a sigh.

"But…I'm sure he has improved with time and as his station has increased. He is apparently becoming quite well known in the medical profession, especially in regards to his work with the savage boy. I wonder what became of that child."

Em did not respond, other than to say, "You have been good to me, Cousin. I will try to remain hopeful, but I cannot promise."

"That is all I ask," Marie said before picking up Albert and exiting the room.

Em became a bit more sullen over the next few days. While she was able to gain more control of her vocal chords, she twitched and jerked uncontrollably for much of the time she awaited the visit from Dr. Itard. Not wanting to damage the lovely castle or shame the lady of the residence, Em confined herself to her room until his arrival. Her greatest joy was the stunning view of the Alps beyond the lake. It was the one thing she never tired of. Something about its stillness and beauty soothed her as if speaking to her subconscious mind to calm down.

When Dr. Itard finally arrived, Em was called down to tea with him and Marie. As the servants put a tea cup in front of him the doctor shunned it away. "So, what is it like, when you have these episodes? Tell me every detail you can think of."

His directness was startling. No exam. No small talk with Marie. Just right to the point. Plus, she wasn't used to being asked questions. It was as if she actually existed as a person, not just a case to be studied.

Em was wringing her hands, barely able to maintain control of herself as she responded to his question. "Well, sometimes, there is an itch in my hands before they fly uncontrollably. Other times, I simply feel a tightening, followed by a release by spasmodic movements that I can't stop. The worst is the words. I am fully aware of the situation as it is happening, but there is no sensation before some words fly out of my mouth. They are vile words that I do not dare repeat."

As the conversation carried on, Marie would occasionally add her observations, Dr. Itard would ask more questions, and Em would answer. While the visit was relatively painless, Em was relieved when it was over. The doctor was unable to stay very long due to other pressing engagements back in Paris.

"When you return home, please send a post to notify me. I will need a few more visits and more research to know what really ails you."

"Well, is there any advice you might leave before you go? Any thoughts or insights? Please, give me something, the days become unbearable when these episodes expand throughout the course of the day. Am I just like the savage child, as they say?"

"My dear, I wish I had more to give you. However, I have seen no incident and am unsure what the root could be. When I first heard of your condition, I wondered how similar you would be to young Victor when he first arrived in my care. All I have seen of you shows the elegance of your upbringing. You hear and speak well, you are polite and thoughtful in your responses. Quite the opposite of Victor. Such a woman would never have outbursts without something very serious going on. I will have to defer any kind of response until we are able to meet again with more in-depth communication and observation."

Deflated, Em rose to bid the man *adieu* as he left to conclude his business in the Swiss Confederation and return to Paris. As soon as the ladies were left to themselves, Em leaned over to Marie with a crumpling sigh. "Marie, I begin to fear I shall never return home."

Embracing the girl, Marie responded, "Well, first of all, it has not been very long. You can't expect to undo a lifetime of disease instantly, even if we did know what was causing it. We first have to figure out what it is, my dear. Then move on to the healing process. Maybe there is another answer to be found during your stay here."

Em looked up at her cousin, still in awe by the love and support she constantly provided her. "Do you really think so?"

"I do, Cousin. Personally, if life doesn't give me answers, it can usually at least provide me with some joy. Methinks it might be time for another outing, my dear. What do you say?"

Em welcomed the distraction from the latest doctor's visit and rushed up the stairs to change her clothes. However, Marie's words echoed through her head in the weeks that followed. She continued her massages and spa treatments, seeking every form of respite she could find.

It was early October when Em was sitting in her room pretending to work on some stitching and trying not to think about yet another doctor's visit that afternoon. There was a soft knock on the door and Em sighed as she put down her stitching. "I'll be down for tea in a moment." As she stood to find a pair of gloves for her meeting, the door opened.

Em stiffened as footsteps came slowly nearer. The servants never entered her quarters. Marie and little Albert were much more boisterous upon entering. Bending to pick her gloves off the bed, Em tried to subtly glance over her shoulder to see a shawl being removed from a shoulder and the hem of an ornately detailed cotton day gown. It looked familiar, but before Em could place the gown, a pair of hands were on her shoulders, twirling her around.

Chapter 9
THE VISITOR

What a thrill! My dear Albertine has arrived in Oberhofen castle for a visit! Now that she is seventeen, Maman thought it appropriate for her to tour various areas throughout Europe and Albie made a detour to come see me. Sometimes I forget the power she has as Papa's heir. I cried when I saw her, I have missed her so. She will only be here a few weeks before continuing her tour of the continent. Her stop will be a marvelous birthday gift! It will likely be the only celebration I have while I am here.

Oh, this has done so much good for my soul. I was beginning to wonder if I would ever see my family again.

With the thrill of my sister the days seem to be running together, together in a flurry of activity. The weeks are only marked by our Sunday services. There is such an increase in joy and levity—I can't express it enough. My sister—my everything! And yet, this entry couldn't be complete without a compliment to my cousin as well. Marie makes our time inside the castle so much fun and always has some new game up her sleeve, whether indoors or out in the gardens—plus Albert (who is starting to walk) is truly a delight. Albie adores babies, and she swears she doesn't mind passing the time indoors because of him. Having Albie here makes my life feel as close to perfect as it may ever get.

Albie was quick to take control and demanded all of Em's appointments with doctors be canceled by the end of her second week. "You are doing so well from what I can tell, even my own health seems to be improving a bit," Albie proclaimed over breakfast, her cheeks flushed, eyes shining, from playing Ring Around the Rosie with Albert. "You can figure out what doctors are even helping later, but I want to be with you for every possible second I am here!"

"I won't complain!" Em said, relaxing a bit into her chair.

Albie put down her tea. "Come! I can't wait a moment longer. You must show me around the *château* and the gardens. Maman told me that you are not to leave the grounds, so I'm sure you know every inch of this place by now."

"You'd think," Em said, taking her sister's hand and leading her toward the grand hall. "And yet, I have not. Every day I seem to discover a new path, a new fountain. Just before you arrived, I discovered an apple tree with the most exquisite flavor. The cooks weren't happy with me, but my stomach was delighted! They weren't mad long–they surprised me with an apple tart on my birthday."

Albie stopped when they reached an intricately carved wooden bench tucked away into an alcove, her eyes large and sad. "I'm so sorry I wasn't here in time for your birthday. The carriage was delayed. Also, I accidentally left your gift at home. You'll have something to look forward to when you return to us."

Em was taken aback at the idea of going home again. It was almost too good to be true. She tucked the hope deep in her heart to not lose the beautiful moment in the present with her sister. "The best gift I received is you," Em said, reassuring Albie the best she could. "I mean it! Shall we explore some more?" she added, to which Albie finally smiled.

As Em slowly walked Albie from room to room, her sister's chatter continued as she fawned over every vase, piece of art, curtain, bedspread and more in each room at Oberhofen.

Albie's eyes lit up in the nursery where she spotted Albert waking up from his nap, grinning and drooling with the joy of seeing his new friend. After that, with the nanny's assistance, Albert followed behind them, babbling and spitting with joy. Marie, who they found in the sewing room, joined in on the tour, answering all of Albie's questions.

"What lake is that?" she'd pointed from a guest room.

"How do you hire the servants for that grand kitchen?"

"What are some other castles around Lake Thun?"

Marie was the ever-patient tour guide, sharing detailed facts about her home and country. Many questions Em had not even considered herself and she learned almost as much as Albie did on the tour.

"I didn't realize there were four other castles on the lake!" Em said, surprised at how much smaller her cousin's estate truly was.

"Yes, this is one of many. With all of the mountains, there is not as much land to spare for sprawling estates. I know it is nothing compared to France, but the castles here are every bit as beautiful in their own way. And so sturdy! The castle walls are over six feet thick!"

Em and Albie looked up, as confused as if their cousin had just spoken in a foreign language.

"Oh, that's right, France uses a different system. It's metric, yes?" Marie asked, always eager to have her cousins understand and be comfortable.

The girls nodded, to which Marie said, "I don't know why France felt the need to be different from the rest of the world, it's only used there. I can only imagine it's because that silly revolution had to turn everything on its head!"

Em and Albie chuckled. Marie was such a good sport, as well as earnest. Her brow wrinkled in concentration. "I think it's about two meters?"

Albie was shocked, "My goodness, are you sure? That's taller than a man!"

"Yes, the walls are thicker than a man is tall."

"What a fortress!" Albie continued, "I suddenly feel so much safer here."

"I feel the same! And here I thought it was because of how welcoming you have been, Marie!" countered Em.

"Oh, you flatter me, my dear." By this point they had walked almost the whole of the castle, both bottom floors, skipping the third and fifth levels of bedrooms, and stopped in front of Albie's bedroom on the fourth level. Marie opened the door and gestured inside as she asked, "What do you say about getting changed?"

"Oh yes, let's!" Em said, a knowing glint in her eye, also gesturing to Albie's room. Albie, however, remained standing in the hall, a confused expression on her face. "Isn't it a bit early to change for dinner?"

"I'm sorry to report that you used up all your questions on the tour!" Marie retorted, before spinning on her heel and whisking away. "Chop chop! We don't want to defy our cousin, do we?" Em playfully pushed Albie inside and shut the door, dashing to her own room to change.

When Em finished, she returned to Albie's room just as Marie threw a round pile of clothes through the doorway, calling, "These should be about your size! Em and I will meet you here in five minutes!"

Albie started to protest, "I brought things with me, you don't have to…Marie, what are these…Marie!"

Em slipped into the room, eyes shining as she watched Albie unroll the bundle. Glancing up from the packet, Albie gave a shout and hid before she heard Em's giggle coming from the intruder. Em gave a little twirl, "How do you like the new look?" Marie slipped into the room moments later as Albie finally gathered her senses.

"Wait until you see what is in store, my dears! We are all in for a treat!"

The trio snuck through the wall right as the fireworks began and emerged into a cacophony of sound and people, none taking notice of what they assumed were servants sneaking out for the festival. Ernestine and Albertine stopped as they stared at the effects of the light display over the waters of Lake Thun.

A small gasp escaped Em's parted lips. She wasn't sure if it was natural awe or her malady, but it didn't seem to matter at that moment. Something about the fireworks was familiar in a way. The uncontrollable power behind each explosion, the anticipation following the boom of sound before the marvel of light was so similar in a way to the itch in her own body that preceded the spasms. The doctors were going to think she was crazy if she explained her disease at all like this magnificent light display.

A few bursts later, Marie snapped them out of their reverie. "We could have done this much inside! We didn't change just to sneak out of the wall, let's go catch the festivities!"

Music flowed through the streets, getting thicker as they got closer to the town square, with several bands combining strings and reeds. Em knew the instruments but had no idea they were capable of such sound! Singers were bouncing their voices in ways the pair from France had never before heard. Young women danced with brightly colored ribbons matching their brightly colored skirts and floral embroidery on white blouses. Men clapped and cheered in their best white shirt, dark slacks, and jewel-toned waistcoats left open.

Em knew they were trying to blend in, but simply couldn't help her wide eyes trying to take in everything at once. The simple joy of each person as they laughed and bounced in time with the music, weaving in and out of the crowds was contagious. She couldn't understand a word that was sung; it was all in German. Yet the streets flowed with something that was simply unique to the Swiss Alps. Leaning to Marie, Em had to shout to be heard, "What is this music? How do they sing like that?"

"It's called yodeling, but I have no idea how they do it. It's fascinating, isn't it?!"

Em could only nod in response as she continued to absorb the scene through all of her senses. There were several stores and booths selling heavenly pastries and the trio simply had to sample each booth's specialty. Once, she bumped into a young man who from behind reminded her of a certain gardener back in France. A blush ran up her cheeks as the young man turned around. He looked right past Em and grabbed the hand of a young maid just behind her.

Albie and Em were unfamiliar with the music, but they couldn't help keeping time with their feet. Albie was even brave enough to stand at the edge of a ring surrounding some traditional dancers and imitating their movements. Em laughed at her sister's attempts, while Marie clapped along with the tune. Surrounded by laughter, music, food, and the warmth of hundreds of bodies lining the street, Em was sure she had never experienced a more perfect day.

It wasn't until the next morning that Em realized she didn't have a single intrusion from her malady the evening before. She was thrilled by this development until that afternoon while taking her daily walk around the grounds. In an ironic twist, she had just begun to tell Albie about the insight from the night before when she experienced a squeak, almost like a hiccup. Her walking slowed to a stop as she tried to catch her breath. She then proceeded into a poor, high-pitched imitation of the singers from the night before.

It only happened for a second or two, but it left her breathless. Seeing her sister's dismay, Albie quickly spoke before Em could, "Well, I see someone is still enjoying the festivities! At least you came to share, but I do think you will need a bit more practice to fit in with the native singers."

Em gave a slight laugh, remembering the joy of the night before. Shaking her head, Em conceded, "It would take years to come close, but I've never had the ear for music that you have."

Without a word, Albertine embraced her sister, giving her an occasional pat of reassurance as tears began to freefall. Neither had the words for much more. After the tears ran out, the pair continued their walk in silence, full of their own thoughts. Em's despairing, Albie's searching for solutions to cheer her sister.

Over the next week, the yodeling impressions were mixed in with an increasing number of inappropriate words and phrases as well as increased tenseness and jerking from her shoulders. Later in the week a new compulsory kicking began. Em spent long periods clutching her arms and rocking back and forth in her chair trying to keep control of her own body. It was decided that Albie would cut her stay in Oberhofen short and continue her tour of European countries and cultures while Em resumed her treatments. Em didn't even trust herself to give Albie a hug or see her off at the end of her stay.

After Albie's departure, Em's weekly massages began again, which seemed to help reduce the tension and physical movements.

But the yodeling and upsetting phrases continued. She was inconsolable with the departure of her sister. Her condition seemed to worsen as she grew increasingly lethargic, spending long hours–sometimes even days–in her room.

Marie could only handle this attitude for about a week. "Come now, Em, you can't spend all of your time in your room. Little Albert misses you so! Daniel will be home this evening and we expect you at the table to dine, no more solitary meals, do you hear me?"

Sighing, Em pulled herself up to sit on her bed rather than spread out, face down as she had been. "I know you are right, Marie, but knowing and feeling are two very different things, I'm learning. I can't quite seem to make myself do much and I apologize for being such a slovenly guest. I'll be down to dine, but please don't ask more of me than that right now. I'm so ashamed and I miss Albie so. Sometimes, this malady just feels so hopeless. I fear you may have taken on more than you bargained for, I'm not sure Maman will ever allow me home at this rate."

Marie gently set herself down next to Em, "Then that is her loss and our gain. We will keep you here the rest of your life if you wish, but I'll wager that you would prefer to be home in France before long. Especially once you realize that you aren't actually ill. I do not know what this malady is, but I do know that aside from these movements and vocalizations, you are perfectly healthy. You are young and have your whole life ahead of you. I hope you are able to create a life you at least enjoy living."

She rose and as she reached the doorway, turned back to Em, putting her hand on the doorframe. "Just think about it, hmm? We'll see you tonight."

Chapter 10
LETTER FROM MAMAN

*C*HÉRE MAMAN,

What a wonderful surprise it has been to have my sister here this week! I thank you for your thoughtfulness! Oberhofen does not have quite the expanse of gardens that we have at home, but we still enjoy our time out in the sunshine. Sometimes I wonder if the sunshine is helping, then wonder if I am imagining things. The malady seems to ebb and flow like the tide, though not as frequent, obviously.

Albie thinks I am getting better. Well, at least she thought so until she discovered that I occasionally lose control of my fork during mealtimes. The doctors have not seen anything that provides consistent results, just a temporary relief. I am still seeing several doctors, though none can seem to agree.

Dr. Andros is convinced I am simply rebelling against my role in society as a woman and marriage would be the most suitable cure, as well as an increased social life. Dr. Klausner agrees with you that I should be kept out of society and my desire for socialization will make me behave. Dr. Shweizer prescribes massages and relaxation techniques, which I do enjoy. I find that my episodes are lessened during these massages, but do still happen on occasion, as he thought they would.

You should know I'm no longer seeing Dr. Wuethrich. Things got significantly worse when he was around and during any treatments he recommended. He was simply awful, Maman! Not only was he incredibly rude, his only course of action was some kind of surgery and the risks were many. One example he gave as a risk was paralysis! I could not bear it and he seemed to make things worse. His techniques seem torturous and inhumane.

I wish things looked better and I apologize for the lack of progress. I wish I was doing better; I truly do! I miss you and Albie and I miss being home. I pray nightly for a cure and to return to you soon. Please continue to pray for me at chapel each day. Maybe I can receive a miracle. Give my love to the family.

As Em's stay at Oberhofen changed from the warmth of summer to the brightly colored fall and into the still-white winter, Em's letters to Maman continued to grow less frequent, and she found there to be no cure for her malady. However, she never grew tired of the beauty that surrounded her and enjoyed the comradeship of the Lady and little Lord of the castle. She never saw much of Daniel, his business often having him away from home weeks or even months at a time. It made the women closer in their intimate discussions of life, running a castle, and relationships. Slowly, the weight of the expectation of returning to Guermantes disappeared. Em determined she must write to invite Albie to come visit again.

By the following spring, before she had the chance to write Albie, Em received a letter from Maman:

My darling Ernestine, Marie tells me you are making wonderful progress with your condition! She speaks highly of your help with little Albert, as well as how charming you are to be around. She tells me you have managed to reduce your episodes greatly with hardly any notice of your condition. I am quite proud of all you have accomplished in your year away. I am quite thrilled and cannot wait to see your progress in person!

We miss you greatly around the castle and wish for your return. Now that you have accomplished what you have set out to do, we can arrange for travel accommodations. I do not wish to encroach upon any engagements you have set, so please write quickly and tell me when you plan to return.

Em was still in shock from the letter when she arrived for the evening meal. Marie noticed that something was out of sorts and prompted the conversation, "What is the matter, my dear? Have you received bad news from home? I surely hope not, but your countenance is so changed this evening!"

"No, nothing is the matter, thank you for asking. Maman says she has heard my condition has greatly improved and that she wishes me home soon to see for herself. I had almost quite forgotten about the possibility of returning. I…I'm almost not sure I want to."

"Oh dear! I have become quite accustomed to your companionship as well." Her eyes welled up with tears.

"Am I not enough for you?" her husband joked, looking up from his book.

"Sadly, no," Marie scoffed back. "But we'll be busy again soon enough." She patted her belly, a knowing smile in her eye. She then turned back to Em who had gotten quite used to the warm affection between Marie and her husband.

"I shall miss you both," Em said.

Marie replied, "Hopefully that won't be the case. You are always welcome at Oberhofen and I would expect nothing less than frequent visits. But for now, we should arrange your travel plans accordingly."

Em nodded in agreement, watching Marie flutter about like a bird, her mind already a whirling dervish. "Shall we make it after your weekly spa treatments and massages? I know how much you love those. We must make the most of what little time you have left here."

Letters were sent to Maman and Albie, arrangements were made, and adventures increased. Em purchased gifts for all of her family members and said her goodbyes to the villagers whose shops she frequented. She purchased a watch for her stepfather, chocolates for the younger siblings, a cuckoo clock for Albie (she was endlessly entertained by them during her stay), and some embroidered handkerchiefs for Maman.

More than once, Em had to remember she would see Albie again to feign excitement about leaving Oberhofen. This place had quickly become more of a home than the one she grew up in.

The morning of Em's departure came quickly. Daniel had said his farewells the week prior due to another business trip, so it was only Marie and little Albert in the courtyard to see her off as the servants loaded the carriage.

As they walked the short distance to the carriage, Marie broke the silence hanging in the air. "Em, darling, it really has been such a pleasure to have you here. I can't tell you how good it was for me to have you around, especially as often as my sweet husband is away. I'm going to miss you so!"

"Oh Marie, I can't tell you how much I've needed you in my life and I am oh so glad for the time we have spent together, I will truly cherish it. As evidence, may I tell you something in confidence? I don't want to go. If I could have Albie here, I would make this my home for always. I'm so scared to face Maman again."

"Oh, sweet child. As much as I would love to keep you here, you judge your mother too harshly. She has been through many hard things herself. I'm sure one day you both will be able to look back and laugh at this time of quarrelling as pure folly!"

"I'm glad someone has confidence in my future, for it looks very bleak to me. Even if I do manage to keep this malady under control. I would receive a lashing if Maman caught me sneaking out, even if I did know my way around the town. You have certainly spoiled me for life in the *château*."

"Nonsense. You are so close to Paris and there is so much to experience there! I daresay your mother would love to join you."

"It seems we are destined to disagree, Marie. Besides, I must be going soon, and I'd rather leave with kind words on our lips."

"How right you are, child. Be sure to write and let me know how you are from time to time. I shall need the adult conversation, knowing I will soon be simply surrounded by children!"

"Little Albert is hardly 'being surrounded by children'... Wait, do you mean??"

Marie nodded, grinning emphatically. "I was going to include it in my first letter when I've seen a doctor, but I'm pretty sure there will be another little one running around Oberhofen soon. Daniel and I discussed the possibility before he left and we were wondering if we could name the child after you? Or at the very least making you godmother?"

It took a moment for Em to find her manners and close her gaping mouth. "Are you sure? Me? I would be a complete dunce to deny you your request if you are certain, but I can't help but question your sanity!"

"Nonsense, my dear. You have been very much a part of this family for the past year, and it would be silly of us to deny that connection we have with you. Not to mention how much you have kept me sane with so much time by myself around the castle. Daniel has promised to start cutting back on trips he must take himself because he has seen how much I've loved having you around. I really am going to miss you!"

The pair embraced while tears threatened to escape from Em's eyes. As they separated, Em pulled out her handkerchief to dab at her eyes, exclaiming, "For heaven's sake, I'll never leave at this rate! I really must be going or I will never leave!"

Marie responded, "I promise to write, and often! Please be sure to return the favor!"

The carriage hitched forward, making Em grab hold of her hat as they pulled out of the iron gates and headed back to France.

ALMOST BEFORE THE HORSES had stopped trotting, Albie was out the door, running toward the carriage. Unable to contain her excitement, Em leapt from it before it came to a complete stop and ran toward the open arms of her sister. Breathless, Albertine's hair and words were flying. "There is to be a grand celebration tomorrow in honor of your return!" she exclaimed.

"Don't you think it would be better for me to adjust to my life here first?" Em replied, taking in the familiar exterior of the house and the winding gardens she had dreamed about so much at the beginning of her stay at Oberhofen.

"It'll be just a simple party," Albie continued. "Food and drink for the attendees, and of course, dancing!" She put out her hand for Em to take and, without another word, the two of them began perfectly synchronized moves right on the gravel, the carriage attendants hiding their smiles at the pair's excitement.

"I'm afraid our cousin has unduly influenced you with your spontaneous outdoor dance!" Em proclaimed upon the last turn into her sister's arms. Albie simply smiled, "I'm so glad! Too bad Maman hasn't spent time with her."

Em looked at her, dismayed.

"I'm afraid Maman is, well, as *Maman* as ever! 'The preparations have to be *très magnifique!*'" Albie exclaimed in her best Maman accent.

Em understood only too well. Each detail had to be just perfect: elegant enough to show the wealth and power of the family, but not so extravagant as to create concern regarding the restoration of the monarchy. Maman lived in a state of constant alarm of another revolution. She had been a child of ten when it began, but the horrors lived with her, and she reminded her daughters often of the caution that should be exercised

"Perhaps Maman will let down her guard a bit when we are reunited?" Em looked at her sister, her eyes daring to hope. The lack of response from Albie was all she needed to know.

Her face a bit more drawn than before Em left, her mother was calm and collected as she descended the large stairway into the court-yard in a simple high waisted gown made of light blue muslin with no pattern, holding her white parasol over her head. Her locks, now showing a hint of silver, were perfectly coiffed with curls framing her face in a simple style as well.

Eulalie de Brisay smiled and embraced Em, but it was somehow different from the embrace Marie left her with and completely opposite from Albie's. She quickly pulled back from the hug. Apparently old habits are not easily forgotten. "*Mon coeur*, a pleasure to see you."

A pleasure? Em thought to herself. *Am I nothing but an acquaintance?* She sighed, before another thought entered. *Why am I even surprised?*

"Nice to see you," Em responded flatly, but not unkind. "How are the party plans going?"

"Quite well," Maman responded briskly, directing her gaze from Em's dress to her eyes. "Especially now that there is no need to worry about any issues, I'm sure?"

"*Oui*, Maman. I am quite excited to be home and there were no signs of my malady throughout the entire journey home!"

Eulalie twitched her lip—not quite a smile, but not a frown either. Em jumped on the opportunity to spin the conversation in a positive direction.

"I hope you are pleased with the results of the past year. And I have such stories and gifts for you all! Even my stepsiblings." She paused, looking round the grounds which, other than a new strain of flowers she had never seen before, hadn't changed a bit. "Where are they?"

"Upstairs with their lessons. I had them continue in order to make sure the welcome was appropriate."

"Oh, I see," Em responded, thinking to herself, *Of course, Maman would want to protect her younger children. Her favorite children. Just in case the demon was unexpectedly unleashed.* Em looked at her sister for reassurance.

"Let us get you inside and refreshed. We have a new gown for you as well, but we need to make sure it is fitted and ready for you by tomorrow."

Em's eyes hit the floor at the mention of the gown. *All the frills in the world can't save my reputation,* she mused. Albie, forever the mind reader, interjected, "Em, wait til you see it! It is lovely! It could easily be worn as a wedding gown when you get married, it is simply divine!"

Albie continued her excited chatter as they headed upstairs where seamstresses were already waiting. Em, though annoyed at the poking and prodding, was simply grateful it wasn't medical instruments touching her. She was also so grateful just to have her sister by her side. She had forgotten how much Maman wanted to always have everything just so. Even though she knew Maman to be the opposite of Marie, she still found herself in a state of transitions, half expecting Albert to run in at any moment and annoy the seamstresses with his unending demands to "use scissors!" What a different kind of mother Marie had proven to be–comfortable with her toddler's messes as well as Em's. Em couldn't help but wonder how bad her malady might be under the loving tutelage of an easy going mother like Marie. But then again, what was the point of thinking? It would not change her own cold mother's harsh glares and words.

The next evening, Maman came in after dressing for the party, her eyes intensely taking in everything from the tip of Em's boot to the tip of her hair bow. "Remember, Em, we have a great responsibility as a member of the Bourbon reign. We have an image to uphold–"

"While maintaining an air of modesty," Em finished for her. "With all respect, I understand."

Maman stared at her even more intently, "It is for your own good, and for the good of the family."

After commenting on various curls out of place in Em's hair, insisting on some buttons to be replaced immediately, and chastising the servant for the wrong shade of blue ribbon in Em's bow, Maman gave her approval and left the room. It was only when she could no longer hear her mother's footsteps that Em let out her breath. She began to rub the back of her right hand with her thumb. She didn't notice until she went to reach for her gloves that her hand began to shake. Her eyes widened and for the first time since coming home, Em began to worry about her condition. "No, no, no," she encouraged herself. "You have gone so many months with little to no incidents, surely you can hold it together for one evening."

Taking several slow breaths, Em went downstairs to the party in search of her sister. Em could already hear the arrival and chatter of guests on the first level and the soft sounds of music floating up the stairs. Praying she wouldn't be too late, Em rushed down the hall to find Albertine greeting another round of guests entering the *château*.

The faces blurred together as Em brushed past ladies in high waisted pastel gowns with elaborate curls piled on top of their heads, and gentlemen in their breeches and fancy cravats tied in fashionable knots. Marquis Sévigné and the same redhead from the last party, now holding his hand, were blocking Em's way. "Out of reach—just like a cure!" Em whispered to herself, so frustrated she could cry. But tears, of course, were out of the question unless approved by Maman which, of course, would never be. She was a lady of prestige. She had to keep it together. Gathering all of her courage, Em smiled and descended the stairs to join the party, determined to maintain control of her body.

Em attempted to answer banal questions about her time in the Swiss Confederation. She feigned interest in a young couple's new baby and even spoke with the village priest who stopped by to bless the new servant's quarters, but as each moment passed, Em could feel her tension rise. She could feel Maman's gaze on her from across the room. It made the space feel so small. There were so many people present, and while she felt so loved that so many would come to celebrate her return, she felt like they all wanted her attention at the exact same moment. It was suffocating. All the weight that had been lifted off her shoulders in Oberhofen seemed to return, twofold. She had forgotten how to live with such pressure and expectations.

The itching in her hands had spread to her shoulders, needing release. She could feel her chest starting to tighten as well. Em remembered these feelings. She knew what was coming. Glancing around for Albie, Em knew she wouldn't make it across the crowded room in time. She wouldn't make it to an exit, either. She felt so many bodies moving in closer around her, squeezing out a cry of "*merde!*"

The clamor directly around her stopped. The orchestra continued to play Mozart's Piano Sonata #16 in C Major at the far end of the room. There were a few whispers heard around the fringe of the room, but Em could hear none of it. All she could hear was the fuming breath of her mother as Eulalie's eyes narrowed.

Em could not wait for her to cross the room in response to her episode. Rather than elongating the humiliation, she bolted from the room, the crowd parting with every step she took, allowing her one step closer to freedom. As she burst from the ballroom out onto the terrace, she let out a loud guttural scream. It lasted longer than she would have liked and took her breath away.

When the scream ended, Em stood, turning, and came face to face with her mother. "Maman! I-I'm sorry! I don't know what happened, I—"

Eulalie sighed. "I thought you were better Ernestine. You told me everything was taken care of. You willful, insolent child. You knew I had hopes for you. This is unacceptable. Apparently, it is not enough knowing that you are of noble birth with responsibilities."

"What does that mean?"

"Enough with the coyness, Ernestine! Return to your quarters. I'll have a servant fetch you to my study tomorrow morning."

"*Oui*, Maman."

Chapter 11
A New Plan

*W*ELL, I HAVE DONE *it now. I wasn't able to go even one day with-out an outburst. What changed? And so quickly? I know they never fully went away, but they were much less frequent at Oberhofen. And much more mild. The gasps, some small twitches. Even the cursing was done under the breath and quieter. Sure, I had the occasional rough moments, but most days I could almost pass for "normal"—whatever that is! I mean, it's not like Marie was a "normal" mother by society's stan-dards. If anything, she was better than normal! She was supreme! I won-der if I had stayed there if I would eventually become good enough?*

Oh, dastardly daydreaming! What's the point?

I'll never be worth anything to Maman! I'll never earn her trust at this rate. She is certainly going to banish me for good this time. Sometimes I wonder, though, does she just expect too much of me? This question matters little in the end. As long as she rules over my every movement, I'll never be able to be free. To be loved exactly as I am.

If I were a man the answer would be simple: This has nothing to do with you, sweet Em, and everything to do with Maman and her own inabil-ity to love herself. Ah! What a revelation! I will simply have to love myself!

But then again, if Maman doesn't change, and she is ultimately in charge, what is the point?

And here we are back to square one again.

The answer—the real answer—the sad, depressing, honest to goodness cold harsh truth is that I have absolutely no autonomy over my own existence. At this rate I will likely be under her care for many years to come.

As I flip through these pages two things are painfully obvious:

1) *I spend an awful lot of time complaining about the same things. How I have no control over my body and my life. No future!*

2) *Albertine is a dear. Marie is a dear. And Théodore…I must flip back many pages…he is a dear, too.*

As long as I can be seen for who I am by a few people who I treasure, then that has to be enough, right? RIGHT! And from this place of gratitude new flowers of hope can grow. Perhaps not a whole garden, but a vase of glorious color nonetheless. I can focus on what IS working—like Albie taking more control of the estate. Has she not stood up for me on many occasions when I was being chastised? Indeed she has! So, things are getting better, right?! Of course, right!

This leads me to my final thought of the morning before my stomach goes into absolute rebellion smelling that fresh bread floating under the door. (The servants are still afraid to even come in—ha! Oh, I can't blame them. They are likely as scared of me as I am of Maman.) I WANT things to change, but I am not sure how I shall make that happen. What would that look like in a perfect world? And then, if the perfect world can't happen on the outside, how can I change my interior world to process the events of my existence—this malady—with more ease?

Since I can't change Maman, I must change myself. My thoughts. My reactions and—at the very least—my location. I'm not talking about this locked bedroom, either. I'm talking about moving. The Swiss Confederation comes to mind. After all, as disciplined as I must become keeping intrusive thoughts at bay, some of them are good. Whole. Real.

I am quite certain that my time at Oberhofen was much better for my condition. Being out in the streets with the common folk, the laughter, the singing, the bright colors. It was all just so happy. It was easy to hide, even if I made an outburst. Here things are so strict and exact. There are so many rules that must be followed to the letter. Not just Maman, but all of the noblesse. *Is that a difference between France and the Swiss Confederation? I wonder what life as a commoner is like here.*

It can't be very good. There is the very real risk of another revolution. I can see why Maman has so many rules for us to follow and so much precision. Maman doesn't talk about the revolution much, but one hears stories of how the streets ran with blood from all the beheadings. I know we are lucky; Maman does remind us of that much nearly hourly it seems. To make a change, there seems to be so much destruction. I don't relish the idea, but if I am to be my own person—unique and free—I must start by destroying old ideas of how I am to thrive in this world. It starts in my head, goes to the pen and we shall see what the future holds.

But first…breakfast!

BY THE TIME EM made it to the study to meet her mother, Eulalie was simply beaming with joy. Em stiffened, unsure of what was about to happen. She was still in trouble, wasn't she?

"Ernestine, *ma biquette.* How lovely of you to join your sweet old mama today. I have some exciting news for you!" She tapped her hand on the chair, flapping it as a bird does its wings. Em, feeling more like a trapped bird every moment, nervously sat down and stared at the cuckoo clock behind her mother's head. *Another caged bird!* she thought. *At least this one can make sounds and not be sent to doctors to suppress them!*

Eulalie flashed a rare smile. "After you left the party last night, I was speaking with the Duchess de Choiseul and she introduced me to a new doctor—"

"And of course you discussed my episodes—"

"Of course!" Eulalie continued, less of an agreement and more of 'be quiet' in her tone. "I told him how much I worry about you…"

Em sighed. If only they knew how overly worried her mother was about her.

"He mentioned some news that was quite encouraging. *Le médecin* said that he has seen such maladies as yours before! Even more exciting, he has seen it disappear!"

Em couldn't help herself. Her spirit picked up and she listened intently.

"He knows of a young woman who walked up and down the street and she was cured within a matter of days! You simply need more time in public, not less."

Em was dumbfounded. From the confines of her room and hiding to going out in public? Was the doctor mad? Was her mother?

"Why didn't those Swiss doctors think of such a genius plan? His theory is that in order to increase your will, you must have sufficient motivation. So, if your will to become a demure woman is too low, we must make you into a woman. Are you even listening, Ernestine?"

Em shook her head in the affirmative.

"Good, because ever since the doctor strongly encouraged this idea, I have been thinking about it. *Ma biquette,* I have the perfect solution for you! His name is Augustin Louis Picot de Dampierre."

"This is the new doctor's name?" Em asked.

"Heavens, no child! Haven't you been listening to a word I've been saying? There is no need for a doctor, I have already spoken with him. We need a minister!"

"So this is the minister's name? We have tried to cast the devil out of me before, but nothing has come of it."

"We will get you out in society more. To do so, we will make you a woman by your social standing as a wife and mother."

Em almost fainted at her mother's last statement, catching herself on the armrest of her chair.

"You must be joking!"

"Does your mother ever joke?"

It was true, Eulalie was not one for frivolity. Em stopped talking as she attempted to process the ridiculous words she was hearing.

"Augustin is the name of your fiancé."

"FIANCÉ?!"

"I spoke with him this morning and he has agreed to the match. Between his status in Napoleon's army and our standing with the *familie de Bourbon,* no matter what party is leading in politics, you and your children will be entirely safe. We will have to speak to the government magistrates to rush the marriage for the sake of your illness and due to you being underage, but then we can get started planning your engagement party and wedding! Isn't it wonderful? I hear…"

Em heard nothing past the word "marriage." Slowly, other words surfaced as well.

Children.

Engaged.

Wedding.

Soon.

"….Ernestine!?"

Her mother's stern voice shook her back to the present moment. "Isn't this wonderful?"

There were many adjectives that flooded Em's mind. "Wonderful" wasn't one of them.

"You seem upset. Pray tell, what could be wrong with such glorious news?"

"Glorious? Mother…I…How is this connected to my illness? A wedding doesn't cure anything."

"Don't be silly, of course it does! When the shock wears off you will see it as clear as the nose on your face, child. Oh! I won't be able to call you child much longer; you will be a real woman soon!"

"Because I am attached to a man?" Em gasped.

"Of course!" Eulalie grinned—one of the first sincere, honest smiles Em had seen on her mother's face when it came to her. "The doctor said that if you truly understood your role in society and had a husband, your desire to please him would encourage proper behavior and you would be cured. Isn't it wonderful? Isn't that what you want? To be rid of this curse that plagues you?"

"I…um, well…isn't there any other option? I don't know if I'm ready to be married." Em fiddled with a ribbon hanging from her waist, tracing the embroidery along the edge.

"Don't be ridiculous. We have tried everything else, haven't we? Besides, this is exactly why you MUST marry. You will simply love Augustin. Don't be shy, dear. I've arranged a meeting with him for you tomorrow. After a quick visit, it is down to the magistrate's office to arrange everything."

Em's body was numb. Which luckily meant no movements or vocalizations. Em stood and turned toward the door.

"Young lady, where do you think you are going? We have plans to arrange."

She thought for a moment for an excuse to leave the room. Giving no expression, Em simply stated, "*Merde*. Oh! It seems I am having another episode. *Pardonne-moi*, Maman."

As soon as the door clicked shut, Em quicked her pace. Before she knew it, she was running. She flew past the old oak tree; that's the first place the servants would look. No, she needed to be alone, to think, and to explode with the nerves of such a large change in her life.

She fled into the *parterre*, hidden by the tall hedges. When she reached the center, Em fell to a heap at the foot of the Montpellier maple, her thoughts racing. The only thing she could think was "why". The word echoed in her head over and over. There were so many questions attached to that one word. Why marriage? Why couldn't she just be normal? Why was she so cursed? Why…why…why?

Before she knew what was happening, tears began flowing. She could scarcely breathe for the wracking sobs. With her entire world turned upside down so quickly, the tree she held onto was the only stable thing in her life. How could things have gone so wrong?

Chapter 12
LOUIS

*W*HAT A DISASTER MY *return home has been! I ruined the lovely party held for me, and just when I didn't think anything could be worse, now I am to be married in hopes that it will cure me!? And they act like I'm the insane one?! Where is Marie when I need her? Why can't they understand that these dastardly noises and movements and words are beyond my control?*

I haven't even been home a full day and already Maman thinks I'm doing this just to spite her. This isn't something I'm doing on purpose. I risk being sent away again and I don't want that. This time it's banishment, I'm sure.

The last thing I would want to do is hurt anyone—even Maman (though in my anger I've certainly considered paying her back with the same intolerance she's shown me). But alas, I could never do that. I certainly wouldn't want to cause such an embarrassing scene. I understand how lucky and privileged I am. I understand the role that I need to fill. And so, despite every fiber of my being wanting justice for what is certainly not of my doing, I can see her point of view. Between the war and society's pressure, it is no more her fault the way she behaves toward me than my behavior itself. I am her daughter, and as such, I want nothing more than to please Maman. But marriage? At my age? That seems quite a high price to pay to earn her good graces.

If only fairy tales worked in real life. If that were the case, I could find my true love and be cured from this devil's curse with a kiss. I am not sure about the devil, but I'm quite certain there will not be a happily ever after for me. I might even be excited about the prospect of marriage if I thought it would work, but that is so unlikely. I would love to tell Maman, "What do I have to lose? Perhaps you are right!" But deep inside I know two things:

1) This malady will never leave me.

2) Marriage is not the answer.

Perhaps I could stomach the idea if we were as compatible as Marie and her sweet husband. The idea of being openly affectionate in our own home surrounded by laughter and children is certainly appealing! But I'm practically a child myself—a young girl full of young fears and naïveté. And questions. Oh, the questions! If only I could share my fears and concerns with Maman. I'd sit by her bedside and share each and every one:

Is he as young as me?

Is he good looking? (Please, let him be good looking!)

Did he fight in the war?

Is he rich?

Does he want kids?

Is he a widow?

Does he have a good sense of humor?

I could go on and on! In my fantasy, Maman would patiently answer each one. She'd hold my hand. Reassure me. Perhaps, if she had a sneaky side like Marie, she'd walk me past his home disguised as a servant so I could get a peek at my future dwelling! But alas, this is not the case. I am, once again, at the mercy of fate. This leaves me with new questions that only time will answer:

What if I can't stand him?

What if he smells, or is toothless, or has a scratchy beard that tickles me every time we kiss!?

What will happen if, after we are married, my noises and behavior become even worse? My ailment indeed seems to progress under stress. If I'm this stressed just with Maman, imagine a life married to someone I don't know?

What is my life to be if I am yoked with a man I despise—or worse—despises me!?

Because THAT is the real fear—the biggest one under all this angst and despair.

Is it possible this man…this husband…(How odd to say the word!)…could even care for me in the first place? I'm not sure I'm all that lovable. Sure, Albie seems to think so, but Albie loves almost everyone. Marie was the same way. Could a man who was, for all intents and purposes, assigned to me, ever really love me? Will he know that I don't mean to be cruel when I say things I can't control? Will he know that I don't mean to hit? Would he love me for who I am?

And then consider children. Whilst part of my duty, what if I don't want them? It's not that I don't like them. Little Albert was adorable. I don't think I would mind being a mother, but what if they are cursed like I am? Illness spreads.

What if it's a family trait like poor eyesight?

What kind of life would they have to lead?

No! I shudder to think about it. I refuse to birth this illness into existence. I will not bear children of my own. I will simply have to spoil any nieces and nephews I have. If only things were different, but they are not. So, I shall attempt to resign myself to my future, as bleak, miserable and dark as it appears to be at this moment.

As Em wept underneath the tree, she felt the trunk shake. It was just for a moment, but she sat up and looked around her. Seeing nothing, she leaned back against the tree. This time when the tree shook, several leaves fell down around her. She glanced up to see a boy jumping from branch to branch, making his way down the tree. Em dried her eyes and stood to leave just as he dropped in front of her.

"Oh! Théodore! It's you!" A blush crept up Em's cheeks and she put a hand over each to hide it. Though it had been quite a while since Em thought about him, his name came rolling off her tongue as easily as air.

"You remembered my name, *Mademoiselle*! It's an honor." And with that he gave a short bow. It was just enough time for Em's cheeks to return to their normal color.

"And why would I not remember the name of the man that almost frightened me to death?"

Théodore smirked, but not in jest. It was, to Em's young mind, in delight. And she wasn't wrong.

"Sorry to disturb you, *Mademoiselle*. I was taking my lunch and noticed you seemed upset. Is there anything I can do for you?"

Em paused, taking in those compassionate blue eyes, as well as his stature that had definitely broadened in the past year. With his longer breeches and form fitting shirt, a strong man now stood before her.

"*Mademoiselle*? Can I help you?" he repeated, still smiling.

"Not unless you are well-versed in removing curses, curing illnesses no one has ever seen the likes of, or how to make things change without changing anything."

"That's quite the request. My *spécialité* is in trees and plants. However, I do listen quite well if you need to talk."

"I'm sure you have much better things to do than listen to me complain about my comfortable life. What could the daughter of a *comte* really lack?"

"Well, your health for one thing. It isn't your favorite thing right now, it seems."

Em gave a loud burst of laughter and responded, "To say the least. But I ask you again, do you know how to cure an illness no one has heard of?"

"That doesn't mean you can't talk about it."

Em sighed in relief. She didn't mean to. She knew it was highly inappropriate to converse with someone so much further down her station. And yet, how appropriate was it for her mother to marry her off so soon? She might not get the chance again. It was Em, this time, that smiled.

"You really think talking will help?"

"I do," Théodore answered. "There's a caveat though. Don't just rattle off symptoms or things you think are wrong with you. You are right, I can't help with that as I've never experienced your illness."

"Lucky you!" Em interjected.

"Perhaps," Théodore responded. "But we all have something, don't we? That's what makes us human. Rich…poor…gardener… daughter of a *comte*. We all have feelings. We all have a heart. We all know what it's like to feel pain."

His words! How they hit her right in her soul. Em found herself tearing up as he continued, staring at her with that old familiar intensity.

"Tell me what it's like to have this condition. Why do you hate it so much?"

"Get back to—"

"And no telling me to get back to work!"

Em just shook her head. This boy…now a man…was sharp as a knife.

"I can work right here in this group of daisies while still listening."

Em looked around, uncertainty written all over her face.

"You don't have to worry, I won't tell anyone. You have my word. Does that suit you better?"

Em nodded.

"Okay then," He picked up his bag and began digging. "What do you hate the most about it?"

"Well, I suppose the condition itself doesn't bother me so much," Em began. "I mean, it *does*, just not the most. I think I mostly hate the look on Maman's face when it happens. As if I'm the greatest disappointment in her life, or like I have failed her. It's only there for a moment before her face quickly turns to anger, which is a close second, though far more dangerous. She is still my mother, you know? I want to please her."

"At what cost?" The question shot out of Théodore's mouth as easily as if he had just asked her for the time.

"I beg your pardon?" Em stammered.

Théodore looked at her briefly before turning his attention to his hands covered in dirt, his expression covered in kindness.

"How much do you want to please her? At what cost to you or your happiness? You are the one who has to live with your actions, not her."

Em felt oddly protective of her mother.

"That's not true! She does have consequences to face as well. She has to comfort all of the guests that I've offended. She has to be seen as an unfit mother. She…well…I'm sure there's more, but, well, I don't know much about what happens after I run off in shame."

"That sounds difficult," Théodore said, before turning back to his gardening. "And I'm sorry if I pushed too hard."

"It's okay," Em said. "I'm not used to talking to people about such intimate affairs…especially men."

"Men you don't know well," Théodore added. "The scandal!"

"It is indeed!" Em replied, laughing as she did so. "I have only met you once before!"

"Well, that's once more than your future husband, then!" Théodore returned.

"How did you…?"

"Servants talk," Théodore interrupted.

"Do you know who he is?" Adrenaline shot through Em's body. "Tell me!"

"I have no idea, I'm afraid," Théodore said, pausing to dig before returning to the daisies. "But whoever he is, I pray he is worthy of you."

"I should think it would be the other way around and you should pray for me to be worthy of him," Em said, sinking back against the tree.

"You're pretty hard on yourself," Théodore stated. "Tell me more. What else do you hate about your illness?"

"Well…I don't like the way most people look at me. There are many faces they wear and I hate them all. The pity, the judgment, the shock. I hate the way people think it's all my fault and that I'm just stupid or obstinate or mean-hearted."

As she spoke her words grew more and more frenzied. They spilled out with increasing force, like the waterfall Marie hiked to with her after a week's worth of rain.

"I hate feeling helpless and out of control. I hate that it pushes people away, makes people avoid me, and makes me feel so lonely. I hate seeing all the doctors that look at me as if I'm broken. I hate that they make me feel as if I am less of a person, like I'm inhuman or some kind of savage. I hate it, I hate it, I hate it!"

Em stopped, realizing that she had raised her voice far beyond the level of a lady. She didn't know at what point she balled her fists or started stamping her foot. All she knew was that it all stopped with a sense of release as soon as Théodore grabbed her wrist.

When she looked at him, she could only see blobs of color, like her painting palette.

Releasing her wrist he apologized and said, "I'd wipe your eyes *Mademoiselle* if my hands were not covered in dirt."

Pulling out her handkerchief, Em wiped her eyes, taking deep breaths to steady herself. "Forgive me, that was unseemly and unladylike."

"I won't say a word to anyone," he said, then added as he leaned in close. "They don't talk to me anyway!" Em laughed and remained in place–so close to him she could practically smell the dirt from his clothes.

He took a step closer, not quite touching, but with an intensity Em felt to her core.

"It looked like it felt good, though."

"You know, you're right. It really did. But it doesn't fix anything."

Em took a step back, but they continued to stare at each other a few moments as a hint of pink rose up Em's cheeks.

"I've got to go," she said, grabbing the handkerchief that had fallen to her feet. "I have a…a…a fiancé to meet!"

She was not quite out of earshot when she heard Théodore's last few words, "Lucky gentleman."

As evening approached, and after processing her conversation with Théodore again and again, Em became increasingly nervous. The moment she stepped back to the *château* she began feeling the old familiar symptoms. In an effort to keep them at bay she began wringing her hands, but to no avail. Her arms flailed. Her back thrust to the left then the right. Her neck twisted. "After two months of practically no incidents!" she sighed to herself.

The only thing keeping her from going into full body convulsions and cursing was the knowledge that Maman had mentioned her condition to her fiancé.

"What a relief I don't have to hide this part of me like at all those parties!" she said to Albie as she dressed for the evening.

"Is that what you are concerned with, dearest?" Albie said, straightening out the bow in Em's hair.

"I want to make a good impression. I'd like to even like the man. Is that so wrong?" Em inquired.

"Not at all," Albie answered her. "But perhaps you should just see what happens! Fear is a terrible liar; and what if he is lovely?"

"Perhaps," Em said before turning to her reflection in the mirror. Her round face from a few years prior had been replaced with a beautiful jawline and flawless skin. If she had to admit it, without sounding vain, she'd be forced to admit she was quite pretty.

"You look exquisite," Albie complimented her. "How can he not adore you?"

"You think so?"

Albie spun her around to face her. "I know so! Just think of it, Em! You are to be married! I am so happy for you! And you are to be married before me, even!"

"That doesn't concern you, does it? I mean, you are the eldest. Shouldn't you be married first?"

"Of course it doesn't! You are my sister, and your joys are my joys!"

"But what if…what if it isn't my joy? What if he hates this malady as much as I do and hates me as a result? He could be cruel, he could be ugly, he could be old. There are so many ways that this could go wrong!" Em said, trying not to cry.

"But there are also so many ways this could go right!" Albie reassured her. "You know I don't mind it at all. Marie didn't. We love you; what if he is the same? Or even better, what if it cures you as the doctors say and you gain that peace of mind?"

"Albie, please don't tell me you believe this is the answer!"

"Don't tell me it isn't, either! Is it possible to not be so harsh and not judge what you don't know? After all, you do not take kindly to people judging you before they truly understand your glorious spirit, do you?"

Albie had a point. Like a velvet hand, her wisdom came crashing upon Em like a welcomed sun after a storm.

"Don't be so harsh to judge just yet. Maybe at least meet him first. Which we will soon. I think I am just about ready, are you?"

"If you mean am I dressed? Then, yes. But if you are referring to my emotional state, am I ready to meet the man who is going to change my life forever and determine my happiness throughout the rest of my life? No, no I'm not quite ready for that just yet. I don't think I ever will be."

"Ah, *ma belle*…how could he not love you and your wit? It will all be well. Let us head down for supper. I thought I heard a carriage arriving a moment ago. Let's go meet your fiancé!"

Em took a deep breath before following her sister out the door and down the stairs to face her future.

As they entered the dining hall, Em's eyes were instantly drawn to the intense brown eyes of the stranger. As he stood, she couldn't help but notice the uniform of Napoleon's army. She was surprised Maman allowed him to enter with such a uniform in the *château*, but he did look quite dashing in it. He stood tall and bowed as the young ladies entered, sandy waves falling around his face.

The man before her was quite handsome, despite being more than twice her sixteen years. His face was rigid, as one would expect of a soldier. Em searched for any hint of kindness that would determine the course of their marriage. She also couldn't help but notice that his eyes went first to Albertine.

A natural reaction, Em knew. While the two girls were close in age and could almost pass for twins, Albie was the more handsome of the two. Simply by virtue of her engaging smile, confidence, and happy manners. Em was more content to hang back in the shadows and was nearly constantly wringing her hands trying to keep them under control.

In a blur of anxiety and excitement, Em followed her mother and stepfather into the dining room. She could hear her stepfather introducing the two girls and even remembered to give a curtsy in acknowledgement of their guest, but she could not tear her eyes away from this man who at least had handsome features going for him. She hung back, worried about their future and how he would change her life.

Em moved to her seat, which was placed next to his. He moved to pull out her chair for her, while her stepfather did the same for Albie. His manners were certainly pleasing. He made easy conversation with the family during dinner, though mostly with Eulalie. The two were first cousins and had played together as children until the Reign of Terror began. It was Eulalie who had made the decision for the match.

The tightness in Em's chest stayed throughout the meal. Though it loosened after a glass of wine after dinner in the library. Her stepfather and Albertine had excused themselves. Eulalie remained as chaperone all the way across the room. Augustin's voice was low.

"You have been quiet, *ma poupée*, you must tell me what observations you have made about your future husband in your musings," Augustin said, his voice low.

Em stole a quick glance at her mother.

"It's impossible for her to hear over this roaring fire," he said.

Em looked at her mother who remained fixed on her sewing and giggled at the boldness of this man and how scandalous it all seemed.

"That's better," Augustin continued, sipping his brandy. "So tell me–what do you think?" He put his hands up, a grin on his face, an open book.

"Oh! Um, well, you see…that is, uh, not much. Forgive me, I am quite nervous still."

"Is it my looks? My charm?"

"You are not helping!" Em giggled. "It's simply I, uh, had imagined Albertine would be married first and this is all so sudden, so I'm not entirely sure, um, what to say. Not that it matters. I've not been very good at social situations anyway, you know. I mean, I- I'm sure Maman told you about my…issues?"

"Indeed, she did. But don't worry if you call me awful things; I'm sure I've deserved it at some point. And I've certainly heard worse hanging around the soldiers. I'm sure we will get along quite well once you are not so nervous." He winked at her and butterflies jumped in her stomach.

"Why would you deserve it? No one should be treated so cruelly, no matter what they have done. I could never dream of being cruel to anyone, Augustin."

"Please, call me Louis. Let's just say war isn't exactly a pleasant experience. I've done my best in the cavalry and as a soldier, but it can bring out the worst in men if they aren't careful. I'm human and I've not been as perfect as I would like. Then again, who is? Most people I know have regrets in some form or another. I just hope you do not come to regret this choice. I, for one, look forward to our marriage."

"You do? But…why?"

"For one, what man wouldn't enjoy being married to a beautiful lady?" He paused to watch a blush crawl up her cheeks as she looked shyly away. "Secondly, I have had enough of war and travel, I would like to settle down and lead a simple life."

"You think I'm beautiful? You are just saying that." Em's thoughts turned to her entrance into the room when his eyes went first to Albertine. Nevertheless, the blush in her cheeks deepened.

"I am in earnest. I have seen many women in my travels. You are simply lovely."

Em made an effort to cover her cheeks as her Maman approached them and sat in a chair opposite them.

"Your daughter is truly lovely," he said, boldly, gently, taking Em's hand.

"She is indeed," Eulalie said, a rare, heartfelt smile on her face. Em couldn't care less if Eulalie's reaction stemmed from being her mother or because of the match. Em's spirit soared, suddenly excited about this possibility.

As the night wore on, and the brandy in the crystal container shrank, Louis spoke more and more graciously about her. His words represented more than kindness. They represented hope. Hope for a happy future. Hope that she could be happy. Hope that maybe, just maybe, this really was what she needed in order to rid herself of her curse.

Fairy tales of happy endings filled Em's mind for the rest of the night. When confronted by Albie that evening, Em was glowing. "Oh, Em, I am so happy for you! He seems like such a gentleman! You will be married so quickly. You must tell me the details as Maman brings them to you."

"I will. I promise!" Em said, her heart light.

"I hope you will stay in the *château*, but what if you move to Paris?"

"Paris?" Em didn't like the sound of it. Her face fell. "You can't be serious!"

"Why not? Paris is a marvelous city! You will be surrounded by such music and art. I will surely have to visit you often so that we may attend the theatre every night."

"Oh! Oh, no! Albie! I cannot be separated from you again. I cannot move to Paris! What will I do without you!"

"You survived a year without me at all, and Paris is MUCH closer. There will be visits in both directions, I'm sure. We have the apartments in town for extended stays, too. Besides, what if you just stay here? That's possible, too, you know. There is more than enough space should you choose to stay here."

"I suppose that is true. I am just so nervous about getting married. I don't know how to be a wife."

"You will be just fine. I cannot wait to be married! How romantic this all is. You are going to be such a lovely bride Em!"

Em wasn't sure if the butterflies were from nerves or excitement.

Chapter 13
The Wedding

*C*HÉRE MARIE,

I do not know if Maman has already written to you, but my return back to France did not go as expected. I am once again at the mercy of the malady. Maman is hopeful though. It seems she has spoken with a doctor who recommended marriage as a treatment. I am now engaged to be married as soon as we can get approval. I'm not sure what that will entail just yet, so we don't know when we can plan a date. But can you believe it? I am to be married! Things can change in an instant.

I'm writing because I simply must have you there! I long to see you and little Albert again. I do hope Daniel can make the trip as well, despite the last-minute notice. I know he is ever so involved in overseeing his business dealings and tending to the community, but I'm sure it will be a welcome escape for all of you. I can't wait to show you around the château and make a trip to Paris with you! Oh, what fun we shall have!

Be sure to keep an eye out for an official date, but feel free to come anytime soon just to be sure. We will have a room prepared for you whenever you decide to come.

All my love,
Em

THE NEXT MORNING, EULALIE informed Em that she would need to write a letter to the Bishop of Meaux. "You are only sixteen. The wedding should happen as soon as possible so we can get you properly healed all the sooner. As soon as we have permission from the Church and King Louis, we can schedule the wedding that same week. We can start the planning now so that all can be ready."

Letters were written. Permission was granted. A date was set in December. Em turned seventeen. The wedding came quickly, and all of a sudden Em was to be a married woman.

There were only a handful of guests present. It was close family only, just in case there were any surprises from Em. Maman was insistent that there be no interruptions that could halt the ceremony or cause any dispute in legitimacy.

So, with a mere dozen attendees in the rows and rows of empty pews of the Guermantes *château* chapel, Em was married.

The wedding happened so quickly, Em hardly realized it was over. It was a small affair, but left her feeling a bit breathless. It was all so surreal: seeing the tears of joy from Albie and Maman, feeling as beautiful as Marie Thérèse, Duchess of Angoulême, the gentle snowfall outside of the chapel. It had an almost numbing effect, trying to wrap her mind around what had happened.

As she stood and faced her family and friends after being pronounced husband and wife, she didn't feel any different. She was happy, yes. She wasn't making movements or noises as if possessed, so that was a good sign. Em couldn't help but wonder if it was a temporary reprieve like her last few months in the Swiss Confederation. How long would it be before she felt like a wife? Before she knew if it had really truly cured her?

Being embraced by her fiancé–no, husband–brought Em back to the present. She thought that maybe she should simply enjoy the day. To not worry about being a wife, her new title and responsibilities, or even about her curse. Today was a day of celebration and moving forward. She hoped it was in the right direction.

That night, there was a celebration at the *Château* de Guermantes to celebrate the wedding. The great hall glittered in the candlelight of four large chandeliers, bouncing off the gilt frames and embellishments that adorned the room. The couple looked stunning next to the windows that showed nature's beauty draped in a blanket of white. The same blue velvety curtains hung beside each window as they had when she was a child. Em was still quite overwhelmed by all the emotions, but it seemed like Louis was in his element. He chatted with guests, laughed, danced with his wife, and drank freely of the wine provided.

Not being socially adept, Em wished she could have spent the entire evening with Albie, Marie, and Daniel. She knew very few of the other guests in attendance. They had been invited by Eulalie and Louis. While she recognized a few faces, there was one in particular that shocked her. Her mother had permitted a nephew of Napoleon Bonaparte to step foot into their home. He must have been an associate of Louis. More than an associate, or Maman would never have stood for it. Shocked by the closeness of their relationship, Em questioned why her mother had approved of this match in the first place.

It was well known that Eulalie de Brisay was vehemently opposed to Napoleon and the revolution that had shaken her world to the core. She never spoke much of the events of her youth, unless it was in lecture. The children must act just so. The clothing must be simple yet elegant. The servants must be treated with respect. Above all else, the part must be played correctly.

The very thought of the younger Bonaparte being in such proximity brought a tightness to Em's chest that took all of the sparkle out of the day for Em. She knew she would have to be on her best behavior to avoid confrontation. Eulalie kept to the opposite side of the room, despite the prominence of her guest.

Em, however, did not have the same advantages or luck as her mother. Louis was attached to her side all night. Em tried to convince herself that she had to simply smile and leave the bulk of the conversation to her husband. Her luck seemed to be running dry. She must have used all her luck obtaining such a handsome and good man as a husband.

As much as she admired her husband, he kept questionable company, connected as he was to the Bonaparte family. She found herself drifting closer and closer to the Bonaparte. Her hands began their familiar itching, threatening to fly out of control. Worse yet, Em was afraid of what she would say if things really got out of hand. She would mortify not only her mother but now her husband as well. She must keep control. All her fears about Louis not being a cure for her disorder, along with the noise of the party, made her anxious. *Not now! You need to behave!* Em told herself. She could feel her body moving uncontrollably already, and she had no escape, making her more nervous.

"Louis. Louis, darling. I need to step outside for a moment, please. I'd love it if you could join me, but it is alright if you would prefer to stay with the guests. Is that all right?"

"But *ma poupée*, I just want you to meet one person quickly, then you may step outside for a bit of fresh air. It won't take long, I promise. I'll be here should you get faint." Turning away from Em, he called out, "Charles! Charles! I present to you my wife, Ernestine Émilie Prondre de Guermantes. Ernestine, meet Charles Louis Napoleon Bonaparte. He is the nephew of Napoleon Bonaparte himself."

Em attempted a quick curtsey, but her shoulder jerked her off balance. Louis put an arm around her shoulder, preventing her from falling over completely. As she attempted to stand and right herself, her neck muscles tightened, pulling her ear to her shoulder. Trying to control her tongue, a gasp escaped her lips. Smiling at her small victory, she dropped her guard and out slipped something Em had never uttered, even in her worst moments. It started as a hiss behind her smile, and came out a soft, "*Sa mère.*"

Em winced, expecting her husband's hand across her face. Instead, she was met with laughter from the very man she had just insulted. His laughter was loud and jolly, turning many heads from the surrounding groups of guests. "Louis, you didn't tell me you were marrying *une rate*. Were we not in a *château*, I would have thought you had abased yourself to unite with *une plouc*."

More loud laughter bombarded Em as she ducked her head, turned, and fought her way through the jeering crowd to the nearest exit. This was far worse than Maman's anger. Anger she had faced, but she had always managed to escape before being so directly humiliated. With tears in her eyes, Em ran out the doorway and down the hall, hoping to reach the outside. She simply wanted a moment of peace. Luck was still not on her side, but Maman was on her heels. "Ernestine Émilie Prondre!! What did you do? What did you say? How could you cause such a commotion and such shame? And on your wedding day no less! If that wasn't bad enough, in front of that ogre?"

"Are you really surprised, Maman? You know I try so hard to contain it. I was so close to keeping it in. I was quiet at least. I didn't capture the attention of the entire room!"

Eulalie, with eyes as dark as night, responded, "No, you left that for that snake who somehow wormed his way into our home. Does your home mean so little to you that you would defile it so?"

"Maman, you know that isn't true."

"Do I? I thought you would hold your husband, your family, or even yourself with more regard than this."

Em tried to speak but could not. She was frozen in fear and shame.

"Compose yourself before you return to the party. Don't be long, your husband is waiting. That is, if you still have a husband after what you pulled. I wouldn't be surprised if he's off to the bishop now begging for an annulment."

Eulalie turned and entered the festivities again, leaving Em not only humiliated, but feeling lower than she had ever felt before. Her marriage wasn't off to a great start. Even worse, her mother still had the power to emotionally destroy Em, just as she had before.

What happened to "the happiest day of her life" and the "life-changing event" that marriage was supposed to be? Not that she really believed in those lies anyway. Alone in the silence, she knew she was trapped behind even more bars than before—not just because of her marriage, but because of her malady.

Perhaps he will come to look for me? Em thought, followed quickly by, *Who am I kidding. He doesn't even know me. I embarrassed him in front of his comrades. I'd be lucky if he even defended me. More likely he laughed right along with them!*

Never had Em felt so alone, rejected, and worthless. What was the point of all of this if she was simply going to be punished and humiliated at every turn? Just then, a breath of fresh air entered the patio in the form of her best friend, her Albie.

"Em! Are you ok? I rushed as soon as I saw you were missing."

"Couldn't be better," Em answered before bursting into tears.

"*Mon chou*, come here," Albie said, holding out her arms to her. Em collapsed into them. Albie held her tightly, stroking her hair as she did so.

"I heard whispers of what had happened while I was using the facilities. I'm so sorry I wasn't there."

Em cried until she couldn't cry anymore. When she finally caught her breath, Em told of their mother's role in the whole escapade. As the story unfolded, Albie grew more and more upset. At one point she pushed her sister away and began pacing in indignation.

"How dare she! How dare all of them!"

"Albie, it's okay—"

"—It certainly is not! You deserve so much better than that! Don't they know how hard you try? They do not know you at all. And I have certainly become disenchanted with your new husband."

Em had never seen her sister like this. She was both honored and terrified at the same time.

"Part of me wants to cry with you, sister, but the other part wants...wants revenge!"

Em was startled at the word. Never had she seen her calm, emotionally regulated sister in such a fit. That was *her* department!

"First order of business: I'm going to have a talk with Maman about the estate and who makes the decisions around here. I'm legally an adult and the heiress of the estate. If she keeps this up, I'll threaten to kick her out!"

"You wouldn't!?" Em was thrilled and aghast all at once.

"Indeed, I shall! I'll decide what is a shame on the family. Oh, I'm so mad I could spit!"

"Do it!" Em giggled. "We can say you caught my malady!"

Em spit across the grass.

"Was that...did you..."

"No, that was just for a laugh!" Em tittered, happy to lighten the mood. Albie, on a rampage like no other, would have none of it.

"I told you when we were children that I would always take care of you. I intend to keep that promise. No one will dare try something like this on my watch!"

"Thank you, Albie. I don't deserve you."

"Nor does that man! That…insolent soldier who thinks he can run France. Just because he is well known doesn't make him any kind of expert on human beings and he has no right to treat you like that. He won't last trying to lead France like that. That's how the first revolution started. Oh, I'd like to teach him a lesson or two!"

Albie paused for a moment and then, in a softer tone, said, "Em, are you sure you are ok? Maybe we should call it a night and get you up to your room."

"No, Maman expects me back at the party. I'm sure my husband will as well. I couldn't let them down and embarrass them further. Disappearing will not make it all better."

"I suppose you are right. The party can't last much longer anyways, I've seen a few guests take their leave. It is getting late."

Turning to enter the ballroom, Em released a sigh. Albie grabbed her hand and gave it a squeeze, walking in with her sister with a look that dared anyone to laugh or bring up the recent event. The pair made their way to Louis, who had returned to his seat to finish eating his meal. After Em sat down, Albie moved toward her own seat, glancing back at her sister as Louis leaned in to whisper in her ear.

"*Ma poupée*, I do hope you are alright. You should not take such things to heart. Charles simply likes his laughs; he didn't mean anything by it."

Em simply gave a half-hearted smile at her husband in response. As he turned away, she muttered under her breath, "Maybe he should find something funny if he wants a laugh."

The rest of the evening passed without incident. The *château* finally quieted down as guests returned home or retired to their rooms. The couple entered a carriage that would carry them off to their apartment in Paris.

Chapter 14
THE HONEYMOON

I CAN'T BELIEVE I'M MARRIED! I find it interesting knowing that everything has changed, yet I feel very much the same. Like I can't quite grasp the changes that have happened. I won't write long, the events of yesterday have me thoroughly exhausted, but I keep staring at the door that separates my room from Louis (my husband!). I'm terribly nervous for when that door opens. I do not believe it will be tonight; Louis had quite a bit to drink. We all did, in celebration. Though what exactly we are celebrating, I'm not sure.

Isn't marriage usually to celebrate the love of two people? Aren't celebrations supposed to be for some kind of success or joyful occasion? This was a desperate attempt to cure an illness. No one throws a party at a hospital.

Now I wish I had paid more attention to Maman. She sat me down to have a talk about this very thing, but I was so worried about my malady ruining the party, I didn't listen as well as I should have. I don't even want to think about it. Being married hasn't done anything for my malady thus far. I'm now just bringing additional shame to my husband as well as my mother. Unless the doctor meant the physical act of becoming man and woman is what would cure me...Do I dare get my hopes up yet again?

After arriving in Paris, it was late enough that the couple simply retired to their separate bedrooms, though they were joined by a door. When Em arose the next morning, she didn't dare peek into his room, so she dressed to head downstairs to breakfast, only to find Louis already at the table.

As she sat down next to him, Louis announced his plans for the duration of the honeymoon. "*Ma poupée*, I have quite the surprise for you. We will not be doing a traditional bridal tour. Most of our family was able to attend the wedding. Instead, I have planned a getaway for us to go south to Nice and tour a little bit of Northern Italy. Wouldn't that be lovely? I could even show you some of Napoleon's famous battle sites, since I was there with him."

Em flinched at the mention of Napoleon but managed to keep a smile on her face. Napoleon was, after all, an enemy to the noble class and her very way of life. She briefly wondered why her mother or Louis had even consented to the match, given their political differences. But class and wealth always won out in the end, didn't they?

Then her thoughts turned more favorably, some travel might be just what she needed. After all, the Swiss Confederation had done wonders for her nerves and even tempered her malady some. Pasting a small smile on her face, she agreed, "A tour of the south would be lovely this time of year. I'm afraid I have not packed anything appropriate for the change in weather, though."

Leaning forward, Louis ran a hand through his hair, "Yes, I had thought that might be the case. We may have to spend a week or two around town while you get suitable clothing made before we set off, but that shouldn't be a problem, I imagine. You have a servant who will be able to attend to you, so you won't mind if I attend to other matters."

Em tilted her head in confusion. "No, of course not. I'm sure I can take Anne with me to get things arranged. But what will you do by yourself? Shouldn't we be spending more time getting to know one another? I hardly know much about you."

Chuckling, Louis leaned back, relaxing comfortably in the chair with his hands behind his head. "Sometimes that is for the better, isn't it? Leaves a bit of mystery if we get along well and delays any unpleasantness if we don't."

The concern on Em's face must have been evident as he continued, "Oh, I'm sure we will get along, you are a sweet enough child, but you are still a child and likely frightened of me to some extent or another. I am, after all, a soldier of Napoleon, not to mention you probably see me as an old man more than twice your age. I can give you a few weeks to adjust to the idea of being Madame Dampierre. Besides, I still have some friends around the city and they as of yet have no wives. I'll not force you to make their acquaintance, they can be quite vile. Especially Charles, as you well know now. No, best to let you do your shopping while I make the travel arrangements and relive my soldiering days. Speaking of travel arrangements, I have a few meetings scheduled and I must be off."

He rose from the table, stood awkwardly for a moment before leaning down to place a kiss on her cheek. "There. You see? I am a gentleman who also must get used to having a wife."

Leaning down, he whispered into her ear, "But I do hope you are ready for tonight. For today you can explore the city and then later, as per your request, we can 'get to know each other'." He winked at her and his smile grew as Em blushed, putting a hand to her cheek to hide her embarrassment. Her mind ran to all sorts of places. She stole a glance at Louis as he stood abruptly.

"I have business to attend to. Enjoy Paris, *ma poupée!*"

However, the thought of such things drove Em to distraction all day. Without Anne and the coachman's help, she never would have been able to find the seamstress her mother insisted she use to acquire every-thing she needed. Luckily, the seamstress had the appropriate materials and styles on hand for travel and Em returned to the apartment in time to change for supper. The fittings would wait until tomorrow.

Louis and Em finished dressing at the same time and met unex-pectedly in the hallway. Offering his arm, the pair walked wordlessly down to the dining room. As the first course was served, Em strug-gled to find something, anything to discuss. How does one speak to a husband they barely know? She still struggled with remembering all of the etiquette and proper topics of discussion based on rank and she was pretty sure none of them had covered "husband".

While amusing herself with the oddities of her situation, she noticed Louis staring questioningly. Turning a shade of red, she asked, "Forgive me, I must have been lost in my own thoughts. Did you say something?"

Laughing (he had such a nice, robust laugh), he responded with, "I simply asked about your day. Did you have much success?"

She mentally kicked herself for not thinking of such a simple topic of conversation while responding, "Yes, quite. Though mostly thanks to Anne. I wouldn't have been nearly as successful without her assistance. It seems I've been lost in my own thoughts all day. How was yours? Were all the arrangements made?"

Louis smirked as he found an opening for his flirtatious nature. "It went well enough, but I'm more intrigued by what has captured your attention so thoroughly. Did you meet another man so soon? Should I be jealous of this new lover? Woe to the poor husband that has not had a chance to yet woo his own wife!"

He laughed as Em protested and her blush deepened. He dou-bled over in laughter when the malady threw in the occasional "*merde*" or "*fou*" with her stammering protests. When her shoulders started to tense up around her ears, Em grabbed the side of her head trying to steady her breathing and Louis's laugh died down. He moved to her side and knelt next to his young bride, rubbing a hand up and down her back. There was still the occasional chuckle as he apologized, "Forgive me, my pet, it was only a bit of fun. You really needn't take such things from me seriously. I did not mean to cause an episode, I forgot all about your malady."

Finally able to breathe, though the twitches continued, Em shot a confused glare his direction. "But this was the whole reason we got married, was it not? How does one forget?"

His hand stopped moving, settling on her waist. Louis responded with a blunt honesty Em was unused to. "Well, that is why *you* got married. I've been needing to settle down for quite a while now. And as my wife, I will be completely honest with you. *I* got married to uphold the family honor. I did my sweet cousin a favor. I'm simply looking for a bit of comfort. I can't be a soldier forever and your portion from your father is large enough to keep us both quite well off. I was in earnest when I told you that you are beautiful, but that is simply a happy bonus in the arrangement."

The surprised look on Em's face was unmistakable. She did manage to keep her feeling of horror in check. Her thoughts swirled as she tried to process this new information. He married her because she had money? She found comfort knowing that it at least wasn't out of pity. She struggled to find any kind of response. Luckily, as her shoulder gave another sharp jerk forward, her malady also took over her, letting out a gasp, with a soft, "*fou, sa mère, mère, merde.*"

Louis covered his chuckle as he continued to kneel beside his wife. He thought for a moment before he added, "It doesn't hurt that you are able to make me laugh in a way few women do. I'm used to this from soldiers, but what a walking contradiction you are! So beautiful and refined, then out comes such words a polite lady has no business in knowing. It's endearing in a way."

He tweaked her nose as he stood, announcing, "I'm going to have my brandy in the library tonight, but I will be by later to visit you."

With a wink, he strode out of the room. Em was left to herself, unable to process everything that had just transpired. Vague ideas circled her head, seemingly all connected, yet with no form to prove it. Thoughts that connected them seemed to be just out of reach. By now her twitches were finally slowing down and she trusted herself to stand.

Moving to take her tea in the drawing room, Em's thoughts swirled. Never had she imagined she would find herself married so young, much less married to a complete stranger who was so different than any man she had ever known. Then again, her list was fairly limited. Her stepfather avoided her as much as possible. Marie's Daniel was charming and provided well for his little family, but she didn't know him very well, either.

Then there was Théodore...Instantly Em felt guilty thinking of another man on what was essentially her wedding night. Her thoughts turned to ways that Louis had shown much kindness, and while he wasn't as affectionate as Daniel or attentive as Théodore, he did at least seem kind. Shaking her head and picking up her embroidery, she decided to turn her focus elsewhere until Louis came to visit her as he had promised.

As the evening wore on, she wondered if Louis had forgotten about her. Had he changed his mind and gone out again with his friends? Standing, she pulled on a woven cord to call a maid to attend to her. When Anne arrived, Em asked if she had seen the master of the house. With a curtsey, Anne responded, "He has already retired for the evening *ma dame*. He went to his quarters shortly after dinner, I'm told."

Em tried, with moderate success, to hide her surprise. It would have been a complete success if she hadn't realized what Louis actually meant. A blush started to crawl up her cheeks. She dismissed Anne and sat thinking about what she should do now.

Going upstairs meant being with Louis as husband and wife, yet she was terrified of the prospect. Maybe she should simply stay in the drawing room all night using her *naïveté* as an excuse. She almost had. However, it was only a matter of time, so why delay? Did going upstairs mean she was taking the lead? If so, she wasn't sure if she was ready.

She finally made up her mind when she realized this was her future. Not only her future as a wife with a husband, but also the possibility of a cure. What if there *was* something that happened in this relationship that could make the malady stop? That was more important than any nerves or uncertainty that would come. Standing, she went up the stairs to see her husband.

Chapter 15
DR. ITARD'S METHODS

*C*HÉRE ALBIE,

I miss you, dear sister! It is incredible to believe that it has already been six whole months since I last saw you at my wedding. Louis has us set up in a magnificent apartment on the Rue de Solferino, right along the Seine. It is fashionable yet quaint with all the most delicious food at my fingertips—so much so that I've had to have all my dresses let out! One of the servants must have thought I was pregnant because the halls have seemed to echo with whispers. The servants point and stare when I walk by. It does not distress me—it's not like I haven't been pointed at in the past. At least they are servants, not the noblesse. I would have to attend social events for that to happen.

To your previous questions, Paris is beautiful. On rare occasions I have gone for long walks up and down the Champs-Élysées—it has the most beautiful gardens. Once Louis took me to see the progress of the Arc de Triomphe. It may have been started by that Corsican ogre, but the craftsmanship is beautiful and it will be stunning when complete.

Meanwhile, my malady continues to come and go. I think this is why we don't socialize much. It appears that Louis, who is not outright dismissive of me, is a bit uncomfortable with my challenges. Occasionally, we get visits from Louis's friends before they head out for the evening, but they tend to sequester in the library. They do not bring wives or women they are courting, so I have yet to make a single friend here. At the beginning of the honeymoon, Louis painted a beautiful picture of all the parties we would have, but he goes deathly silent when I bring up such topics now, so I stopped asking.

Oh, how I wish you would come to visit soon! It's only been a few months, but it feels like it has been ages. Time passes so slowly here. I feel so bored trapped inside all day and surrounded by so many buildings and strangers.

I have, however, been loaned a fascinating book with no author to name. I'm sending you a copy, I think you might enjoy it. I read Orgueil et Préjugés *at least three times. Shame no one seems to know who the author is. It must be someone Maman knows, for it seems the mother in the novel is just like her at times! I long to be one of the sensible sisters, but you absolutely remind me of Lizzie. Sometimes Jane, too. I'm sure you will love it. It gives me comfort when I miss you most terribly.*

Anyway, please come soon so we may go out. I have hardly been anywhere except my daily strolls in mostly empty gardens. Write to me of your plans!

Your loving sister,
Em

AFTER SEVERAL MONTHS OF marriage, it was clear that this was not the cure they were looking for. In fact, Em seemed to think that she was more often on edge trying to keep things under control than before, but with less success.

One morning over brunch, Louis broached the subject and mentioned a fantastic doctor he knew from his days as a soldier. "I know a fantastic physician, maybe you should give him a visit."

"I have seen so many physicians, remember? I went to the Swiss Confederation for a *year* trying to find some kind of cure."

"True, but speaking with your mother, it doesn't seem as if you have met with Dr. Itard. He was the man who took in that wild boy, the one from Aveyron. He made marvelous progress with the child, I hear."

"Itard? I did meet with him, actually. He was passing through the Swiss Confederation while I was there and stopped at my mother's request. He wished for me to notify him upon my return to France. However, when I returned, we had thought I was cured. Then the idea for the wedding came up and moved forward so quickly. So, nothing further came to pass."

"He's conducting research…" Louis said, at which her mind went blank. Research meant potentially uncomfortable medical procedures and exhaustive psychiatric evaluations, but it also meant she wasn't alone with the disorder. *Could there maybe, just maybe, be others like me?* she thought, a bit of hope rising in the solidarity of others with a similar disorder. It hadn't ever really crossed her mind before. She was intrigued at the possibility of knowing more about what was happening and why. It wasn't until Louis mentioned fixing this so they could attend more parties and gatherings that Em snapped back to the conversation. The comment suddenly led her to a fury she hadn't known before.

"So that is why we never go out in public? I should have known!"

Louis put down his fork, shock in his eyes.

"Am I really that disagreeable that I have to be cured for you to really see me?"

Louis went back to eating and smirked, "You must calm down, child—

Standing, Em shouted, "CHILD?! I am your wife! And I have tried to be everything anyone has ever asked of me! I do my best to obey the rules of society, yet no one sees any of my efforts. No one sees how hard it is to simply smile and partake in normal conversation. I have tried extra hard to compensate with talents–the music lessons, the painting, the embroidery…" Collapsing into her chair once again, her voice softened. "Has it not been enough? Have *I* not been enough?"

Louis simply rang the bell. A portly servant picked up his plate and walked away.

"I am done eating. Are you?" He got up and head toward the door.

"Please!" Em said, bolting from the table and blocking his way. "The only answer I seek is why I am considered so unlovable. Have you ever once considered this malady from *my* point of view?"

Louis tried to dodge to the left, but Em took hold of his arm, preventing him from doing so. A mix of incredulousness and anger crossed his face as he stood there; a stalwart soldier, blocked by a petite young woman in the epitome of high fashion.

"The doctor can't be called soon enough. A sedative perhaps—"

"No! I am not broken! Broken-hearted maybe, but *mon dieu*, has it really come to this? To be poked and prodded and examined simply as a curiosity for the rest of my life? Am I no better than that wild boy? Would you sell your own wife to whom you promised to love and be bound to til death to the highest bidder? No, instead, you would rather pay them for such an honor. You seek your own comfort and ease rather than my well-being."

Louis remained with his mouth gaping open. Even the swearing was nothing like this. The vehement passion behind her words, the hurt in her eyes.

"How had I never considered how taxing this must be on you?" he said, compassion in his eyes.

"You would not be the first!" Em said, then broke away, crossed back to the table and slumped in the chair. She stared down at her plate, then covered her face with her hands, while her husband kept talking from his place near the door.

"But surely you mind how you respond in public? It leads to such shame and embarrassment that is beneath you."

Em put her hands in her lap and let out a sigh. "I'm sorry. Of course, I mind. I want to be a good wife. I know this is my lot in life. I just don't know how to do it!"

Louis walked up behind his wife and gently placed his hand on her shoulder.

"You're doing fine, Em. You are. But you deserve peace. We deserve peace."

His words softened her. Louis might be gruff at times, and he certainly drank more than she cared for, but beneath his tough exterior was a man with a soft heart.

"I apologize," Em said. "I don't know what came over me, making such a big deal of this. It would be wise for me to see Itard. His research could find the cure we are looking for."

Louis walked around to her side and lifted her chin, searching for a response. Em's smile didn't quite reach her eyes, but it was enough for Louis. "Excellent. I shall write to him directly and arrange a meeting. Perhaps until then we can take a jaunt into the city? We have a new horse I've been meaning to train with the carriage, and the shops have beautiful displays this time of year."

That's when Em really smiled. An outing locked in a buggy wasn't a perfect solution to her woes, but she wasn't having to dress in gardener's clothes and walk through a forest to get there. Plus, it meant her husband wasn't completely tired of her. It would have to do.

THE TIME LEADING UP to the scheduled meeting with Itard passed much like the initial visit back when she was in the Swiss Confederation. Em holed herself into her room with no public appearances. Despite the one day spent sightseeing through windows around Paris by buggy, she saw her husband for the morning meal, but not much more than that. Her only company was from Albertine who finally came for a visit. The timing couldn't have been better.

The stress of marriage and isolation had taken its toll on Em. Her movements became unbearable. Not only were they constant, but they were starting to cause a lot of pain throughout her entire body. Even Albie's soothing presence did little to calm the quell of the curse. The convulsions became so intense that Dr. Leroux, the family physician, was sent for. He issued her a few tinctures of laudanum to help calm her nerves and relax her spasming muscles. The reddish brown liquid was bitter, and Em pulled a face the first time she tried it. But it was remarkable how well and quickly even one drop of the medicine worked.

The laudanum made the last few days leading up to the meeting much more bearable. When Dr. Itard was finally available, Em requested Albie's presence on the ride to the office building he was using for his practice. Louis opted to allow the sisters privacy while he stayed home and waited to hear the results upon their return. When the carriage stopped in front of a large brick building, Em grabbed her sister's wrist and froze, staring at the staircase in front of the building. Her last dose of laudanum had long worn off so that the doctor could see her unbridled condition.

"Perhaps I made a mistake, leaving additional tincture at home," she whispered to Albie as her body twisted and convulsed on her way out of the carriage.

"Take a few breaths, sister," Albie said. "He's a doctor who has studied this. He is going to help you. Nothing is too shocking for him."

Em calmed down and, slipping her hand in her sister's, headed up the stairs to the office. Each step felt heavier than the last. When she finally reached the top, she couldn't bring herself to knock on the door.

Instead, it was Albertine who raised her hand to the door to announce their presence. The large double doors swung inward to reveal the distinguished Dr. Itard himself. "You made it!" he boomed, his wild curls making him look a bit mad. "It is good to see you again!"

Em nodded. It took everything she had to sit down on the chairs he pointed to. Albie's hand on her elbow helped keep her grounded while she rubbed her right hand to quell the familiar itch.

Em may have been a married woman, but at this moment, she very much felt like a child. Something about this visit just felt like it was important. As if it would change the course of her life. She uttered every prayer she could remember, hoping that this man could find a cure for her.

Dr. Itard brought the pair into a second room with several medical instruments lying on a table next to a small leather notebook. He sat them down to explain the procedures and tests he would give, but Em was hardly listening. She was too busy focusing on anything but the good doctor. She could hear a dog barking somewhere in the house, heard the maid scuffling around as she cleaned the upstairs rooms, and felt her body temperature rising.

Her face began to flush, and her clothes seemed to weigh at least five times as much as they usually did. *This must be what it's like to be underwater.* Finally, Dr. Itard stopped talking and turned to reach for the first instrument while Albie leaned over and whispered, "Are you sure you want to do this?"

With only a look of confusion as a response, the doctor began his first procedure. He ran routine physical exams, each more uncomfortable than the last. They were not very different from the tests run in Oberhofen with other doctors, though. Em was so nervous, she was unable to contain a few jerky movements of her hands and shoulders. A few gasps and only one soft *"merde"* escaped her mouth. Overall, Em was fairly pleased with how well she was holding inside her bundle of nerves. After every test, Dr. Itard made notes. "Interesting, very interesting," were the only words he uttered during the examination.

The girls were unsure about what was so interesting since he had so far only performed routine exams. At least, that was until he bound Em's hands and feet. Calmly, Dr. Itard mentioned to her that she needed to still for the next bit, for her own safety. He picked up a knife from the table and started to walk toward her.

Maybe it was something in the way he smiled, or the glint in his eye. It could have been the slow, menacing walk. Her first clue should have been how tightly he had bound her in a way that was uncomfortable. It was likely a combination of all of this that threw Em into a state of absolute panic.

She began to scream and fight against the bindings, her wrists raw and smeared with blood. The doctor took a few more trance-like steps toward her until Albie started to yell as well. Albie's voice was at least coherent. "You mentioned nothing about this, sir. She is frightened; let's stop here for today."

"But my dear, it is a simple and routine bloodletting. I am a surgeon, this is all perfectly safe, I assure you."

"Absolutely not. I have NEVER seen my sister in such a state. Are you completely daft?"

By this time, Em had stopped screaming and regained her senses. She was fully aware of the pressure in her chest that was about to explode in her verbal assault. For once, she wasn't upset at them and let them fly at him unbridled as they bubbled up her throat. *"Itard, 'Bâtard! Merde, putain de cochon!* Stay away from me! I'm done with this, please just let me go home, Albie, please, let's go!"

Her neck twitched as she gave a final insult, *"Itard en retard."* Then she spat at him, landing it directly in his eye. Turning to Albie, Em leaned in and whispered, "That was new, I didn't mean to spit!"

"I'd spit if it happened to me, too!" he said, his face red. Neither woman expected that answer, and Albie suppressed a giggle as she quickly loosened Em's bindings while the doctor cleaned himself up. As soon as her limbs were free, Em seemed to lose control of them, twitching and wiggling through the rest of the conversation.

"I must say, *ma dame,* that is not the first I have seen such a display, but it is the first time from a woman of your station. Tell me, how much of that was intentional?" He had taken a seat and pulled his seat closer with his plume in hand and eager eyes.

"What? What do you mean?"

"You had mentioned outbursts like this, but it all seemed fully coherent. I was hoping the stress of the situation would prompt an outburst like this, so we could really see what you are in control of."

Albie's face turned red with anger. "Are you mad? How could you do such a thing? That was cruel. You could have gotten that answer simply by asking questions!"

"I did not know. When we met in Oberhofen, you had no outbursts and I needed to experience them to really understand them the same way that you do. I was nervous that there would be no reaction."

Em was incredulous at the boldness of his statement, "So you thought *you* were nervous?"

"I could never treat a woman with such cruelty. I simply needed the answers I seek. I apologize for the extreme manner I had to take. But please, tell me what you were aware of during that episode, you thoughts, your movements, etc. The more detail the better."

Em turned her head to the side, glancing at him, contemplating whether she should respond or not. However, this may be the only chance she had to get some kind of cure. She finally relented and answered, "I was aware of all of it. It's not as if my brain could turn off, or I fall asleep. I am fully aware; I just have no control to stop it."

"What parts? All of it?"

"No, I was obviously struggling against my bonds, but you had seen my movements before. I chose to tell you to stay away and cry out for my sister. The rest, including the spitting, were not of my volition. Now you have your answers. Albie, may we leave now?"

"Say no more; we are homebound," Albie said, gathering their coats.

"Wait, please! There are still more tests I must administer to fully understand!" the doctor said as he put down his notes. "Once I understand, you will have the cure you seek. I have seen others with similar conditions cured."

Em put her hand on Albie's arm to pause her.

"Cured? But, how? What cured them? And why perform tests if you have an answer?"

"The difference is that they were lower class. They could be cured simply by giving them the exposure you have had since birth as a Bourbon. One woman required only walking up and down the street in a higher-class neighborhood to see an improvement in her condition. They were obviously in stark contrast to your background, intellect, and refined manners."

Both sisters looked at him, nodding for him to go on.

"You, Ernestine, are a very special case. Very unique. You have had the right upbringing, had roles of responsibility, and even have changed your status to that of a married woman. And married to a Marquis, no less! Yet you still have these outbursts. We must find out why. If we can figure that out, you will surely be the case that changes history."

Em became more despondent as he spoke. She knew what had really happened to those that had been "cured." She had done it many times herself. Holding everything in until she was out of sight. She doubted they were really cured. These cases were simply hiding from the shame and embarrassment of their "treatments" and "cures". This doctor was a complete hoax. Looking at her sister, Em shook her head.

It was Albie who spoke. "You will not have any further access to my sister. You have quite traumatized her enough. Do not contact us, for there will be no more visits. We bid you a good day, sir."

The girls could not leave fast enough. Em could feel her muscles relax the second they walked out the door, despite a few extra twitches. Albie was the one who broke the silence. "I do believe there are some divine bakeries around this part of town, are there not? I simply must have some madeleines. Those always were my favorite."

A smile crept up Em's face as they continued down the stairs. "They were not. Those were my favorites and you know it. You always had to have one of everything."

By the time the pair were climbing into the carriage, they had agreed to find a local bakery. Em did indeed purchase a few madeleines while Albie purchased a few *maccherones*. "Wouldn't it be divine to have some kind of jam between two of these? Maybe you were right, and I have to have everything combined into one grand dessert."

The pastry melted in Em's mouth and seemed to melt away the stresses of the morning as well. "I could eat these every day and never tire of them. They are perfect as they are, no combination needed!"

During the carriage ride home, they agreed to tell Louis and Maman that Dr. Itard had no conclusions and that there would be no future visits. Em was relieved and grateful to know her sister was there supporting her every step of the way. Knowing Albertine was in charge of the estate kept her mother on her best behavior and brought so much relief to Em.

Albie would always be there for her, and this brought more hope and comfort than Em had felt before. She fell asleep that night without the help of a drop of laudanum and felt peace for the first time in weeks.

Chapter 16
TUBERCULOSIS

WHAT A RELIEF. I am so glad that things are finally getting better. Things were getting just about unbearable. Louis is a kind man. Paris is diverse and entertaining. It has been wonderful having Albie here. We've been to the opera, out to lovely restaurants, as well as a few parties. I have fewer outbursts these days.

Sometimes I wonder if Maman is the cause. Well, obviously not the cause, or I wouldn't have done them in Oberhofen, or here. They still happen, just less often and less…dramatic. I am not causing scenes when I am out with Louis and Albie.

Even when Maman is around, I do them less. It might be the laudanum. It could possibly be because I know I have Albie to protect me. I don't know what I would do without her by my side. I wish I knew what the actual reason for all of this was. I wish I had a bit more control. When the outbursts do happen, I'm usually at home.

I'm starting to not mind big crowds so much. However, even though my outbursts are fewer, there are still occasions that betray me. Just this past week at Sunday services, I let out a high-pitched screech. Most of the congregation jumped. I probably woke many sleeping members. Father Chapelle is not the most invigorating of preachers, to say the least. However, there were no more outbursts and everyone was looking around to decipher where the sound had even come from. It was almost comical watching the confusion on their faces, while I turned my head this way and that as if also searching for the source of the screech. Humor is beginning to be the best cure I've come up with so far—and I didn't even have to go to medical school to figure it out!

In addition to not taking myself so seriously, I also saw such success in calming the outbursts with the laudanum that Dr. Leroux provided before my visit with Dr. Itard, that we have continued the course of treatment. They never seem to fully go away, but they do seem to help decrease the frequency. Not to mention I feel so much calmer. Who knew that all along, this was the medical cure we were seeking?

IT WAS ONLY A few short weeks later that Em received a letter from Maman stating that Albertine had fallen ill with tuberculosis. Em rushed home to Guermantes, longing for nothing more than to be by her sister's side and nurse her back to health. Maman forbade Em from going anywhere near Albie's room. After all, Ernestine and Albertine were the only children and inheritors of their father's estate. The bloodline must continue, regardless of the outcome of Albie's illness.

For weeks Em prayed that it was not as bad as her mother claimed. Of course, Albie would get better. She spent many hours at chapel, knowing that somehow God would hear her prayers and heal her sister. Life without Albie would be impossible.

In the first week of Albie's illness, Em started showing more symptoms of her malady. Em began attending church more regularly to pray for her Albie, but her screeching was not as accepted as it was in the past. The leader of the parish had to ask her to leave on more than one occasion. That didn't matter to Em. She spent long hours in the pews alone. *It's more peaceful anyway without the people around,* she thought. *Oh, Albie! If only you were here to laugh as the sounds of my noises reverberate from the top of the ceiling to the stone hard floor!* Talking softly to Albie and praying for her sister calmed her down. It filled a space in her brain normally reserved for shame and guilt.

And yet, there was stress. Each passing day that Albertine did not show signs of improvement increased Em's nervous episodes. Maman tried to keep the girls apart for the health and safety of each, so Em spent more and more time at the chapel. After a few weeks, Louis came to join her, since she was no longer returning home to their apartment in Paris.

As the episodes increased, Em increased the amount of laudanum she was taking. It took more in order to simply cope. It not only helped Em's uncontrollable and unknown condition but helped her escape from the heaviness that had settled over the *château*. It was a different place without Albie's laughter throughout the halls. Her smile that was once so infectious now seldom graced her own room.

Not that Em could see if Albie's grin was there or not. She hadn't seen Albie since she left Paris. It felt like years. *Le médecin* came and went daily to check on the condition of the heiress with no change reported. Occasionally, there was an update, but it was usually to say that she had only become increasingly weak. Those days Em took an extra drop of laudanum.

One day, Em paced the floor in her favorite room inside the *château*. It was just a few doors from Albie's room, but it was the closest she could get. Albie had been sick for several months. Em would have felt more comfortable outside, but she needed to be closer to Albertine. The room was built to imitate the Hall of Mirrors in Versailles; the paintings may not have had the same historical significance as their counterparts, but they were no less stunning in appearance. Every gilded frame reminded Em of how much she had to be grateful for. And she needed something good to cling to.

Albertine was not recovering the way she needed to. Em wanted to send for every physician in the entirety of France, if only they would cure her sister. Each step Em took up and down the hall only increased her worry and helplessness. The individual details in the room mocked her, flashing that their wealth and status could do nothing to bring back Albertine's health.

"*Merde, merde, merde.*" Spoken by choice, Em attempted to pray for some kind of mercy. Albertine was the one person who really loved her from the beginning. The one she could trust with her secrets, her true thoughts and feelings, and really be her comfortable self. Em needed her sister.

"Please don't die," Em would pray, day after day. "I can't lose you."

What kind of God would take away the one person willing to come close to her without trying to fix or change her? Every muscle in her body tightened and Em's neck twisted her head up and to the left, then down and to the right before flying back and snapping back in place. The tension flew out of her body as quickly as it took over, and she fell to the floor, unable to stand up. How could she survive moments like this without her sister?

She grabbed her bottle of laudanum and fiddled with the cork. She desperately wanted some of it. But she needed to be coherent to hear the latest update from the physician who was letting blood yet again. Besides, it wasn't time for her dose. Bloodletting hadn't helped thus far and Em was livid that she was powerless to stop it. Maman insisted it would help, yet with every letting, Em lost more hope. If it was helping, she would be with her now, sitting under their tree sharing afternoon tea with madeleines.

Why wouldn't her family let her sit with Albertine? It seemed as if all of the water in the reflecting pool began to flow from her eyes with no warning. Collapsing the rest of the way to the floor, Em didn't see the servant enter, standing above her. The irony was not lost on Em. Even a servant seemed to have more respect for herself, standing tall above her.

After a moment, the servant lowered herself to kneel beside Em. Extending her hand, she spoke. "*Ma dame?* Your sister wishes to see you. She doesn't have much time left and it is among her final wishes to see you. Will you go? Will you let me help you stand?"

Despite her complete exhaustion, a surge of dismay rushed through Em. Her right hand flew out of control, just as it had during her writing lesson all of those years ago and many times since. It knocked the servant's hand, who instantly recoiled. Reaching toward the servant, Em tried to apologize. Just then her husband entered the room.

"*Mon Dieu* Ernestine! You should know better than to apologize to the servant! Do you never learn?" Sighing, he walked over and pulled Em to her feet.

"Anyway, I have news of your sister. She's gone. The disease has taken her. You cannot risk getting even more ill than you currently are. We don't know how your malady will react if you also get tuberculosis."

Em shook for a moment as she tried to understand what her husband had just said before going limp in his arms. Placing her on a stool at the side of the room, he continued, but Em didn't hear a word. She had expected to feel empty, but she didn't. Looking around

the room, it was still full of sunlight from the double French doors on either wall. That meant it couldn't be true. Could it? Life couldn't just continue when the most important person in Ernestine's world had disappeared. Her sister was fine. Her husband always had the worst timing anyways. Albertine had just asked for her, she couldn't have gone that fast. She had probably fallen asleep and Louis assumed incorrectly.

Standing abruptly, Em rushed out of the hall toward her sister's room. She didn't care if she got sick. Behind her, Louis shook his head and turned, walking slowly in the opposite direction, allowing Em the space she would need to grieve. He had seen enough of death and grieving in his lifetime; he needed a drink.

Em shoved the door open as the physician pulled the sheet over the pale face of Albertine. Em rushed forward and ripped the sheet away from the face of her best friend. Falling to her knees, she placed her hands on Albertine's cheeks, Em noticed they were cold. Too cold. Wide-eyed, she turned to the physician yelling, "*Salaud*, fix her. Fix her!" A string of obscenities followed as the fear increased. The tension threatened to close her windpipe as she held back her tears. Tears were for the dead and Albertine wasn't dead.

The physician stood unmoving behind Em until he reached forward to put a hand on her shoulder. "You should leave *ma dame*."

Chapter 17
ALBERTINE

*HE IS GONE. My dear Albie is gone! What will I do now?*

"HOW DARE YOU," EM whispered.

"Pardon, *ma dame?*"

"How dare you, *putain de cochon.*" Em could not control the shaking in her voice. She was furious. Not only was he clearly incompetent at his job, letting her sister die like that, but she was so tired of being told what to do. Albertine had asked for her, and she wasn't there. Her mother, her husband, and the physician all had told her to stay away. She had failed her entire life at keeping everyone else happy. She had failed to live up to everyone's expectations of what she should say and how she should act.

The one person she had never failed was dear Albertine, mostly because Albertine did not expect behavior that Em was unable to give. Sweet Albie had never asked anything of her. The one time Albie asked for something, Em wasn't there. It was the one moment when it would have mattered to her the most. Em should have been there. She should have been there the way Albertine was for her. She should have been there.

"I will stay with my sister until the coroner comes for her."

"But *ma dame*…"

"You are in no position to speak back to me. I stay with my sister. Your services are no longer needed. Please leave. I will send payment for your services in the morning."

"I…*Oui, ma dame.*"

As the doctor packed up his things, Em released the expletives that had been building up since she entered the room. Hastening his pace, he shut the bag and dashed out the door as quickly as he could to avoid the appearance of wrath. Her eyes rolled at his actions. She wasn't saying these things on purpose. Just like every other time in her life, she couldn't stop it, no matter how hard she tried. And today she didn't have the energy to try to hold back.

Em was tired. Physically exhausted from the uncontrollable movements and keeping watch over her sister, yes. But she was equally tired of having no control over her own life. What could she really do? Sure, she was accomplished from her tutors…and always followed every other person's wishes for her. She was trying so hard, yet always seemed to fail.

Her uncontrollable words were so inappropriate for polite society and her unusual movements were embarrassing. She was never good enough for her parents, for her husband, for the doctors, for friends, and for society in general. She wondered if she was even good enough for God. After all, God didn't listen to the many prayers on Albie's behalf.

But what more could she have done? Em's tears flowed freely as she remembered happy memory after happy memory with her sister. When she snuck treats to Em when she was confined to her room in punishment. Laughing under the oak tree together. The fire in her eyes as she got protective over Em.

There was a hole in her soul that felt like it took up her entire body. She was simply a shell of a person without Albertine by her side. How could she live in a world without her? Life suddenly felt so very hopeless. Not only had she lost her best friend, but who would be in her corner now when dealing with this awful malady? Who would stand up for her against her mother? She could do nothing but collapse into a chair and sob.

When the coroner came, a pale man with a frown as dark as Maman's, Em ran to Albie's bedside, grabbing her beloved sister's hand.

"*Ma dame*, you must go," he said, not with anger.

"No. I–I can't. You don't understand." Tears streamed down Em's face. "I'll never see her again."

With a look of pity, the coroner explained, "She is already gone, this is just an empty shell of who she used to be."

Em continued to hold Albertine's hand, now heavy and growing colder. Glancing at her sister's face, she noticed the delicate cameo necklace–the face of her great grandmother in alabaster. It dawned on her then that she had never seen her sister without it.

Leaning forward, Em gently removed the necklace, placing it around her neck. The coroner watched with gentle eyes.

"Shall I also give you the signet ring?" he asked, then pausing. "Actually, perhaps your mother will need it for estate business."

"My mother is not here," Em said, releasing her sister's hand and to stop his movement toward Albie. "I will deliver it to her."

After a few more moments of disbelief, determination set over Em's face.

With that she pulled the ring off her sister's finger. It wasn't difficult as Albertine had grown so thin the past few weeks.

Em gave a small sigh as she slipped the delicate accessory onto her own finger. To her surprise it fit perfectly. *Just like you did, Albie. Just like you,* she thought.

"You may take her now," she said to the coroner. "And thank you for your kindness allowing me a few more moments with my sister. I am indebted to you."

"Of course. I am terribly sorry for your loss. Men?" Within moments three other men, dressed in black, rushed into the room. Em stepped aside as they carried on with the business of death.

They shut her eyes, placing coins on top.

They tied a scarf around her mouth to close it.

On the count of three they hoisted her, bedsheet and all, on top of a rolling cart and, in perfect unison, carted her away.

Why isn't my mother here? Em thought to herself as she eyeballed the empty room. *Where is my stepfather? Where is my husband?* All she could see was a housemaid coming in to clean up.

"She's gone, *ma dame*," said a servant as she began gathering the quilt and pillow off Albie's bed. "Do yourself a favor and take a break from this place. Find some space."

Grabbing a flower from Albie's bedside, she walked as quickly as she could to the Hall of Mirrors and grabbed her laudanum. The little bottle always left her feeling a bit more in control of her life. Each sip brought a bit more of its calming influence. Thank goodness for pain relievers, because this pain was far more than Em could bear.

It only took a drop before the warmth and numbness spread all the way to her fingertips. Em needed air. She stumbled across the room, bumping into the door frame on her way outside. Once she was free from the walls containing all of her misery, her pace quickened until she reached their tree. The tree where Em and Albie would meet as children to discuss their deepest secrets.

She sat completely numb from the shock and the medication. She didn't even hear the rustle of the branches next to her, or notice Théodore as he sat next to her until he spoke. "You doing alright m'lady?"

Slowly, Em turned to face him with wide eyes. He was sporting a slight beard which just accentuated his strong jawline and tanned skin. "Théodore! You always seem to show up at my lowest moments."

With a shy smile that had just the smallest touch of mischief, he looked down before looking at her again, "Yes, that would be me. I'm at my highest as you are at your lowest." He pointed to the tree and made a slight bow. "Is your sister—"

"She's gone," Em said, sitting down against the tree.

"My lady. I am so sorry."

"Thank you," she said. Not unlike her medication, she could feel this man's warmth finding its way to her soul. And yet, also like the medication, it wouldn't last long. It couldn't.

Even if I wish it could! she thought, then quickly chastised herself for even daring to have such ridiculous notions. She stood up in a jerky motion and backed away a few steps.

"I'm married now!" she said, as much for her benefit as his.

"I heard," he said. Em thought she saw a hint of disappointment in his eyes but couldn't be sure. She didn't want to be sure.

"Turns out my fine husband can win wars but he can't beat this disorder," she said. "Neither could any of the doctors in the Swiss Confederation. I may not be possessed, but I am certainly cursed."

"Is that what you think?" Théodore said, not breaking eye contact with her.

"What else can I think? God must be punishing me for something. First the twitching and the words, now my sister."

"Thank goodness we have hope," Théodore said.

"Hope? Surely you jest."

"I do not, dear lady. Though I do not make light of your troubles. Please know that." He looked worried, as if he had offended her.

"Théodore, I don't know you well, but I believe you mean no harm. What I don't believe is that I will ever have hope again."

"That's not true, *ma dame*," he said. "You will. I used to feel like that–leaving my parents and starting over in a country where I was seen as second to the citizens here. Poor. Uneducated. Lonely. But I found hope."

"How?" Em said, grateful for a break from her own troubles.

"In the new friends I made. The simple roof over my head. The gardens. In God–"

"Humph, God indeed. God has rejected me!"

"I see," remarked Théodore. No judgement, only a statement.

Em was surprised not just at what she said–a thought she'd been considering for quite a while–but also at Théodore's calm reaction. She always forgot, until she was in his presence, how non-judgmental he was. How wise. How easy to converse with.

As a breeze began to blow, she placed her arm on the tree, feeling a bit unsteady.

"It's just a light wind, *ma dame*," he said, eyes twinkling. "I don't blame you for feeling tired, though. You've just experienced a difficult blow, no?"

"Indeed," she said, sliding down to sit against the tree once more. "I'm also tired. The laudanum I take…a medication I use… makes me sleepy. Warm and cozy, but sleepy."

She shut her eyes. "Perhaps this God you love so much will grant me the dignity of a sleep where I perhaps don't wake."

"I know you don't mean that, *ma dame*," said Théodore, concern filling his face.

"I don't know anything anymore, friend," she said. Théodore smiled at the last word. He might have said something more, but his friend had long since fallen asleep.

Théodore stood watch over her as she dozed until the sun reached her pale face. One of the stable hands passed by at a distance near enough that Théodore was able to ask him to fetch someone from the house to take care of Ernestine. Shortly, Louis came out to find his sleeping wife and take her inside to bed.

The next day when Em awoke, she ran into her mother meeting with the local seamstress. Other than wearing black from head to toe, one might think she was planning a party instead of a funeral—the only giveaway being the gray and black fabric she was going through.

"Mother, there you are!"

"And here you are. Someone had to pay the servants; they would riot if we were late in paying them their due," Eulalie responded, before turning to the servant. "We need darker thread. This will not work!"

As the servant rushed from Eulalie's side Em approached closer. "Maman, must we already discuss the funeral? Do you not feel any pain?"

"What sort of question is this?" Maman said, not looking up from the lace samples she was sorting.

"You have an odd way of showing it!" Em said, putting her hand over her mother's to stop her work.

"Child, I adored Albertine. You know that. But the funeral won't plan itself and no one else is going to do it. Unless you'd like the honors?"

Em just stared at her mother, releasing her hand from the fabric.

"I thought so," Maman said as she walked briskly past Em. She slowed her pace and stopped before turning to face her daughter. With a deflated sigh she whispered, "Besides, I've planned enough of these in my lifetime, what's another?" Squaring her shoulders, Eulalie continued as if with a renewed purpose, "I made an appointment for you with the seamstress after lunch. You'll need to dress accordingly."

"I doubt Albie would care about such formalities," Em retorted.

"Well, your sister isn't here anymore, is she?" Eulalie said. "Do it. Understood?"

Without waiting for a response, she exited the room. Em's neck tightened. A quick shake loosened the tension and Em walked trance-like back to her room. The portraits were blurry. She didn't pay attention to the servants. Even the cat, a stray they had allowed into the *château* months ago, appeared to be nothing but a limp rag doll sleeping in a potted plant.

Em went inside her old room—the same one she had been locked in for days at a time. She hated it then, but now she relished the solitude. Before long she heard a knock at the door.

"Em!"

"Please leave me, Louis."

"I'm your husband and—"

"—you were not around when I needed you most. You are gone most days, in fact, and only making an appearance for the sake of pretenses."

"Em that's not true–"

"It is. We both know it. So, you go back to that double room we share and I'll stay here and we will both be better for it."

"As you wish, my dear," he said, the sound of his footsteps showing his obedience.

"I wish you were gone instead of Albie!" she said to the door before throwing herself on the bed and collapsing. She stayed there the rest of the day, not even leaving for meals. She had no appetite; what was the point, anyway?

The next morning, in a trance-like state, Em heard bits and pieces of information about the funeral from the servants' conversation outside her door. When breakfast arrived, she again refused it. Sustenance mattered little when her life as she knew it was over. She fiddled with the signet ring. "Oh, Albie, what will become of me now? Who will protect me? How will I go on without you? Where will my doses of kindness come from?"

Glancing out the window, she saw a few gardeners trimming the *parterre* and she remembered parts of her conversation with Théodore. He had shown her kindness. More than once. Her husband wouldn't like her talking with a servant. Neither would her mother. Smiling at herself, she thought that sounded just about perfect. She would have to find a way to get to know this gardener better.

Chapter 18
BETRAYAL

DOES IT EVER GET any better? Will this ache ever go away? I'm tired of hurting. I'm tired of being afraid of a future without Albie. I'm tired of hiding. I need to remember to find Dr. Leroux and procure more laudanum. I'm going through it so quickly these days. It's interesting how this little drink lessens the physical pain, yet the emotional pain from losing Albie has only intensified, not dimmed. I wish it would do more for my emotional pain.

It does help me to forget, even if just for a moment. I forget that Albie is gone. I can see her waltz in through the door, ready for some new mischief and adventure. Albie never hid from anything. She probably would drag me out of this room by my toes if she knew what I was doing. I suppose, for her sake, I should at least get up and go to the funeral.

But I'm not wearing the new dress Maman made. I shall wear Albie's old one and no one will dare say a word.

After a week of letting the shock and despair fully consume her, Em started to gain some coherency. The funeral was today, but somehow, she couldn't remember what time it was supposed to be. She wasn't sure that the maid had told her, so she went in search of Louis or Maman. Surely one of them knew.

She found Louis first. "Ah, *ma poupée*! I have been looking for you! We simply must have a chat about what we can do about your malady during the funeral. We have some time before the funeral starts; shall we chat in our room?"

"I suppose. This way the servants can't say we are never together."

They did not speak as they walked, Em supposed he simply had a lot on his mind. She certainly did. As they reached the doorway, he gallantly beckoned for her to enter first. Once she crossed the threshold, she heard the door creak. Whipping around, she saw the door closing as her husband said, "Please understand. Your behavior has grown more and more unpredictable these days. We cannot risk you in public during the funeral."

The door slammed shut and Em heard a key in the lock. Em stood frozen in disbelief. She stared at the door for several minutes before she was able to understand. They had locked her up like a caged animal. She would not be allowed to attend the funeral for Albertine.

"Open this up immediately!" she yelled, pounding the door as she did so.

No one came.

Em crashed to her knees in a scream that could be heard throughout the entire wing of the *château*. Her body shook with uncontrollable sobs. Unsure if there was even anyone left in the manor to hear her, she didn't bother to bang on the door. Everyone loved Albertine. Of course they would all be there. Her convulsions began, accompanied by a series of vulgarities and hiccups that she had never heard herself do before. She didn't care. Why stop them? The physical pain seemed to match her feelings. The loss, compounded by the betrayal.

Had there been any witnesses, it would have seemed Em was truly possessed, for her body was not her own as she continued to kneel, unable to stand. Her head and neck rolled in a half circle along the right side of her body before snapping back into place. Her shoulder hugged her ear and dropped suddenly in uneven intervals. Her left arm, hand, and fingers curled and uncurled. Her toes couldn't stop wiggling. All while tears ran down her face and hiccups and obscenities flew.

When her eyes ran out of tears to shed, she glanced around the room. There. Louis had at least been kind enough to leave a fresh bottle of medicine on the nightstand. She could barely stand from grief and barely move for convulsions. She made her way over on her hands and knees, stopping when her convulsions wouldn't allow forward movement. When she arrived, she uncorked the bottle and took a drop of laudanum. Then a second. And a third. After that, she was quite comfortably numb and crawled into bed.

It was around suppertime when there was a knock on the door, waking Em from her slumber. The room looked completely different from when she fell asleep. Darker, with long shadows from the fading sunlight. Her husband entered and Em instantly scowled. Before either of them uttered a word, she was up and running out the door.

"Em! Return at once!" Louis bellowed. But she was too fast to hear him.

Down the hall, past the great hall and out the door, she ran until she found herself yet again at the mighty oak that Em had shared for years with her Albertine.

For once, she actually wished she was possessed by the devil with a witch's power. She would simply love to put curses and hexes on many around her. Em had no idea if it was Maman's idea, or her husband's. Either way, they would have been her primary victims. After giving the tree a few good kicks and muttering about the cruelty of those closest to her, Em whirled around and found herself face-to-face with Théodore.

"I doubt the tree committed such crimes *ma dame*. It doesn't deserve your fury. Might I suggest throwing a few of its acorns instead? Still gets a bit of the anger out, don't you think?"

Em's right shoulder shrugged and dropped dramatically. "*Ducon.* Sorry. You know I don't mean it. Of course, you are right. But oh, if you knew what they have done! I'm so angry! I can never forgive them."

"What have they done? And who is 'they'?"

As Em unfurled the events of the morning, Théodore reached through the bushes and after a moment brought back several small, though ripe, mulberries. Em's mouth watered for the fruit, remembering she hadn't eaten anything all day. There was something soothing about the presence of this man, and he seemed to know almost by instinct what she needed.

The sweet berries on her tongue brought a small smile and a few tears to her face as she remembered all the times she and Albie had picked berries here through the years. It felt good to be here. She could almost feel her sister near as she continued to converse with the gardener with a listening ear and kind smile.

He may have been the opposite of Albertine in many ways. He was quiet most of the time, always so thoughtful and almost wise beyond his years. Yet there was also a familiarity in the kindness that he showed to her. Despite her odd movements and involuntary exclamations, he was ready with a quick, shy smile.

Before she knew what was happening, words and stories began to fall from her lips. Like the time Albie found a squirrel that had seemed to be injured. She had snuck it into the *château* to nurse it back to health. But it hadn't been sick at all. Every single servant had to chase it before it was caught. Or what a shameless flirt Albie became when she turned fourteen years of age.

Sharing stories of her and Albie's childhood with Théodore was therapeutic in a way. No one in the house was willing to talk about her at all. Em shuddered, unsure if it was her malady or the loneliness. She was very grateful to have this friendship.

Em wanted to remember all of the goodness that her sister encapsulated. She wanted to feel it surround her like one of Albie's hugs. She found herself longing so much for one of her sister's hugs that she noticed she was leaning toward Théodore, who was covered in dirt as he continued to pick berries and trim back the bushes. She quickly reminded herself of her posture, sitting up straight as she noticed the sun starting to fade from view behind the *château.*

Lights began to flicker on in the windows and Em heaved a heavy sigh. "I suppose I should return inside. But thank you so much. I needed this and I appreciate the time you have given me."

"But of course, *ma dame.* I am at your service. Please let me know if there is ever anything I can do for you."

Em considered this as she picked up her skirts and ran inside. The gardens had always been a sanctuary for her. A place where she could hide from her mother, the place where she and Albie shared their most intimate secrets and playful moments, and this was a place where she could think clearly and reflect. It would do her well to spend more time here. Especially with someone like Théodore.

Théodore was probably the one person left on earth that didn't think she was possessed. She had always thought Albie was the only one who wasn't afraid of her to some degree, but Théodore didn't seem afraid. In fact, he seemed incredibly kind and welcoming. She remembered the first time they met and how much he had given her to think about and consider.

She would have to find ways to spend more time out here. Out where she could relax, where she didn't seem quite so agitated…where she was more in control…where she could be herself.

Chapter 19
RESPONSIBILITIES

Chére Marie,

Words cannot express how grateful I am for your letter. Losing Albie has certainly been a huge shock. It seems like everything is suddenly changing. The worst part is, I don't seem to be keeping up with the changes. I can't function properly anymore. I can't even remember how I spent my morning. The only record today will hold is this letter to you, my dear cousin.

Even my malady seems to be simply exhausted by the day to day. That or the laudanum is working extremely well. It has been doing wonders for the pain caused by my movements, sometimes it even helps with the pain of losing Albie.

There is good news. I believe I have made a new friend. At least, I hope so. It might just be that he is tolerant or trying to gain some kind of favor. He is a gardener at the château…

As SHE MADE HER way back to her room, she found several letters sitting on her bed. Three, to be exact. One from Louis, probably offering some form of apology. Em was far too upset to read it and tossed it to her nightstand. Another was from Albie. Simply seeing her familiar script of her name across the front brought tears to Em's eyes. She couldn't handle that right now, either.

"Leave it to you, my dear sister, to leave some sort of goodbye note."

The final letter was from Maman. She wasn't particularly in the mood to read this one either, but it couldn't be a scolding, Maman did those in person. In fact, Maman hardly ever wrote letters, and it seemed to be quite short. Her curiosity got the better of her.

Ernestine,

You really haven't changed at all, child. Hiding away whenever you are upset does not accomplish anything. I must speak with you regarding running the château. *I have spoken with Louis and the two of you will move in immediately. I expect to see you at breakfast so that we may go over the details.*

Maman

Oh. Em hadn't considered that part. With Albie gone, Ernestine would be the sole inheritor of her father. Her first instinct was to write a letter back to Maman.

Dear Maman —

In order to run a château, *I would have to stop being locked in bedrooms.*

Em

With that fantasy set to the side, reality set in. She had no idea how to run a *château*; that had always been Albie's role and included in her training from the time she was a child. Em knew nothing of the sort. She suddenly felt very small and highly insecure. She could add it to the list of ways that she did not measure up. She was suddenly exhausted from the events of the day, and despite sleeping for most of it, fell into a very fitful sleep.

The next morning while dressing for breakfast, Em was simply overcome with dread. She did not want to meet with her mother and was overwhelmed at the thought of having so much responsibility placed upon her shoulders. "My constantly moving-out-of-my-control shoulders!" she bemoaned to herself. Overseeing finances and tasks for the servants was more than she could handle. She didn't even know the role of most of the servants!

By the time a servant named Nicole started working on Em's chignon, Em couldn't stop thinking about another servant; one in particular. She knew her friend was a gardener, but what did he really do all day? It might be helpful to spend some time and learn more about the gardens and his role. What a lovely excuse! She could get to know him better while still learning about the *château*. Plants seemed much better company than figures in an office all day. She must speak to Théodore right away.

Em couldn't wait to get outside. She ate her breakfast as quickly as possible and endured her meeting with Maman. She ran upstairs for her daily medicine to keep her under control, and the first moment she could, she dashed outside to her tree. She sat and waited for a while, before realizing that Théodore wasn't there. Which made sense, it's not like he spent *all* of his time waiting around for her.

But she'd had an idea as she was dressing and was eager to discuss it with Théodore. She wandered the grounds and found herself in the *parterre*. Entering the maze, Em wandered until she found a stone bench and sat down. She began to wonder if she had overstayed some kind of welcome with her last few visits. He was someone she needed, but he had a job to do. Possibly a family of his own to take care of when he wasn't busy.

Despondent, she wandered back to the oak. Her idea had distracted her during the morning hours, but without being able to share and act on it, her emotions were starting to catch up with her. Sometimes the grief was so physically painful and overwhelming that she couldn't breathe. Em had done a lot of moping as of late, and she was tired of it. However, she couldn't quite manage another emotion until just this morning.

She needed something to do. Something to keep her hands and mind busy. She hoped if she ignored the pain, it would eventually get softer. Then again, luck rarely ever favored her, why would it start now? Em shed a few tears for her sister before standing and heading back toward the house. On her way back, she managed to cross paths with Théodore.

Em could hardly contain her excitement upon seeing him. "Théodore! You said yesterday that I should ask if there was anything you could do for me. Is this true?"

"*Oui, ma dame.*"

"Wonderful! Will you please teach me?"

"Teach you? What could I teach you that you do not already know? You have studied far more than I."

"But no one has ever taught me about the gardens and the plants. Your work is so magnificent. These gardens bring me so much solace. Not to mention that I need a distraction and something to do with my hands. I would love to learn if you are willing to teach me."

"As you wish, *ma dame.*"

"You are certain you have the time? With your duties? You don't mind the extra time with me?"

"I have the time. I do not mind at all."

Em arranged to have daily lessons from Théodore around the gardens, shadowing him as he completed his duties around the property. The gardens were expansive and caring for them was no small feat. The family employed several gardeners, but none seemed to have the passion for it that Théodore had. Em was grateful and excited for the opportunity.

At least, at first she was. With time, it began to be more and more difficult to get excited about her lessons. Unlike with writing and music, Em did not have much of a natural knack for the skill. It was still a welcome distraction, so the lessons continued, but Em struggled to understand more than she cared to admit. But she did like the small feeling of control it afforded her to be in charge of such a beautiful life.

Em loved the look of the irises and hoped to have some inside for her to enjoy when she couldn't be outside. Within the hour, there were shoots moved into the *château*. Em was thrilled to have this little piece of the gardens with her when she couldn't be out in the sunshine. She made sure to put the pot near a window where they would receive sunlight. These lovely little shoots became her focus whenever she was indoors, and she was determined that they would do well under her watchful care.

As the week progressed, they didn't bloom, even though the plants outside began to thrive. In fact, the leaves began to turn yellow. Assuming they weren't getting enough water, she increased how much water she gave them daily. But seeing them grow weaker absolutely broke her heart. It hurt to look at them. She had enough heartache after losing Albie; she couldn't bear to lose the irises, too.

One day during her lesson with Théodore, she mentioned how sadly her poor irises were doing in the house. "You are really watering them every day? *Ma dame*, no! That is too much. Flowers are not like humans; they do not need constant care and concern. They just know what to do. We cannot force the buds to grow or force them open the same way we can use force on humans to do our will."

This was news to Em. "You mean, I can just enjoy them without all the work?"

"*Mais non*! They still require work and tending to. They do need water, but only once per week. They need sunshine, so if they are in the shady side of the house, they should be moved. After the blooms die, they will need to be trimmed off. It just doesn't need to be so constant."

After receiving instruction from Théodore about how to change the soil so it wasn't so wet, Em raced inside to care for her little pets. *En route*, she ran into Maman. "Ernestine, *ma biquette*, where are you going in such a rush? And the wrong way, too. You have some company you must attend to."

"*Oui*, Maman, I will be just a moment, I have to change the soil for…"

"Soil? You cannot play in the dirt when you have duties to attend to! You are filthy already. Good heavens, child! I can make a quick excuse while you wash up, but don't dawdle, hurry! Albertine would have been clean. You always manage to get into such a mess! Hurry, but don't run, it's not fitting for a lady of your station."

Em felt as if she had been smacked in the face. As she turned to freshen up, she considered what she had just heard. She did have a lot to measure up to with Albie gone and having to lead the estate. She had been neglecting her duties in order to spend more time in the gardens with Théodore. She might have to limit herself. Weekly rather than daily might be a better option.

She would tend to the irises after her company left. Surely such visits wouldn't take long. A quick visit to check in on the grieving family, offer condolences, and they would be on their way.

After a quick change of clothes and washing of hands, Em was soon with her neighbors. She was not expecting them to ask after her husband and his whereabouts. Having spent so much time with Théodore, Em was unsure where he was.

She tried to ignore Maman's shocked look of disapproval and the glare she felt rather than saw for the duration of the visit. As soon as the company was out of the door, Em dashed away, ignoring her mother's orders to stop running and to come back. But Em didn't feel like another lecture so close to the last one. Besides, her irises needed her help, or they would die of overwatering.

By the time Em had reached her room to grab the pot of flowers, she turned around to find Eulalie in her door frame, blocking the exit. "Put the plant down."

Her icy words froze Em to the core. Making no sudden movements, Em slowly returned the plant to its original position. With the confrontation that ensued, Em felt herself shrinking little by little under her mother's glare. "What has gotten into you, child? Have you forgotten your new role and responsibilities so quickly? I have hardly seen you at all the past few weeks. And when was the last time you saw your husband? You have responsibilities there, too, don't forget. The family line must continue through you. You need an heir. Especially with Albertine gone."

Em felt the familiar tugging at her shoulder as she listened to the rest of her mother's lecture. She was right, of course. Em had been quite careless as of late. It was about the only happiness she had managed to find, but was happiness really the point of life, anyways? She had certainly never seen her mother happy, least of all with Em.

"Ernestine! Are you even listening?"

Snapping her fingers, Eulalie got her daughter's attention. "Did you hear me? I want you to find your husband! The three of us must have a chat about your actions as of late and what must be done."

Stepping aside and pointing out the door, Eulalie barked, "Now!"

It was all Em could do to get her feet to move. She didn't even know where she should look. She knew nothing about this man that she had joined her life with. He was not to be found in the study or the library, his quarters, the kitchens, or any other room in the *château*. They didn't even share a room. She did know that he was not one to spend much time in the gardens. At least, she had never run into him in all her time there.

Enquiring at the stables, she found he had taken a carriage into town to visit with a few friends. He was expected to return to the *château* just before supper. Now Em was in a predicament. What would she tell her mother? By this point, Em's nerves were so frazzled, she was unable to contain the shoulder and hand movements. "*Fesses de singe enflammées. Singe, singe, singe.*"

The word felt oddly good on her tongue and Em could hardly stop saying it. Well, she certainly couldn't talk to her husband in this state. She felt out of control and decided she would need another dose of laudanum for today; her daily dose didn't seem to be cutting it anymore. On her way back to the *château*, "*sa mère*" joined the throng, making an odd little song. "*Singe sa mère, singe sa mère.*" She ran into Théodore along the path to the *château* while singing her little song.

She wished she had gotten to her medicine to get rid of this before facing him. Laudanum worked quickly. "Oh! Théodore! *Singe sa mère.* I'm so sorry! *Singe, singe.* I can't seem to stop. *Sa mère.*"

Théodore simply smiled. "That's quite the tune. How are your blooms faring?"

"Oh. I mean, they're fine. I think. *Singe. Merde.*" At this, Em started to bite the tip of her tongue to ease the itch of s's in her teeth. "I haven't had a chance to change the soil just yet. *Sa mère.* Maman pulled me aside for a chat, I've been running around trying to follow through with her requestsssssss*sa mère.* They might not make it; I might need to start over with a new set of blooms. I have failed this batch."

"No such thing *ma dame*. The timing on this might be off and I apologize, but are the blooms dead? If they are simply sick, there is a chance to save them. Do not give up on them just yet. You are still learning. Do not be so hard on yourself."

"I…I suppose you are right. I should go do that before I forget again. And I still have to find my husband. Have you seen him return by any chance?"

"I have not seen him, my apologies."

"Well, then I must be off. I will see you at our next lesson!"

Em ran off to her room to take care of her blooms and await the return of her husband.

Chapter 20
THE DEVIL'S VIOLINIST

I HAVE REALLY DONE IT now. I have never been so terrified of Maman. Louis isn't home yet, and I don't know what to do. I cannot continue my lessons with Théodore, she is watching like a hawk. I doubt she would like me to go out in public in order to find Louis. Where is he? How is he spending so much time away from the château? And in the country no less! What could he possibly do with his time?

Maman refuses to let me out of her sight, I feel lucky to have quill and ink and paper right now. She glares as if she doesn't know every facet of my life and is trying to see into my soul for some great secret. Maybe she can find a cure while she is there. What is taking Louis so long? Ah, the twitching becomes too great, I will stop for now and continue writing an update when Louis returns.

WHEN LOUIS RETURNED, THE servants informed him that Ernestine was looking for him. He went in search of her, finding her still in her quarters.

"You wished to see me *ma poupée*? Is everything alright?"

Now that her apprehension around her mother had subsided and the wind had blown out of her sails, Em was no longer sure what to say to him. Feeling keenly the awkwardness of such a moment, she stumbled to find the right words. "Well, you see, I uh, well, Maman said, that is…"

Seeing him struggle to hide a slight smile was both endearing and incredibly frustrating. There was a wave of bravado to cover her hurt pride. "Where were you today? I needed you and you failed me. You didn't even tell me where you were going. Do you loathe me so much that you have to run away and hide your location?"

"Not at all, *ma poupée*. I simply went to be with some friends who were passing through. We stopped at the local bar for some drinks and to visit. Why, did you miss me horribly?"

"Truth be told, I wouldn't have noticed if Maman hadn't brought it up. She thought to blame me for your lack of attention. It seems she is eager for an heir and a grandchild to dote on. She didn't use those terms exactly, but I wouldn't be surprised if that was actually her agenda."

"So, you are saying you want more attention and a baby?"

"Don't be so crass."

"What are you saying you want? In YOUR words."

Em had to stop and think for a moment. Most of what she wanted didn't really involve Louis at all. He had just kind of happened in her life. She had dreamed of getting married and the fancy wedding party. She had never considered what comes after.

"Well…we don't have much time before supper and we both need to dress. Shall we consider this conversation later?"

"Of course, *ma poupée*."

After dinner, however, Em managed to find convenient excuses to stay away from Louis. She didn't quite have an answer to what she wanted from him. Or from life in general if she was being perfectly honest. It had never really crossed her mind. The most she had ever considered was to cure this ridiculous mystery illness. She just wanted a name for it. That was always the first step. But what came after that? Worse yet, what if it never happened?

Louis managed to corner her on her way to her quarters for bed. He seemed to have gone overboard with his alcohol during and after dinner and he smelled strongly of whiskey. "So, *ma poupée*...First you want to see me, demand attention, then avoid me? It was your idea to talk, so let us talk. Shall we head into your room or mine?"

Disgusted by the overwhelming stench and the crudeness of manner, Em pushed him away. "You wouldn't even begin to understand what I was trying to say in a state like this. Would you even remember tomorrow?"

He threw his head back and laughed loudly. "There are certainly things I would understand. It's only natural, after all. Though you have a point, I have no thought of tomorrow in my head. Just what I need right now."

"And that is sleep, sir. Sleep is what you need."

Lucky for Em, Louis turned away in a huff and staggered down the hall to his room. "Fine. Keep your secrets then, I'll discover them sooner or later. Though it would be much easier if you would just tell me what you want. You can't hide from your own husband."

Turning back toward her room, Em heaved a shaky sigh of relief. She had too many questions on her mind to consider right now. She felt heavy and overwhelmed by life. She wished—and not for the first time—that it had been her who had passed instead of Albie. Albie knew what she wanted in life. She was vibrant and fun and even more important, not plagued by some unknown illness that affected so much of her day.

Now that Albie was gone, Em had received none of those same gifts, yet still had the weight of responsibility to figure out how to lead the *château* and make some kind of life for herself. She felt stuck. With the household responsibilities, with a husband, with an unknown illness, and stuck with numerous questions. The questions of the evening kept coming back and repeating their demands for an answer:

What does Ernestine Prondre de Guermantes, Picot de Dampierre want from her life? What would she do once the condition was discovered and finally cured?

Most terrifying of all, what would she do if that never happened and she lived her whole life with this curse?

As she lay under the sheets, alone as usual, Em tossed and turned with these questions on her mind. She needed something to calm her mind. Turning to her bedside table, she took a large dose of her beloved laudanum. She knew it wouldn't solve her questions, but it would solve one—her need for sleep. Hopefully, she would think more clearly in the morning.

When the morning came, however, the only answer she received was a throbbing headache. She still didn't have any idea what she wanted, other than a cure. This just seemed so impossible. Em wasn't sure if she considered herself lucky for the distraction or unlucky when Maman entered her room shortly after Em was dressed.

"*Ma biquette*, how is the laudanum treating you? It has been helping immensely, no? We must make sure you are on your best behavior tonight for the party."

"Party?"

"*Oui*, remember I told you about it yesterday. Speaking of, did you find *ton mari* and chat with him? I'm sure you did; you can be such a good girl when you want to be."

"Louis and I are getting along quite well," she said. "You'll have another grandbaby, maybe with a condition like mine, when God finds time to bless us."

Her mother winced. Em knew it was a cruel thing to say, but she didn't care.

Every once in a while, Em felt guilty about not loving her mother more. Today was not one of those days. She couldn't quite understand why her mother was so kind-hearted sometimes, and other times she would hold a grudge for weeks on end. She never quite knew what to expect from Eulalie.

"I'll be sure to take my laudanum before the party, Maman. I will do my best to keep my tongue in check and not bring any further shame upon the family," she said flatly.

Albie would never stand for this, she thought to herself, but Albie wasn't around to speak up for her and she didn't have the energy to start another fight with her mother.

Maman always wins anyway, she mused. *She always has the last word, the last laugh, and always gets her way.*

"Is there anything else before I begin my party preparations?" Em inquired. "I'd like to try a new style in my hair tonight and it will take time. The images seemed quite elaborate, but Anne seems confident she can manage it."

"Nothing, dear," her mother said, truly smiling. "I daresay it's lovely, and high time, you took an interest."

There it was. A compliment based on Em's false self with a passive aggressive scolding in between.

On her way out the door, a thought, seemingly out of nowhere, stopped Em in her tracks. She couldn't help but wonder if it was Albie visiting her—it was not something she would admit to herself without her sister's strong support.

Maybe the one thing I want out of life is to stop being so afraid of Maman for once…to have the final word on a subject. Any subject.

She smiled at the prospect. Her grin faded as quickly as it arrived, however. It didn't seem like the kind of thing she could tell Louis, though. Her mother had more of a history with him than his own wife did. It was a nice wish, though.

As flowers were arranged in fresh vases and the cooks dashed in and out of the kitchen with more food than Napoleon's army needed, Em's nerves increased in anticipation of the party. She wasn't sure who it was for or why she had to go, but her questions weren't important. She had no choice in the matter. As the sole heir, she now had the reputation of the *château* to uphold. Em was still missing her sister so violently that she wasn't sure she would even be able to hold a decent conversation. That was assuming she could keep her curse in check.

Em couldn't bear to be considered obstinate in addition to all her other shortcomings, so she donned her gown–approved by her mother, of course–and put on the best smile she could manage. She decided against anything new and kept her hair in its traditional fashion. From her view on the landing into the grand hall, it wasn't long before she noticed that this gathering was quite different from the few others she had attended. There was no way for Em to tell if the crowd parted when she walked by because of the little black cloud of grief over her head or if rumors of her "possession" had spread even farther than the house servants.

Either way, she didn't mind. She was not feeling like a socialite this evening and was just fine spending her time with her thoughts and observing the crowd. Slowly she made her way down the stairs and into the ballroom. She found herself slinking her way over to a secluded corner to watch the festivities as her senses were overcome with silk and perfume, and suits of every fashion. She couldn't help but notice her mother animatedly talking with a new woman recently married, or her stepfather making a rare appearance and shaking a banker's hand. And then there was Louis, laughing and dancing with other young ladies as if it was the most natural thing in the world to him.

He's touching them more than he's ever touched me, she grimly thought. Louis sure didn't have any qualms with dancing with other young ladies. Em was sipping on her drink when a shadow on the wall seemed to stop right in front of her.

It was a man's shadow. He wasn't particularly tall, but considering his slender frame and proportions, he seemed to tower over her sitting frame. Turning to face this slender shadow, she almost saw the exact replica of the shadow in three dimensions. He was dressed in all black from head to toe. She might have believed him to be the shadow if it wasn't for the stark contrast of his pale skin stretched across hollow cheeks.

The shadow incarnate bowed deeply and spoke to her with an Italian accent marking his French words. "Good evening *ma dame*. Forgive me for being so forward and brash for introducing myself. My name is Niccolo Paganini. I couldn't help but notice we seem to share the same ability of parting a crowd and I simply had to know the young woman with such abilities for myself."

"You said Paganini? I've heard of you; you are the devil's violinist!"

With a slight bow he responded, "In the flesh. Rumor has it you may also be possessed. What a delicious trait to have in common. What did you do to become the local devil?"

"Oh, but I'm not really. At least, I don't think I am. We have tried being blessed by the priest and exorcisms to no avail. I just feel like it's some kind of curse. No doctor can name it as an illness."

He was tall with shining eyes and a buoyant disposition, Paganini instantly put her at ease.

"And where science fails, the church prevails, yet again. But that isn't always the case. I did not sell my soul to the devil for my talent, I assure you. I have worked very hard to get every piece perfect. I work incredibly hard to make my compositions appear as if they fell together with ease."

"They are delightful and masterful in every way, Sir," Em gushed in the presence of such a master.

"I'm not here for praise," he said. "But simply to say that most people don't have the dedication or work ethic to truly make themselves great. Since it is something they can never achieve, they spread false lies out of jealousy."

"Why are you sharing this with me?" she said.

"I suppose I'm wondering if you must do the same to keep all your magical pieces in check."

"Magical?" she laughed. "I wish I had the same explanation for the rumors about me. There is only pity or disgust on the basis of my own rumors. It is impossible to be jealous of one so inappropriate."

"Ah, but that is where you are wrong! Who wouldn't love to speak their mind as freely as you are able? It is likely only your claims to not be in control of what you say that makes you appear possessed. Then again, that is just the opinion of a crazy musician. What do I know of humanity?"

As the conversation progressed with talk of travels, human nature, and the transcendence of the arts, Em began to appreciate the knowledge this composer had. He was about the same age as her husband, and was a shameless flirt throughout the conversation. He was Italian, after all. Under normal circumstances, Em might have found excuses to leave the conversation in search of more proprietary company.

However, there were few options for conversation among those labelled as possessed, so the two remained in conversation throughout the duration of the party. Em considered what types of art she could create on the same level as Paganini. Her music skills were passable, but nothing extraordinary. While she loved to listen to music, she never was one who cared for practicing. Her painting skills were not particularly wonderful, and she didn't mind it, but wasn't very passionate about painting, either. But what else could she be passionate about if not the arts?

The very thought of Paganini's many radical ideas and passions brought nervous itches to Em. Not just the pre-movement type of itches, but the actual fire of an itch crawled over her ears, her eyes (which brought on excessive blinking in an attempt to scratch it), and her throat. She managed to keep a few choice words fairly quiet, so as not to disturb the party, but Em was grateful she brought a small dose of laudanum with her. She might have to use it soon. Luckily, Paganini made no response to her movements and soft mutterings when her illness did appear.

Paganini was full of incredible ideas that could come across as him being out of touch with reality, and it affected every aspect of life. It even touched on politics. He had radical ideas that went far beyond Napoleon or even the Royal Bourbon line. "I would love to visit the new country in America. They seem to have started something that has all of the theory correct; the question is if it will work in practice. They are not the same, you know, theory and practice. Only time will tell if their experiment will work. But what an exciting idea. I'd love to think that France could be just as enlightened in their political practices, but what a mess you have here.

"It gives me hope for my home country. Monarchies make people hungry for power and split things into smaller regimes. Napoleon has the right idea of unification, but also cannot expect every human to respond the same way. No one form of government will work if it is so absolutist. Unified groups like the theory America is testing is my favorite option. Hopefully, Italians can be unified in such a way without so many people and countries fighting over them. Down with Napoleon!"

Em noticed a few heads turning at his shout against Napoleon. It was a bold move after all; one never knew who was for or against the Corsican. Heads tilted together in whispers and stares at the pair. Em needed a distraction and returned to the conversation. "You seem so well informed with current events. There are whispers of Napoleon attempting to escape. Do you know anything of these rumors?"

"Not specifics, just that people are trying to gain support for him to return, so it seems that an escape plan is in the works. But never fear, there are still those who oppose such foolhardy actions."

"You seem to know something."

"You seem interested. Are you asking to be involved?"

"Well…maybe? I need some kind of distraction from the constant letdown of not finding what is wrong with me."

"Well, good news, you might even find a use for this thing you call a curse. Meet with Pierre at Le Pavillon de la Reine. He can give you more information if you really wish to take part in the underground. Though it would absolutely solidify you as a demon. I dare say you might quite enjoy it if you lean into the title. I must turn in for the night. I'm off to Paris tomorrow, but I do so hope to see you again."

The second his back was turned, Em downed her small bottle of laudanum. She instantly felt warm and lighthearted after such a

serious conversation. She smiled whenever she caught someone looking her way, but heads turned quickly and no more conversation was
to be had.

Chapter 21
REPERCUSSIONS

*T*HAT MIGHT BE THE *first party that I didn't make a complete social embarrassment of myself. I didn't have any loud outbursts at all! There were a few small ones, but none that turned heads. I was enough of a spectacle just being there. It was weird to watch the path clear before me, no one wanted to talk to me at all. How different things are without my sister.*

Oh! I got to meet the famed violinist Paganini at the party! He came over and introduced himself. He's about as possessed as I am. He was wonderful to talk to, and so intelligent, even if he is a shameful flirt. I can see how many women would fall for his charms, though. He is so passionate about everything he does. I hope to find that kind of passion someday. Like Théodore and his gardens.

Maybe I should begin violin lessons again. No. I really don't care for it. Certainly not the way Paganini does. He is a master at his craft though. I wonder if there is anything that I will be known for the way Paganini is known for his musical abilities. To have my name echo through time as I'm sure his will…

THE NEXT MORNING, MAMAN called Em to the study. By instinct, Em started to go over the events of the party to see what she had done wrong. *There's always something,* she thought, taking a breath before entering the study.

Em was surprised to find both her stepfather and husband already in the study. "Ah, Ernestine, good. We may begin with the calendar for the estate. With last night going relatively well, we need to make sure we are all on the same page for future engagements, as well as making sure they are all quite successful."

"Em, *ma biquette,* you really need to loosen up a little. You won't make the connections we need for the estate if you continue to be such a wallflower and let only one man monopolize your time. Especially a man such as that. He has a known reputation for being highly improper in manner, especially in regard to young ladies. You must know who you are talking with at all times. And regardless, one young man should never take all of your time; it is highly improper for a young lady to spend so much time with one man that is not her husband."

As Maman continued, Em glanced nervously at the men in the room, lazing in their chairs. Both had their eyes fixed on her. Shifting nervously in her seat, Em could only nod and occasionally murmur the same phrase she had repeated since she was a child. "*Oui,* Maman. *Oui,* Maman."

Even without any loud outbursts, Em couldn't seem to get the etiquette correct. Em was so overwhelmed by the disappointment she felt in herself that there was no room for the onslaught that came from her mother. Tears welled up in the corners of her eyes and her shoulders couldn't seem to sit still.

"Ernestine! Would you stop moving?! Can you not even sit without causing such a scene? Really! What will I do with you? How can you be so inconsiderate of others? And in front of the men, too! I was hoping their presence would remind you of your role and prevent such thoughtless manners. You really have no shame at all, do you?"

Em glanced over to the men, hoping to see some kind of solidarity, or at least pity. But their faces were unchanged with the exception of the occasional nod along with Eulalie's words. The tears threatened to spill as the corners of her mouth pulled. She clamped her mouth shut tightly, fighting the movement. She refused to give her mother more ammunition against her. Eventually, she could no longer stand the stares and lectures. She stood abruptly and ran from the room.

The tears were flowing quickly now, inhibiting her view. She bit down on her lips, still refusing to allow the words to exit. She could taste the blood from her lip as she continued to bite down. She felt lucky she was at home and knew these halls and rooms so well. She only hit one or two corners as she continued to run toward the gardens. She wanted to be lost in the *parterre* and never be found again.

As she reached the edge of the *parterre*, she bumped into someone. Looking up, she saw Théodore. She jumped back quickly and attempted to clean up her tear-stained face. Théodore spoke first, "I take it we will not be having a lesson today. Seems like there are much more important things going on."

Em did her best to wipe her tears and stand tall, pretending nothing was wrong. "No! I mean, I want to have a lesson today. Walk with me through the *parterre*?"

As they started to walk, she took his arm. He stopped. "*Ma dame*, is this wise?"

"My husband prefers the company of dancers. I am about to run this estate, so I say 'Yes, it is perfectly fine!'"

"I cannot argue with that," Théodore said, once again beginning to walk with her.

They soon entered the garden maze.

"I wish…I wish…" Em stuttered a bit.

"What is it, my friend?" Théodore said.

"It's just, my life resembles this maze. It's beautiful in some ways, but there are so many twists and turns. If only I could walk through the winding paths of my life with someone that makes me feel as comfortable as I do right now."

Théodore gazed at her with a look that wasn't quite flirty, but wasn't lust either. It was simply a sweet understanding that made Em feel dizzy.

"I've said too much," she said "I am… ridiculous."

"Hardly," he said. "We all want that. Me, included."

A pause ensued as the two friends just stood together, enjoying the effortless companionship.

"Tell me," Théodore said, breaking the silence. "What happened this morning?"

After a few deep breaths to compose herself, Em began, "It's…I don't know why it bothers me so, I should really just expect it at this point. I know if Maman is going to summon me that it is likely not going to be a pleasant conversation. I try so hard to behave how she wants me to, I really do. But even when I am able to prevent loud outbursts, I'm still wrong. Even worse, today she told me all the things I did wrong in front of my stepfather and my husband."

Théodore released her arm to begin tending to some Astrantia as he casually mentioned, "That sounds rough. Here, they need more water."

Em bent down and put her hands in the dirt as well.

"I just wish for once that there was someone on my side willing to stand up for me the way that Albie did when she was alive. I have you and I know I can confide in you, but I can't expect you to stand up to my mother. She holds your job in her hands, and I know how much you love working in the gardens here."

Théodore simply continued to tend to the flowers as he nodded. She did not see him occasionally sneaking glances her way, so she did not notice the furrowed brow. She only glanced over as he returned his focus to his work. But he did not stop her to offer any kind words of sympathy or advice. Which made Em furrow her brow as well. She wondered if he simply didn't understand how cruel her mother could be.

Em continued to rant about how unfair her mother had always been from the beginning, how angry she was about being sent to the Swiss Confederation, and the many injustices she had to suffer. Théodore continued to simply care for the flowers in the *parterre* with gentleness. The contrast was sharp between the two as Em grew more and more agitated thinking about her mother and all the things she had suffered.

She knew Théodore was listening. He would nod as he listened but gave no wisdom or advice. Pausing, she hoped the break was what he needed to give voice to his thoughts, but the only response was more weeds tossed into the wheelbarrow at his side.

The silence that was once so comfortable between the pair was suddenly fueled by her anxieties. "Surely, you must agree with me, Théodore. I don't understand how she could treat me so. Her own daughter! What more could I do that I have not already done?"

The soft sound of weeds falling onto the discarded pile seemed to echo in her ears. She pushed a little further, "It's like she isn't even listening to me. I know she hears me but blatantly ignores me."

The pause this time was deafening. Em was no longer focused on the injustices she suffered at the hands of her mother. "Théodore! I thought you were my friend! Are you going to speak up for me?"

With gentle eyes, Théodore turned to her, "But you said yourself *ma dame* that I could lose my position here. I cannot speak against her."

Rocking back, Em straightened and brushed the dirt off her hands. "But you could at least agree with me that she is a horrible person and unfit to be a mother! Are you that spineless that you could not even agree with me when we are not in her presence? Oooo, you make me so...so..."

"Mad?" Théodore offered.

Affronted, Em stood. Her eyes seemed to burn through the truth he just stated. "So what if I am? I have every right to be mad when my mother treats me like some kind of wild animal to be tamed and the one person I considered a friend won't even speak to me in my torment!"

Théodore turned just enough to look up at the figure towering above him and only long enough to respond, "But I have been speaking with you."

Yelling in frustration she ran off, leaving Théodore with his Astrantia. She didn't see his small smile or hear him whisper to his precious buds, "I don't think she gets it yet. Don't worry, she will."

As Em stormed off, her head swam. Needing to release some of the anger she had been holding in, she headed for the stables. Em usually preferred walking for her daily exercise, but today she opted for horseback. She found her favorite horse, a male named Zephyr who was gentle but strong. The stable hands were quick to prepare him for a ride. Before long she was galloping away from the home she felt so burdened by. The house faded away as trees and roads came into view. She made a left on a cobblestone street and kept riding. Maybe she would even ride as far as Paris, who knew?

It was a few minutes later when she finally stopped to give the horse some water near a running stream when she realized she would probably calm down with some laudanum, but that was still in her quarters. Besides, she was running low. Maybe she would see the doctor while she was in town. Assuming her mother didn't have some kind of arrangement where she controlled that as well.

That woman had a hand in everything in Em's life. She was taking lessons from Théodore behind her back, but that was really the only joy she gave herself, not daring to risk too much of Eulalie's wrath. Everything else was influenced by her mother. Maman controlled the menu, the social calendar, Em's lessons, the doctors. She was a force to be reckoned with; there was no doubt about that.

After the horse had its fill she continued riding. *Will I ever get my life in my own hands?* she worried. *Will I ever control my body and words or forever be at my mother's mercy?* She was still furious, but less so. In time, she calmed down, only feeling the strong horse beneath her and smelling the beautiful air on the warm French day. Her mind turned to what life would be like if she lived on her own–in charge of her own home on her terms, not someone else's. No husband. No mother. Only Théodore.

Théodore! she mused. *Not only is that a fantasy but I have been so unkind.*

Remorse fell over her like the waves at sea. She was so absorbed in guilt she didn't even notice she had somehow stumbled upon a little hotel: Le Pavillon de la Reine.

She looked up and stared at the sign for several minutes. She went back and forth on whether she should enter and why. Was she considering this because of her mother's hatred of Napoleon? Was she doing it simply to make a choice on her own? Would she be considered reckless involving herself in such a scheme? Would it be dangerous? She hoped so. If she had no control over her life, she might as well have some fun with it. Maybe it would be a way to take a bit more control.

With that, she stepped inside.

Chapter 22
MEETING PIERRE

CHÉRE MARIE,

You would be so proud, I attended a party the other night and was able to maintain my composure throughout! There were a few instances where I lost control, but they were small and quiet. Hardly anyone noticed. For once, I did not turn heads by outburst! The crowd did often part for me and there were plenty of whispers. They were likely only exacerbated by my conversation with a man that I met there.

Yet how could one not enjoy the company of the great Paganini? He was an intriguing fellow. He spoke with so much passion about everything. He spoke of some new compositions he is working on that seem simply impossible for anyone who does not practice as he does. There are weeks on end when he will practice for eight to ten hours per day!

Do you have anything that you love that much? Aside from Daniel and Albert, of course. I can't seem to think of anything that I am that passionate about except for finding a cure for this malady.

For someone who has felt wrong her entire life, at least now I can put that label on Maman because marriage certainly has not made my condition any better. Dare I say the stress of being "happily married" for the public has made my insides even more knotted than before. At the same time, maturity has given me a bit of perspective on myself, too. I am not fit for society, perhaps, but I'm starting to love myself anyway. What an extraordinary thing—to have compassion for oneself when judgement used to prevail. If this is the outcome of my little malady, perhaps I am not so bad off for it in the end. As I learn to let go, like the autumn leaves on the maple outside our study, life is more bearable and serene.

In conclusion, I am not in bliss, but I am not in the depths of despair either. Despite uncertainty and a body that has a mind of its own, I find myself in peace. This shall have to be enough—and I hope the same for you, too, my dear cousin. Give my best to your sweet husband, Daniel, and little Albert.

Em

EM FELT THE BUTTERFLIES in her stomach leap to life as her shoulder muscles tensed. She tried very hard to keep them still so that she wouldn't stand out. This was supposed to be a secret rendezvous spot. No one should know she was here. She had no idea how to find the man Paganini had told her about.

She also was suddenly unsure who she was supposed to meet. Was his name Paul? Perce? It started with a 'P', of that she was sure. She had spent the rest of the evening of the party trying to hide her need to repeat the sound, usually in the form of "*Pute*". Not something to scream at an inn, to be sure.

Em had to bite her lip to keep it from escaping just at the thought of it. She tried to focus on the intricate designs in the thick, velvety curtains or the various perfumes of the guests milling about. A young man walked past, gently brushing her arm as he moved by. He called out, "Pierre!"

Yes! Pierre! That was the name. She turned to see a man about the same age as her husband sitting at a table against the wall with a single candle for light. His dark hair fell into his eyes as he studied the documents in front of him. Every once in a while, he would take out a quill and write in a notebook off to his right. The young man that had brushed past her joined him and started talking emphatically with his hands. There were a few nods from Pierre before the young man nodded and ran off.

She approached the table slowly. She sat down at the table behind him, unsure if she should join him. She asked softly, but as loud as she dared, "Have you ever met the devil's violinist?"

He turned quickly to face her. Hearing his movements, she did the same. He asked, "You know Paganini?"

"I met him yesterday. He is quite a unique individual."

"Indeed. He most certainly is. What conversation did you have?"

"Well, he mentioned that I should find you here, if that is what you are asking."

"It is. Marvelous, he knew what I needed, you must be exactly who I am looking for."

"Who or what were you looking for, sir?"

"Please, call me Pierre and join me at my table."

He stood up and pulled a chair out for her. Awkwardly, she sat down.

"Thank you," she said, clearing her throat and taking a deep breath. "I was unsure what the protocol was. All of this seems so secretive."

"It is for now. It was wise of you."

Em's heart doubled in size. No one had ever called her wise before. It felt nice to receive such a compliment. Pierre continued, "The tales of Napoleon's escape appear to be true. He is planning to return to power. He has his followers paving the way for him. Our goal is to counter efforts to recruit and downplay support for him. We plan to do this by making sure the whole country *knows* what a scoundrel he is. The Bourbons are infinitely better suited to rule than he is. Though to be perfectly honest, I'm not sure how long that will last, either. Most groups vying for power are united in the cause to defame Napoleon and prevent his return to power."

This was all certainly news to Em. Her mother, the constant doctor's visits, marriage, and Em's general inability to socialize had kept her fairly naïve as of late. Napoleon had only been on Elba for a few months. She had heard of his exile during her stay at Oberhofen. Was he on his way to Paris? Maman must not know, she would be simply livid. Possibly even terrified. She still spoke so often of the Revolution when she was a child.

"Forgive me, *monsieur*. Pierre. I do not understand what I can do for this cause. Yet, you said that Paganini would have sent me as the person you are looking for?"

Pierre picked up a cigarette, lit it, and inhaled deeply, sending out puffs of smoke as he spoke.

"We have many among our ranks who are helping in many ways across the country. What we do not have is any connection or word from the *noblesse*. We need information on who is for or against Napoleon, as well as someone to defame him and his family."

Em's eyes widened. She knew where this conversation was leading. She wasn't sure whether to be terrified or honored about the information being disclosed to her.

"Napoleon may not rule, himself. If he does not have the support, he will try to seat his son or his nephew for ruling France and whoever else he can conquer. There is no limit to the greed of this man and he must be stopped. Will you join our cause, *Mademoiselle?*"

"*Ma dame*, for I am a married woman."

"You are so young! Surely you are not even of age? Forgive me, I have overstepped my bounds. I do not even know your name yet."

Em said nothing, still processing what this stranger, friend of another stranger, was sharing with her.

"You may give an alias if you prefer," Pierre continued. "It might be safer with the messages we shall be passing back and forth. Pierre is actually my alias; I keep my name out of my political affairs. How shall I call you, my dear?"

"Um…I have no idea. I suppose it would be dangerous to even use the name of a family member. I have never even given any thought to what I would name a child. Well, I suppose I could use… um, Jeanne?"

"A fitting name for the cause. A nod to Jeanne d'Arc would absolutely be perfect. When you have information on the political stance of the *noblesse* families, please address them simply to Pierre at Le Pavillon de la Reine in Paris. I will tell the hotel to watch for letters from you. And how do we reach you should we have information to convey?"

Em wrung her hands and bit her lip. Her life consisted mainly of her apartment in Paris and the *Château* de Guermantes. Surely both would be too obvious. "Well, I…I am unsure."

Pierre lightly knocked his knuckles on the table. "Not to worry, direct communication is most discoverable in any case. After your first letter, we would have to find another route. Be sure to send me your first missive before the end of the week."

Standing quickly, Pierre explained, "I must be off, we have been too long together. I would see you home, but further association could prove perilous. If we do our jobs well, we will see you soon *ma dame*."

The gentleman stood and went up the stairs to his room. Em was left to sit and process the amount of information she had just received. There was certainly a lot more than she had been aware of. But how could she accomplish the tasks that were set before her? She certainly questioned Paganini's choice, considering the party last night where everyone avoided her. That was a large issue she would face often, she was sure. Everyone avoided her. But she was committed now. She would simply have to find a way.

Suddenly aware of how late the hour was becoming, she decided she would need to get going back to the *château* and endure the repercussions for leaving unannounced for the day. She had missed a few visits from the doctor. *The Doctor!* she thought to herself. She was going to stop by the apothecary for more laudanum. She had kept the twitches to a minimum during her visit with Pierre, but there was a mounting pressure wanting to be released.

She rushed out the door wanting her medicine more than anything else, and she would need to restock before heading back to the *château*. Em walked quickly through the streets, glancing at the shop windows as she did so. Dresses. Meats. Fabrics. Leather belts… all on display for the curious observer to daydream. Em had no time for such fantasy, however. When she saw the white coat hanging off a chair and the tableau of empty pill bottles, she darted inside. There was no line, and within moments she had a full bottle of laudanum in her front jacket pocket. As she walked out the door, she considered taking one right there and then—in front of the carriages and the shoppers and the young boys selling newspapers, but she didn't dare. She wanted a clear mind to consider the tasks she had received from Pierre. Yet her mind kept returning to the bottle in her pocket and her hand kept finding its way back to the small glass vial.

"Are you okay, sweet one?" she said to her horse who had been patiently tied up about a block down. "It's time to go home. We have much to discuss!"

She untied her mount, hoisted herself up into its gleaming saddle and headed away from town.

About halfway through the journey home, with the day turning into the evening, she considered her husband's connection to Napoleon and how this would affect his status–and hers by extension. She was so busy mulling everything over she was caught off guard by a tall man who grabbed her from behind and pulled her off her horse. He spun her around to face him with a grin on his face. "What have we here? Out after dark, and by yourself? Seems the nice rich lady could use an escort."

The sudden rush of alarm took over Em's ability to hold in her movements and she started violently shaking. With the rush of adrenaline and movement came a slew of every inappropriate word she had ever heard and then some. The combination didn't allow much breath, so every break in words, she took a deep gasping breath. Em was fascinated as the man slowly let go of her, smile fading from his face. He backed away slowly as she continued to curse and shake. His eyes became larger and larger until he turned and ran, calling for a priest and crying "Demon!" while making the sign of the cross.

The cursing stopped as he ran away, but the shaking continued. It took a few tries to get back on her horse with all the fearful quivering, but she made it up. Little by little her body returned to a state of stillness as she journeyed the rest of the way home. By the time she reached the *château*, what little shaking remained was that of excitement. She escaped! All on her own! Well, with the help of her curse. Maybe it wasn't so awful after all. It had essentially saved her life. Closing the door behind her, she leaned her back against it to consider the night's events.

How she wished Albie were still here; she would have loved to hear of this. She would have called it an adventure. Em couldn't quite call it that. It had scared her witless. However, she was incredibly proud of making it home safely. She remembered the laudanum in her pocket and pulled it out for a quick sip to calm her racing heart. Maybe this malady wasn't as bad as she had always thought. With a smile to herself, she pushed herself off the door and ran in search of someone to tell of her success.

She ran into her husband first. "Oh! Louis! You will never guess what has happened to me tonight. I went out for a ride, you see–"

"Yes, I noticed. You haven't been anywhere to be found all day. First, you shift blame to me for not being more attentive, then run off the day I spend time around the *château. Mon Dieu*, what do you want from me?"

"Well, I was upset. But let me tell you–"

"Oh, the poor little doll. You were upset? As if no one else ever has been upset before."

He took a few steps toward her, closing the space between the wide hallway. "I have also been upset, but no one ever seemed to care. Ever watch a soldier die in front of you? Mighty upsetting. The world doesn't stop though; we keep pressing forward. We do what must be done. I've done my duty in marrying you. I was even willing to spend time with you as per your request. Then you run off because your poor little feelings were hurt? You will receive no sympathy from me, *ma poupée*."

He continued down the hall toward his quarters. Em stood there for a moment, completely dumbfounded. She hadn't meant to be insensitive. All the excitement she had a moment ago had completely disappeared.

She had finally done something that she was proud of. In an instant, it was completely gone and uncelebrated. Oh, how she missed Albertine. She had no friends inside the castle. Maybe she could tell Théodore tomorrow. He seemed to be the only friend she had left in the world.

Slowly, she finally started moving again. She went to her quarters and refilled her medicine bottle, but decided she might need another dose before heading to bed. It took her several drops before all of the many emotions she felt disappeared. She crawled into her bed and quickly fell asleep. Maybe tomorrow she would be able to understand the chaos she left behind.

Chapter 23
A Visit and A Choice

I did something I was so proud of today, and no one would listen. In fact, I was chastised for my reckless behavior. I think Albie would have been proud of me. It was probably the first time in my life I did not have to depend on anyone's help. I did it all on my own. Sort of. What an interesting dichotomy that my curse saved me.

I've spent so much of my life hating whatever this is and searching for a cure. Maybe it isn't such a bad thing, though. What if it is some kind of blessing in disguise? It's a really good disguise, that's for sure. Dressed as a demon or witches' curse. It's not as if there are many uses for it, but it does make me wonder if there are more possibilities that I have not yet seen? And how can one utilize something that has no consistency?

THE FOLLOWING MORNING, EM arose with an awful headache. She had often heard her husband complain of headaches after long nights full of excessive drinking. She concluded her laudanum must have the same effect. She would need to temper how much she took before bed in the future.

Once she was dressed, she went down to breakfast, hoping the food would soothe the effects of the previous night's events. Still a bit groggy, she sat down with her mother and Louis at the table, murmuring a soft, "Good morning," which was met with silence. Glancing up, she saw the fire in her mother's eyes that she usually only saw after her failed attempts to control her malady. Stealing a glance at her husband, she found him to be staring intently at her, poking at his food, but she was unable to read his expression.

With an excessive amount of forced sweetness, her mother asked through gritted teeth, "How was your evening, my child? I trust it was uneventful?"

Taking a quick bite of the nearest slice of bread, Em chewed slowly. She knew her mother probably had some complaint, but the way her head was pounding, she could not figure out what crime she had committed now. Her head throbbed with each new thought that tried to enter her mind. When she finally swallowed, she had decided upon the direct approach and simply asked, "What have I done now?"

Eulalie scoffed at the simple response. "Really, child," she patronized, "you think that no one would notice the absence of an heiress for several hours late at night, knowing only that you rode off alone on a steed? Goodness, anything could have happened! What if you had another episode and this one caused injury? What if you had been robbed?"

"What if I could take care of myself?" Em countered.

As she related the events of the evening, Em was met with just as much criticism as her post-party meetings with her mother about her etiquette. "Ernestine! You are proud of such foolishness? Why were you out that late after dark? Why didn't you have an escort? Do you realize what could have happened? You tell no one else of your shameful behavior! Foolish girl. First, it was your shameful etiquette at parties, must you now be under constant supervision?"

"But I thought—"

"No, you most certainly were not thinking. Even if you were picking up more medicine, we have servants for that Ernestine! There is no excuse you can give that will make all of this better. What a stupid mistake. Don't get me wrong, *ma biquette*, I am very grateful you weren't hurt and that you are ok, but please let this be a lesson. No more running around after dark, especially without either your husband or a servant attending to you.

"And that's another thing! Your husband spent the entire day looking for you around the *château*. He was trying to be a good, attentive husband, and you left him all alone. I really don't know what to do with you, Ernestine. How could you disregard your position and your responsibilities running about like that? You never give me a moment's rest."

Louis gave a small smirk, but said nothing. The rest of breakfast passed in silence. Her mother was not wrong. She knew she shouldn't have been out after dark without an escort. That wasn't the point of her story! It was as if they didn't want to hear anything good about her illness. The only thing good they could see about it would be a cure and for her to be the perfect French *Comtesse*.

Long after Louis gave her a perfunctory kiss on the cheek and exited with her mother to discuss the hiring of new servants, Em sat at the table alone, thinking about her life. It was true—she didn't know how to be perfect. Em couldn't even manage normal on a good day, much less perfect. It all felt so hopeless. She just couldn't manage to get anything right. *Maybe Théodore would appreciate it?* she thought. Before long she found herself walking toward the gardens, thinking of the young gardener as she did so. He was a lot like Albie in many ways. He was supportive and encouraging. *Maybe he can find a bright spot in all of this?* she mused. *Surely, he will not chastise me. He is a servant after all!*

She only waited a few moments at their traditional meeting spot before he arrived.

"You are back," he greeted her.

"I am," she said, suddenly shy as she remembered how their last conversation ended.

"Let's get to work then, shall we?"

He handed her a hand trowel. They worked without words, just happy to be in each other's presence. In time, however, small talk about her irises eventually transitioned to politics. It was then that Em related the story of last night's escape to Théodore. She focused on the work in front, unable to look at his face for fear of disappointment. She didn't need to see it; she could hear it in his voice when he spoke. "*Ma dame*, I wish you had taken me with you."

"I was upset with you, remember?"

"This is true. Was there no servant you could have taken? I am not in a position to criticize *ma dame*, I am simply worried for your safety. I couldn't bear to lose you. You are easily the closest thing I have to a friend that isn't a plant. I am grateful you made it home safely."

Em couldn't hold in a sigh and her shoulder started to kick forward in a most painful manner. "That might have to be all for today, Théodore. I need to take some of my medicine for this shoulder."

Em stood up and took her leave. On her way to her chambers, she ran into her mother. "Ernestine! How do you always seem to be covered in dirt? You have a household to run and appearances to keep! Go wash up this instant. You are unfit to be seen in public. What must the servants think?"

Eulalie's criticisms didn't stop as she walked away, but they did fade as Em briskly went to her chambers to wash and change. As she strode through the halls, Em could feel the tension creeping up her shoulders and longed for the release her medicine would give her. As she reached her room, she strode first to her bedside for the little glass vial before washing.

Drying her hands, she couldn't bear to face the unfriendly faces of the *château* staff and especially didn't want to face her mother. She needed solace. She needed a friend. With another drop of laudanum before leaving the room, she found the courage to do something else she had been putting off. Em decided it had been long enough; she needed to see her sister.

As she meandered through the cemetery, she contemplated the many lives of those laid to rest in this place. What of their lives? Did they struggle so? Maybe one of them had a similar curse. Who brought the curse upon the family? Well, obviously not the whole family. She was the one who was out of control. Though her mother did have to raise an uncontrollable daughter. She was reminded daily of her mother's "curse".

By the time she reached Albertine's grave with traces of grass starting to fill in the freshly turned earth, Em was quite upset. Even angry. Em wasn't really sure who she was the most upset with. Albie for leaving her alone with no one to depend on. Théodore for caring for his garden more than her. Maman for almost every interaction they had ever had and for caring more about appearances than building Albie a proper mausoleum. Louis for being so disinterested. Altogether, Em was simply furious.

Em wanted nothing more than to scream herself inside out. Instead, she collapsed on the nearby bench and cried. A lot. Afterward, she was simply exhausted. Em felt so empty without her sister. As a hollow shell, what impact could she have? She had never felt more lost. She had lost her freedom between her marriage and her mother. She had lost her sister, her only friend and confidante. She had lost purpose in giving up on finding a cure, and in so doing, felt she had lost herself.

Then again, Albie did always love a blank page. After all, it meant you were free to create anything you wanted. The problem was, Em didn't know what she wanted. At least, not specifically. Right now, all she wanted was to stop hurting. She knew she wanted to be free to make her own choices. She wanted to do something that would influence others beyond her life. She wanted to be loved. Then again, who didn't want those things? They felt so very common, yet also so far out of reach. How could she ever hope to obtain any of them?

She ached for another dose of laudanum. These questions and emotions were simply too much for her to carry. Her medicine not only reduced her outbursts, but brought a moment of pure ecstasy, letting everything else fade into the background. But that wasn't much of a life. It didn't help her really do anything worthwhile. While she longed for the feeling her medicine provided, she also wanted the passion for something that Paganini had shown her. The two didn't really go hand in hand, did they?

Em wasn't sure why she was sitting on this stone bench. It's not like her sister was here. Albertine wasn't going to magically appear before her like Cinderella's fairy godmother to fix everything and make everything right. Maybe she was afraid of thinking in her room, too close to her laudanum. She had already used a large portion of what she had gotten yesterday. Even though she still had outbursts with about the same frequency, she was taking more and more of it.

She didn't fully understand that, either. It helped before a party, to be sure. It just didn't stop them the way the doctors had hoped.

She had discovered that she could hold them in for a while. Maybe she could work on that skill until they stopped completely. If not completely, at least when she needed to put on a calm front. The only way to make her mother happy and to help the resistance was to act the part of a good high-born *comtesse*. No one else could fulfill this role; it was her responsibility. Em decided she would play the game and see how well she fared.

She would learn to keep these outbursts under control. She managed to hide them well enough during her meeting with Pierre. At least until the highwayman had come along. It was better than nothing, though. She had to try it. Anything was better than this.

Things would be different. Yes, she had tried to fill this role and be a "good girl" before with no success, but this time, she had a rea-son. She had a mission to accomplish. Find the names of those siding with Napoleon among the *bourgeois*, and find ways to gain the favor of the well-to-do so she could discredit Napoleon. She knew it would take time, but what else was she going to do with herself?

Yes, she had made up her mind. She would go right to her mother with a request for a party. Or whatever Maman had on her calendar already. She would also have to look into whether there were any art competitions coming up that she could enter and possibly win. She was accomplished, but an award would certainly raise her status in the eyes of others. She would do her best or die trying. She didn't fear death anymore. It couldn't be worse than life as it was now. Maybe then she could be with her Albertine.

She rushed back into her room for her medicine and took a quick swallow for courage as she approached Maman. Eulalie, of course, was beyond thrilled for this new attitude from her daughter. Finally, all of those lectures and instructions were beginning to yield results. There was already a party scheduled for that week and Eulalie hoped her daughter's resolve would last at least until then. Preferably longer.

There was also a fair coming up in the next few months. Em could prepare a few entries in the horticulture exhibits thanks to her time with Théodore. With his instruction, she must be able to win something. Things were finally looking up for Em and for the first time in her life, she looked forward to the coming days and weeks with excitement and joy.

After the conclusion of the audience with Maman, Em ran outside to find Théodore. She was simply glowing with excitement when she arrived. Théodore smiled at her as she approached. He didn't even have time to ask what had happened before she started asking him questions about the Astrantia he had pointed out the other day.

As he explained how to care best for this perennial, Em calmed. Something about this flower stirred her almost as much as the iris. She mentioned this to Théodore who seemed unaffected by her comment. "Well, that makes sense. All plants have symbolism. I told you they bring me closer to God, and that's in part why. When I see these plants, I'm reminded of what they stand for, and it's like God is speaking right to me.

"Take for example this Astrantia. Sure, it's a pretty flower, but it is so much more. The color is also important. So, this red one is usually a symbol of courage and strength. But a white or pink one can change the meaning. The iris that you are so fond of and have in your room, that is the inspiration for the *fleur-de-lis* and is widely recognized as a symbol of the French monarchy. Again, it has a deeper meaning. They are a symbol of faith and hope. I would imagine this is why monarchs have used it in their emblems for centuries.

"Or take that old oak tree you love to sit under so much. It also has a symbol. They stand for strength and stability. So it makes sense that it is often where you run to when you have a bad day. I'm not sure why you chose the *parterre* today. But I am glad. It meant I could run into you sooner. I'm sure you are bored with my long-winded speech. I tend to ramble on when I get excited like this. This is why I love the gardens so much. Forgive me for my overindulgence."

"I like it. That's why I wanted to ask you a favor. No one knows more about plants and gardens than you do. There is a fair coming up and I wanted to submit a piece of horticulture from the things I am learning from you."

"You want someone to judge if your plants are good enough? That doesn't make any sense."

He had a downcast look that Em had never seen before.

"No, it's like a competition to see who raised the best plants."

"That makes even less sense," he retorted, voice flat. Dare she say, cynical? "You already said that I'm the best you know, so why are you trying to be better than others?"

Em tried to respond but he uncharacteristically cut her off. "*Ma dame*, I just shared with you how this growth is an act of God and you turn it into a game? This isn't a game. This is my life and my heart, and you would degrade it so? This isn't about awards or showing off. The opinions of others don't matter here. Isn't that why you felt safe here to begin with?"

Em was dumbfounded. "No, of course not! Théodore, I do love this. You are right; this is why I've felt so safe and comfortable here and with you. But shouldn't a gift like this be shared?"

"I do share it. With you."

Théodore turned, paused, and before walking away said, "I think that is our lesson for today. I do not think we should continue them."

With a quick bow, he turned and walked toward the servant's quarters. Em was completely dumbfounded. She had never considered that Théodore would say no, much less that he would discontinue their lessons. He left her. He had slowly become the best friend that she had, yet he could walk away so easily.

It was a slap in the face, not just to her connection with Théodore, but also to the one thing that had started to really make her feel like she had a purpose and something she could do to make a difference. Now how would she gain any kind of favor with the *noblesse*? How would she make any difference in the Revolution? The world that had just started to finally make sense was turned upside down so quickly.

Her first thought was of the tenseness crawling up her arm, then of the laudanum sitting on her bedside table. She was suddenly right back where she started, completely overwhelmed and feeling inadequate. She would never be able to accomplish this task. Yet the drive to try was still alive and well. After all, she could die trying or having done nothing at all.

She ran inside to take her medicine before the spasms could start. There had to be other options that she could use to study and further encourage her love of flowers, even if Théodore had turned his back on her. There were plenty of books in the library, surely there must be a few that would be able to help her in some way.

It quite possibly meant more time around Maman, but she could keep up the *façade*. They were on the same team now, right? Surely her mother would welcome such an accomplishment. It would all be worth the effort, she was sure. First, however, she needed a nap.

Chapter 24
THE PERFECT PARTY GUEST

Isn't it strange how laudanum works? At first, it worked extremely well. However, I have noticed I need more and more doses just to function. I feel like I need it on my person at all times. It makes me increasingly tired and I have some of the strangest dreams. I have never been one to do so, but the more I take, the more I find myself almost as if I'm in a waking dream and it is all so increasingly odd. Sometimes even disturbing.

I know there are some crazy stories that play out in my head as I sleep, but I don't always remember what they are. I've also noticed I start getting more upset if I go too long without my laudanum. It's almost like I need it, not just for this malady for which it was given, but also just for my own sanity. It is an odd happenstance. The important thing is that it is helping, regardless of the other changes that seem to happen.

Without Théodore's sweet company, Em began spending more and more time with Maman. What she didn't anticipate was the increased involvement her mother would want to have in her life. "Ernestine, I love how dedicated you are to your studies and how much you have changed in the past few weeks. It really is quite remarkable."

Em glowed with the praise she had worked so hard for her entire life, even if a small part of her felt as if it was due to her hard work over the years trying to earn approval. Not for the mere fact that Em was her daughter–worthy of love and honor just for being her. *Théodore always liked me for me,* she thought, quickly remembering that this would not be the case anymore. "Thank you so much, Maman. I am so pleased that you are happy," she replied, grateful for the praise regardless of its intention.

"I am quite. The only thing that would make me happier would be to see your marriage thrive as much as you have on your own. Tell me, dear, how are things with Louis?"

It was Saturday. Much of the help had been released from their labors to attend a local fair. Eulalie and Em were sitting in the parlor, dining on leftover quail with roasted potatoes and vegetables.

"I can't complain much, Maman. He is a good match," Em replied, stabbing a carrot with a shining silver fork. "This year's crop has been exceptional, has it not?"

Eulalie put her utensils down and folded her hands in her lap. "My daughter, I won't be distracted so easily."

Em smiled at her mother's shrewdness. Eulalie was tough, but it was admirable that she never missed a trick.

"So…Have you been spending more…time together?"

"Oh yes, much time. Lots and lots of time. It's been fairly exhausting but delightful if I do say so myself," Em said.

Maman's eyes widened. While Eulalie might be cunning and direct, Em was forever the victor with her wit and sass.

"That's…wonderful, Darling," Eulalie answered. "I would so love to see a baby running around the *château* again!"

"How many would make you the happiest?" Em asked, her hands crossed across her chest.

"As many as it takes," Eulalie said. "But one will do as an heir for your fortune and the *château*. Based on your…eh…reports…this shouldn't be too difficult, then."

Em looked down. "I am tired, Maman," she said.

"Perhaps this is good news then?" Maman said, clapping her hands together. "How long have you been…not feeling quite yourself?"

"Good question," Em paused for dramatic effect, then added, "At least the past two minutes since your interrogation began."

And with that she stood up, placed her napkin on the chair, and walked over to her mother. "Thank you for your concern," she said, kissing her on the cheek and exiting the parlor.

THAT EVENING, AS SHE dressed for bed, Em was flooded with thoughts of the earlier conversation. It wasn't the first time the topic had come up. While she felt a bit guilty for playing with Maman so, she couldn't indulge her either. The idea of having children still seemed like a ridiculous notion. Not while she was cursed. *If Albie were here, she'd understand this. What would my child's first word be? 'Merde?'* She laughed at the audacity of such a thought. She wished her mother could understand this, but of course she couldn't, so Em kept her feelings to herself.

As the competition came closer and closer, Em stayed busy studying the various plants and how to care for them. She even found a book on floriography. She was fascinated by the symbols and the extensive history through various cultures around the world. She had so many questions, though. A few times she caught up with Théodore in the garden, hoping he might spare a few minutes to talk to her, but he always found an excuse to leave.

Her heart broke a little knowing Théodore had the information so vital to her winning. But more than his intellect, she missed his heart terribly. She felt no different than the roses who simply could not bloom under the shade of the leafy oak. How she longed for the sun and the warmth that Théodore had always carried with him. She felt withered without him.

"Maman, I've learned something from you," she said to Eulalie one night on a moonlight stroll. "You might have endured a lot of heartache of war, but you persisted, and so shall I."

"I am so proud of you, my dear. Your condition will not keep you from finding happiness."

"What about if a man will?" Em said, stopping at a small lake with stars reflecting off the glass-like surface.

"Are you having a lover's quarrel?" Maman asked.

"Perhaps," Em said, "Nothing major, but…I miss how we used to talk. Do you have any suggestions?"

"Of course, my dear," Eulalie said, taking her daughter's hand "Put it out of your mind, stay busy with what you can do for you, and he will come around."

Em smiled. This actually made sense to her. The next few days, when she bumped into Théodore she kept to herself. "Excuse me," she said, before walking away.

By the third day in a row of this happening she could have sworn Théodore was about to say something but did not. She still missed his words, but the knowledge that she still had an impact on him dulled the pain of their conversations. Besides, she really did have much to do! Between the various party preparations, gown fittings, gathering intel for Pierre, and wondering if she should enter the competition, she wasn't sure how to even begin a conversation with him again.

Before she knew it, the day of the party arrived. She had been practicing all the time around Maman, and Em was confident this party would go over much better than previous outings she had been to.

She entered the ballroom with her head held high and she was instantly greeted by her friend Paganini. "Hello, beautiful lady! How are the demons treating you?"

Em gave a small curtsy as she replied, "Very well, sir. They seem to be behaving as of late. It has been very beneficial to the harmony at the *château*."

"Pity. They are lively and exciting. One needs a sense of adventure and the unknown from time to time. And harmony can be overrated. I've been composing some lively pieces and had you in mind as I wrote one of them. I will play one for you tonight. I'm sure you will recognize which piece was composed with you in mind."

With a wink, Paganini turned and disappeared into the crowd. As the evening progressed, the tune caught Em's attention instantly. It was incredibly moving, starting out slow before gradually building in speed, with several quick and bouncy embellishments. Then it suddenly changed to almost exactly how Em felt when she was itching all over before her convulsions began.

She didn't know how he managed to capture so much of her daily emotions in one song, but there it was, displayed for all to see... and people loved it. She wasn't able to speak with Paganini afterward; she was too busy trying to work her way into the crowd instead of being the wallflower. Still, she wished she could listen to it over and over again.

Speaking with a few people during the party, there were a few gasps she couldn't keep in, but they were luckily well-timed and fit in well with the conversation. She had spoken fairly minimally by usual standards, but it had been more conversation than she had with any-one besides Théodore, Maman, Albie, or even Louis. Em was proud of herself for how far she had come.

Oh, how Albie would have loved this party. She was always the center of attention wherever she went. So vibrant and full of life! Em thought of her often throughout the evening, trying to imitate what she would have done. It was bittersweet to think of her so often, yet have to hide the tears in addition to her outbursts. Somehow, Em had managed.

The only downside to the party was running into Charles, that terrible, cruel man. Em hated that Louis always insisted he come to their events. She crossed the room to be with her husband at the request of her mother and for appearances' sake, only to find him with Charles. With a heavy sigh, Em pressed on, determined not to let that oaf of a Bonaparte get the better of her. Plastering on a smile, she approached the pair and looped her left arm through her husband's.

Em could already feel her shoulder creeping up toward her ear and the muscles in her arm tighten. She feared it was only a matter of time before she had an outburst. As Charles boasted of his latest travels, Em's face began to contort. Quickly, Em pulled out her fan and turned her head as if to speak to the woman to her right.

It didn't seem to matter how well Em did at hiding her out-bursts, Charles somehow knew just how to make her a target and a laughingstock. He joked, "Louis, when will you leave this wife of yours for a real woman? There are many I could introduce you to. She can't even manage to give you an heir like a proper wife, much less spend time among polite society!"

Louis let go of Em's arm to roughly grab Charles' arm and moved him toward the balcony, leaving Em standing alone trying to hide behind her fan. Despite how much it hurt, Em kept a smile on her face. She couldn't quite manage to laugh along with the joke, but she still considered not running away a success.

The rest of the party went off without a hitch. By the time she made it up to her room, it was very late, but still she did a little dance of joy. However, the movements seemed to trigger all of her usual itchiness and she began to convulse much more severely than she ever had before. Her jaw tightened and the only way to loosen it also released a string of vulgarities. Many she had said before, but there were a few new phrases in there as well.

She couldn't even hold still long enough to pour her medicine. She didn't dare try. When the movements didn't stop as they normally did, Em ran to her door and tried to call out for help. Louis had been walking past and stopped when Em stumbled out of the doorway. "Laudanum. Please."

She couldn't say much more due to the constant movement. Em had never felt so out of place in her body. Louis rushed into the room to help her since her hands refused to unclench. When she had taken a few drops, Louis helped himself to a couple of drops as well. "So, this is where you keep the good stuff."

"No! That's my medicine! I need it! Please, another." Louis prepared another dose, but she finally had enough control of her hands to take another portion by herself. The convulsions slowed to a stop over the next several minutes, while Louis helped himself to another serving as well.

"Thank you, Louis. I have never seen them quite so intense before!"

"Well, that's good to know. I'm glad this isn't a common occurrence when I'm not around. I might really begin to think you possessed if I hadn't seen the doctor's medicine work so efficiently. Then again, it works wonders for me as well."

With a smirk, he took another drop. "And with that, I'll bid you good night my dear. That stuff is potent! Especially after a lovely night full of fantastic wine. Wouldn't you agree? It was high quality, if I do say so myself!"

However, instead of rising, he curled up against Em's pillows and quickly started to snore. *My husband is a drunkard and opium-eater. My medicine is not for recreation. What luck I have.*

Grudgingly, Em pushed him aside and curled up next to him. After all, Maman had been pushing for this. Not to mention, she was far too exhausted from the episode and laudanum to think of anything besides sleep. Once her head hit the pillows, Em was asleep almost as quickly as her husband.

Chapter 25
RECONCILIATION

I HAD KNOWN THAT LOUIS drinks a lot of wine. I just hadn't pieced together just how much and how often. He is good at putting on a show, but he drinks wine the way I take my medicine these days. Sometimes I wonder if it is too much. Not just for him, but for me as well. It has increased so much. I used to take one or two drops, but now I am taking several drops per day. Probably closer to six or seven. Maybe eight on rough days. Is there such a thing as too much medicine? If there was, I'm sure the doctor would inform me. He knows what is healthy, right?

Being a drunkard is different. There is easily a limit to how much he should consume. I wish I had the ability to keep him in line. A wife should know what is good for her husband. Maybe Maman is right, I really should pay him more mind. Then I can help him with things like this. Drunkenness can lead to all sorts of scandal, and we already have enough of that, thanks to me. Yes, I need to be more attentive.

THE NEXT MORNING, WHEN she awoke, Louis was already gone. Then again, between absolutely exhausting herself at the party, her after-party attack, and the laudanum, she slept much later than usual. She had the most atrocious headache. A dose of medicine would be sure to help.

As soon as she opened her door, a servant informed her that her mother was waiting to see her. Apprehension instantly gripped Em and her shoulder somehow had the energy to twitch up toward her head. "Alright, I will dress and be right down."

Em took another quick dose of her medicine to calm her nerves as she prepared herself and got dressed. She stopped at the door of her mother's study for a deep breath before entering. "You wished to see me, Maman?"

Looking up from the book she was holding, a genuine smile lit up her face. "Ah! There she is! *Mon Bijou*! Darling! I had so much fun last night, didn't you? I just needed to tell you how very proud I am of you. I knew you had it in you all along."

"Thank you, dear Mother." Em curtseyed deeply, rising slowly so the blood didn't hurt her head more than it already did.

"It was only a matter of time before you stopped being so stubborn. I had so many come up to me and tell me how changed you are."

"Is that so?" Em said, taking a seat opposite her mother.

"Yes, my dear! Several haven't seen you since the wedding, and they say that Louis has done you well. My Ernestine, it was a true success! Did you enjoy it as much as I did?"

Recalling her promise to herself, Em forced a smile. She wasn't expecting to feel so hollow after getting the praise she had always wanted and yearned for. Maman's words felt so empty. For the first time, Em noticed that even with her compliments, Maman managed to push Em farther away. Yet, for the sake of her mission, she couldn't just walk away with her thoughts and sorrow. "Of course! It was the most fun I'd ever had at a party!"

This wasn't a lie. It was certainly much better to laugh and smile and be admired by others than to hide against the wall in fear. Even if it was just a front. It was a lot of work, but Em did enjoy the attention. She was still reeling over the idea that Paganini had composed a song about her. Of all people! And she loved it. She didn't dare share this with her mother; Em was not about to be called a liar when Maman was finally starting to give her a break.

Maman chatted gaily for the next hour, with Em responding when appropriate. While she loved the attention, she didn't see the need to chat about the gowns, the food, or the gossip. None of that was information she was looking for in regard to her mission.

At the earliest moment she could, Em took her leave and, swinging by the kitchen for some madeleines, ran out into the gardens. She found her favorite tree, grateful for some peace and serenity, allowing her space to speak her thoughts out loud as they came.

Em knew she needed to speak with Louis. There was a lot going on there that she didn't want to face. Em didn't want to even think about starting a family, or politics, or what they were to each other, or what their future was going to look like. She wanted to consider new ways to avoid him, but instead tried to think of ways to initiate a conversation without feeling afraid of where the conversation would go.

Em hadn't reached a conclusion about Louis before her soliloquy turned to Maman. After all, she had just realized that getting what she had always wanted from her mother didn't feel quite as she expected it to. There was still a void in her heart. She had wanted it for so long, hoping it would fill the hole of loneliness she felt. She was still so lonely in this struggle. She missed Théodore.

With that thought, she stopped. A few tears started to form and threatened to fall, when she heard a rustling of leaves. Around her the bushes were still. Suddenly, Théodore dropped to her side from the treetops. "Hello, *ma dame*."

Em was speechless as red crept up her cheeks. "Were…were you up there the whole time? And do you always just spend time up in trees trying to eavesdrop on unsuspecting maidens?"

"Yes, I was up there the entire time, trimming off a few dead branches. I should have come down sooner, but I didn't want to interrupt your thoughts or drop branches on your head. However, it sounded like you needed someone to talk to. Also yes, I do spend a lot of time climbing trees. It drove my parents mad as a child. It seems to help me think about things more clearly, just as it seems to do the same for you."

"Except as a lady, I am not to be climbing trees," laughed Em. "I did not realize you were up in the tree or I would have been sure to remain silent."

Théodore blushed. "I was actually thinking about you. I was wondering how upset you were with me and how we could be friends again. I've missed your company."

"Really?"

"Yes, *ma dame*."

"If we are friends…how come you are still so formal with me? Will you call me Em? No one calls me Em anymore. It's always Ernestine or some other formal title. I miss the sobriquet."

"Of course…Em. And in return, please call me Théo."

They smiled at each other for a moment. Each was unsure how to break the silence. Em decided she needed to start taking charge of things and began to broach the subject of their disagreement. "Are you still upset with me about the competition?"

"Well, yes, actually. But just like with gardening, I cannot control all the factors. I can't control the weather, and I can't control you. I am still hurt by the idea, and I could never do it. But that doesn't mean that you can't. I just don't understand it at all."

"I'm sorry that I hurt you. I can respect your decision not to help me specifically to win the competition. You did make your feelings very clear. I do need to do this, even if I am uncomfortable with it myself. I'm terrified to put myself out there like this."

"Then why do you do it?"

"Well, there are a few reasons, really. I've lived my entire life simply searching for what illness I have and how to cure it. I want to do more with my life. I want to do something worthwhile, something that makes me happy. If I am lucky, I want to do something that will have a lasting impact. Some kind of legacy after I am gone. I want to prove to myself and others that I have worth, despite this curse I carry. I want to be taken seriously instead of treated like a child both in the *château* and in society in general."

Théo looked at her intently. Of everything she had missed, it was those big blue eyes she missed the most. They were captivating. Compassionate. She felt understood in a way only he made her feel.

"Go on," Théo said, after a minute of pause.

"Yes, of course…it's…This might not be the route to get me all of those things. However, I must try if I am to ever know. Just like what you heard a moment ago when I was talking about Maman. I wanted her praise and affection. Yet now that I have it…it's just not what I was hoping for. I didn't actually know much of my mother aside from her discords with me. We have nothing in common. Had I not achieved her confidence that allowed me to see her as a person, I would have kept searching and wishing for it, you know? I have to try and do things to find what I'm searching for."

"What exactly are you searching for? I'm still not sure I understand that or how this will help. You don't need to have anyone else's approval."

"It's not so much approval…I want a purpose; to know I've made a difference, and to be loved. Who besides Albie has really loved me? You are important to me and I love our companionship, but I don't even know how you feel about me."

"You know, I love this oak tree. I come here anytime I have a spare moment. I have been climbing the branches of this tree for years, ever since I was first employed here as a gardener. I remember the first time I ever climbed the branches, I felt like I was flying. Like I was finally free from the life I had been raised in.

"Once as I rested up there, I suddenly heard two young women approaching. One of them was crying, while the other gave comfort and advice. I wished to wipe the tears from the young lady myself, but didn't dare give away my position. The young ladies were my employers and I didn't dare risk such a job as this.

"That night, I was so struck by the humble nature of the girl. What type of girl is able to create such a bond with a sister? The way the elder spoke to the younger showed an incredibly deep love and devotion. I longed to know how the younger sister felt. I had to know more about this lady and how I could be the one to wipe her tears away for the rest of her life."

Upon hearing those words, tears began to fall from Em's cheeks. Théo's hands approached her eyes and slowly, gently, he began to wipe them away. Em did not resist. Never, other than Albie, had she felt so loved by another person. So healed by someone's touch.

"Em, I've loved you since the first moment I saw you. I had to arrange a meeting that night. I had thought after your time in the Swiss Confederation you would have forgotten about me and I'm so grateful that you have come back into my life. I am honored to be a part of yours."

Once again, Em was left completely speechless. She felt a blush rise in her cheeks as she contemplated if she felt more joy, relief, love, guilt, or embarrassment. She was, after all, a married woman. Despite this fact, she couldn't stop a smile from spreading across her face. "Really? Cursed, married, and confused me?"

"Beautiful, thoughtful, considerate, capable you."

Em bit her lower lip with pleasure, unsure of what to do next. She had never had any kind of admirer. She went straight to having a husband for the sake of her curse. "I don't know what to say…"

"There's nothing to say. I've probably said too much. But…perhaps like your condition, I couldn't keep it trapped inside anymore."

"Oh, Théo, what would I do without you?" Em smiled. "I… appreciate your words more than you know. They calm me. They keep me grounded."

"And you allow me to soar among the clouds and dream that more is possible."

Unsure of what would be appropriate, she leaned over and kissed him on the cheek before getting up and running back to the *château*. She was already overwhelmed by her emotions and could not handle much more. Especially considering she had a husband. She glanced back once at Théo to see him standing, watching her with a smile on his face.

When Em got back inside the *château*, she ran into Louis. "Oh! Louis! I was hoping to run into you. If you have time, could we maybe have a talk? There have been some things on my mind."

"*Ma poupée*, but of course! However, not right now. I am headed out to meet up with a few friends for drinks. That is, unless you care to share the good stuff you have hidden away in your room, hmm?"

"But that is my medicine! I need more as it is, you almost finished it off last night."

"Alright then, your questions will have to be answered tomorrow. I have an appointment to keep."

With that, he waltzed out the door. Speaking of her medicine, Em should probably have some, she could feel the tension rising in her shoulders. She went up to her room for a dose and to think about what she should do regarding her husband and Théo.

Chapter 26
Too Much

❧

*C*HÉRE MARIE,

Forgive me for skipping the pleasantries, but I have some questions and I believe you are the only person I know who will be able to answer them. It's obvious you love your husband with all the affection, the kind words, and I once saw you kissing behind the carriage right before Daniel left for Vienna. It was a long kiss, too! And you seemed to enjoy it, as did he.

My questions are two fold—first, how did you gain such a relationship? I would love nothing more than to have a husband I am close to, but our circumstances were such that I fear I may never find such joy in wedlock. I'd even settle for mere affection as bliss seems not to be our path.

Secondly, forgive me if I'm sounding forward—I don't mean to—but I am so very curious as he wasn't present much at Oberhofen. You certainly didn't seem distraught at his absences—you are so strong! And yet, you always appeared overjoyed upon his return, often spending one or two days in his room with nary sight nor sound of you.

Your Daniel is so engaging. So kind. So considerate. I can't imagine him refusing anything from you. He is always so ready with a warm embrace or a flower. He's so eager…so genuinely interested in Albert's and your days.

I'd like to think I'm making up a story, but no. I am doubting myself so much less these days. My very soul believes that there is true love between you. I can feel it. I can feel this emotion even between the servants. Even Anne blushed scarlet when Henri, a carpenter who lives in the lodges on our property, slipped a note of adoration into her apron last week. She hasn't stopped talking about it since—and Anne is usually far too busy gossiping about others to speak of herself.

These occurrences give me pause when it comes to my own husband. Louis is nice enough, but I fear I've made a mistake. We haven't shared a bed but a handful of times since our honeymoon. We don't share conversations. He is more interested in his wine, my laudanum, and his friends than me. How can I spend the rest of my life with someone who seems to view me with such disdain? Part of me wants to love my husband. Louis, while indifferent to me, seems like he could be a nice man. He has only once really hurt me, back when Albie passed away. (Oh, how I miss her!)

Maybe I could forgive him for that one crime. I do seem to be stuck with him, after all. We are married, and I would love to have a happy marriage like the one you have, like the one I dreamt of as a younger girl. Though I more often find myself wishing I had never married the man at all and could still choose someone I could love.

And yet, my dear Marie, I have a confession to share which I know you will keep close to your heart. You see, I have this friend. Sadly, he is not of noble rank, but he says he loves me. Right now, he is my favorite person. He is someone safe, who pushes my way of thinking to new dimensions. I feel so stuck. I rarely see Louis and don't miss him one whit. I spend so much time with my friend and yet, parting with him, even for a second, leaves me longing to return to him. What of love, dear cousin? What am I to do? I fear this has become an even more important question to me than how to cure my condition. My malady is certain to be constant, but a real romance with my friend shall not be. For that, I am heartbroken, Write back soon!

Em sat on the side of her bed and took another dose of laudanum. She was feeling very down and missed her sister dreadfully today. She would need an extra dose to bolster her spirits. Wanting to feel close to Albie, she grabbed a stack of letters from the top drawer of her writing desk. Just holding them helped her feel closer to her. Most of the letters were from the year they spent apart, though there were also a few notes left for each other and a few plans concocted as children.

As she reached for the last of Albie's correspondence, another letter fell to the floor. It was the letter Louis had left her right after Albie's death. She had skimmed it then, but in her distraught fog, she didn't remember much. It only served to bring back memories of betrayal and loss. She could not bear the weight of such thoughtlessness, even still, so she set it in the bottom of a drawer she rarely used. She would need another dose of laudanum to cope with the anger so she could be properly sad when reading Albie's letter.

After taking her third dose of medicine, she read Albie's letter, tears filling her eyes. Even seeing her sister's scripted hand resulted in so much pain, Em could not manage to fill her lungs with some much needed air. Her breath became heavy and labored. Maybe she could not read it today after all, and Em needed a distraction. Remembering she had arranged a meeting with her mother to discuss the needs of the estate, Em's emotions went from bad to worse. Louis and her stepfather would be present again. The very thought had Em so nervous she could hardly see straight.

Maybe this meeting would be different, though. Maman had acted very differently toward Em since the last party. Hopefully, Em would be able to continue her ruse. With her medicine and remembering the love and strength of her sister, the meeting had to go better.

But she took another dose of medicine just to be sure. It was only her fourth that morning. Or was it the fifth?

Feeling the floor roll upwards underneath her feet, Em tripped on her way to the meeting. She would have to mention to a servant about how unlevel the floor was, she didn't remember that being there before and it must be fixed. Better yet, she could mention it at the meeting. Surely her mother could make the floor stop moving.

Em was the last to arrive at the meeting. She stumbled to her seat with a giggle. Noticing the three sets of eyes on her, Em realized the serious nature of the room and stopped giggling. Eulalie cleared her throat and began by pointing out Em's role as a *stagiaire* and learning the ways of the estate. But what a funny word!

Em found herself giggling again. She had to repeat the word. She did it quietly, almost under her breath, but loud enough to feel the vibrations as she said each individual sound. *Stagiaire.* Sta. Gi. Sta. Gi. Sta. Gi. Aire. She loved the way it felt in her teeth. Em glanced up to find everyone staring at her again. "Oh, forgive me," she giggled, "but what a funny word! Isn't it a funny word, Louis?"

"Ernestine! What is the meaning of this? What has happened to you?" Eulalie demanded.

"I was nervous, so I took some medicine for my nerves. It wasn't helping, so I took a bit more, and then a bit more. Look, Maman, I am in complete control of my body! I'm not saying *'Putain,'* *'bâtard,'* or even *'enculer!'* cried Em, waving her arms and falling backwards into her chair, narrowly missing the large vase and bouquet on a pillar behind her.

All three leaned in, hand outstretched, attempting to catch the vase should it fall, pulling back as Em tottered forward. "Oh my! I do apologize, but apparently, my hand still moves on its own accord!"

Em's hand shot out like a canon, sweeping forward and waving and pointing at the three solemn faces in front of her. Eulalie watched the bouquet fall to the floor. Her eyes narrowed as the vase shattered.

"Ernestine! This is all highly inappropriate. Go to your room at once and sleep this off!"

"It is still early in the evening, Maman, I'm not tired at all! Is there no ball to attend after this meeting? Surely some fancy dinner party would do nicely."

Louis jumped in the conversation, "*Ma poupée*, I can't help but agree with your Maman. Even I do not drink this much when there is a meeting about estate affairs."

"Ha!" shrieked Em. "It would be a rare day to find you sober."

Maman and her stepfather gasped. Louis just smiled and stood up. "Clearly you are not feeling well. Come, let me escort you back to your room."

On his way around the table Eulalie gushed at Louis. "Oh, thank you, Louis darling. What a gentleman you are."

Louis bowed grandly and, once behind Em's chair, placed his hand on her shoulder. Em jerked her shoulder, a sullen, childlike expression on her face.

"My body doesn't seem to care for Louis," she said, half serious, half with levity.

"Ernestine Émilie Prondre. Stand up at once!"

Sighing and flailing her arms, Em awkwardly rose from her chair. Once on her feet she turned in the opposite direction of Louis.

"Heaven! I wish this daughter of mine could appreciate you more."

Louis forcefully spun Em around to face him. Em burst out laughing.

"What a spin, my husband! Are we dancing…which would be odd…as you never dance with me at balls and prefer the company of your friends and other women to me."

"Out!" Louis barked, this time with a hint of anger. Em dragged her feet, making it nearly impossible for Louis to guide her.

"I guess we'll have to do this the hard way," he said, swooping her under her legs and carrying her toward the door, all the while she was throwing her head back and waving her arms. "I feel so free! Can we go on the roof and fly away from here, just the two of us?"

Louis, by this point, had carried her to the hallway. Various servants, including Anne, stood like tin soldiers on either side watching the spectacle.

"Anne! I bet you wish your Henri would be as brazen as my husband here!"

A young man gasped and dropped an armful of wood on his feet. "Ow!" he said, his face reddening.

"Ah, yoooooooou must be the grand suitor. Good looking if I do say so myself, though I shouldn't say, since I'm currently in the arms of another man who, despite being a bit of a drunk, is quite good looking in his own right."

"Pardon my wife!" Louis stammered, carrying her down the rest of the hall and up the stairs toward her bedroom.

Once outside the room as Louis attempted to open the door, Em continued, "I wish you would find us a nice place to settle down where we didn't have to listen to that *poufiasse* I call a mother. Wouldn't it be nice if the two of us could just go away all on our own? I'm sure Théo would make anywhere we live just as beautiful. Oh, you don't mind if he comes too, don't you, dear? I do admire him so, he makes me happy."

"How did I get so lucky to be stuck with you then?" Louis scoffed, as he continued to fight with the doorknob. "Anne!" he screamed. "Open this door at once!"

Out of breath, Anne came scurrying toward them, opening the door quickly for the married pair. "I shall take it from here," Louis said, entering the room.

As Anne backed out with a soft, "Yes, sir," Louis kicked the door shut with his boot.

He carried her all the way to the bed, dropped her on her back, and picked up her laudanum, still open on her side table. "Listen here, *ma poupée.* You will not be having any more of this without someone watching how much you take."

"What about you? Who will be watching how much you take?"

"I refuse to take what you are saying seriously. You are out of your mind—"

"But I *need* it. I can't handle this life we have here. Unless we fly away. Then you can have all of my medicine. As long as I can *fly—*" Em threw her head back, outstretching her arms as if soaking in the sunshine on a warm spring day.

"We will not be flying away; we are to stay here. This is where your livelihood is. This is where the money is."

He stopped abruptly, realizing how he must sound.

"What I am trying to say is that you must stop abusing your medication. You need to steady yourself if either of us is going to… make any success of our lives."

Plopping her hands into her lap, she stared intently at her husband. "You mean, 'if any of us are to see the money.'"

"Say what you want–you won't remember it in an hour."

"You are upset."

"What's upsetting is seeing how hard you have worked to gain your mother's trust and affection, just for you to blow it like this. Do you not care about your future? Do you not care about mine? What about your precious Théo?"

Her eyes quickly narrowed at the mention of the gardener. "Don't try and talk to me about Théo."

"Why shouldn't I? Do you not consider his livelihood? *Mon dieu*, Em!" Louis sighed and glanced back at the door as if ready to escape before facing his wife once more, "Listen, I have to get back to your mother. I'll try to smooth things over, but do try to abstain and fix this mess you've gotten yourself into."

With that, he was gone. Em attempted to respond, but a darkness fell over her eyes and, within moments, she was asleep, dreaming of Oberhofen, Albie, and a wedding kiss with Théo under her favorite tree, stars of silver and gold winking their blessing above.

It was late the following morning when she awoke. Anne had even left a breakfast tray on the table next to her bed, a sure sign that the meal had passed.

With a sigh, Em plopped back onto her pillows, trying to remember why she felt so unsettled about the day before. She pulled the blankets closer to keep out the chill with a gasp and a sigh from her malady. Groggily, she attempted to piece together bits and pieces from the night before. With little success, she decided it was probably long past time she dress and show her face in public. Ringing for Anne, Em leaned over and began to pick at the bread and cheese on the tray at her bedside, hoping it would alleviate the throbbing in her head. Anne arrived all too soon and with one last shiver, Em rolled out of bed.

Once dressed, and as Anne arranged Em's hairstyle for the day, Em silently tried to figure out the best way to ask the servant girl what had happened yesterday. She had overheard enough whispers of her own condition to know there was probably some kind of gossip going around. The few bits and pieces she could remember weren't pleasant, so she knew there must be something significant that had happened.

As it turned out, Em didn't need to initiate anything, Anne was more than ready to start off the conversation, though it was not at all what Em had hoped for.

"Forgive me, *ma dame*, I do not wish to intrude, but is there a secret admirer I should be aware of? I assure you I can be discreet."

Em whirled around to face the maid exclaiming, "Why Anne! Whatever would give you such an idea?"

Bobbing a quick curtsy, Anne rushed to defend herself. "I mean no disrespect, it's just that you and your husband do not seem on the best of terms and well, you received this note from a messenger this morning. He would hand it to no one but your lady's maid. He seemed so passionate that you receive it immediately, and well, I did not know what else it could be."

Snatching the note from the trembling girl's hands, Em noticed the seal was from Paganini. Turning back to the mirror for Anne to continue her hair, Em broke the wax seal and opened the letter. A smaller folded square fell into her lap. She turned her attention first to the larger and open letter:

To the Beauty Who Haunts Shadows and Dreams:

Though my fingers are famed for dancing across strings and precision connected to the devil himself, they tremble at the thought of your eyes upon this very page and hands caressing where mine have inscribed these words.

Enchantress, I have missed your engaging conversation and stories of your "possession" for they were a sweet aria in a time when so many whispers seem to disrupt the opera of life.

As a musician, I know the power of timing. One note too soon or too late and the melody is lost. So, too, it is with fate. What sad fate is mine that I was too late to win your affections! However, I am not too late to share other aspects of my life with you.

I wish for you to remember this phrase: Il tamburo dorme, ma sogna la marcia: *The drum sleeps, but dreams of the march.*

My lovely daemon in lace and satin, not every note sings the first time it is played. The notes require reflection and repetition for them to sing and be truly understood. Ideally before the curtain rises on the world.

Until your eyes meet mine again,
Niccolo

PS, As with all good compositions, sometimes the most vital theme lies not in the first movement, but tucked quietly within the pages of the symphony. I trust your eye is as keen as your ear.

As Anne pulled and tugged at Em's curls, Em's hands relaxed, placing the letter in her lap. It felt far too early to attempt any kind of understanding of the letter. Not to mention the terrible headache she felt. It was certainly no letter from an admirer, even if it would appear so to another. Paganini was certainly well-known as a flirt and a rake, but during their conversation, he had been nothing but genteel. This letter was so brazen, so forward. Yet if he felt the need for this *façade*, then Em would continue it.

Again, Anne was the first to speak, "*Ma dame*, you look troubled. Does the letter contain bad news? I was so certain this would have had you full of smiles and giggles. Is it not from an admirer?"

Em scoffed and rolled her eyes, but offered no response. Anne continued to prattle on about her Henri and what a romantic he was and how Anne could hardly keep from smiling at his attentions, but Em could not hear a word of it. Picking up the letter again, she read it over trying to understand why Paganini would have even sent a letter.

Em was certain he had female attention enough wherever he was. Snapping her head around to look directly at Anne, Em nearly shouted, catching herself at the last moment to demurely ask, "Was there a location to send a response to?"

Anne's eyes widened with realization of her own *faux pas*. "Oh, uh, no *ma dame*. They did not say where to send a letter. I had assumed you would know where to send it. Was it not an admirer of yours?"

With an awkward laugh, Em returned to facing the mirror. "It was indeed from an admirer, but he travels and I do not know where he is headed next. Are you nearly finished? I have matters to attend to regarding the events of yesterday."

Anne simply flushed and quietly finished her work, giving a small curtsy on the way out the door. Noting this, Em could only conclude she had done something to the poor girl, but it was of little importance compared to discovering the secret behind Paganini's letter. As she stood, the smaller square in her lap fell to the floor.

Stooping to pick it up, Em noticed a much more detailed fold. It wasn't very often she saw a diamond folded letter. They generally took more time, but it was more secure. Especially to fold it inside of Paganini's letter. Someone must have wanted to secure the letter, as this was also sealed in bright red wax. Her fingers fumbled as she tried to remember the way to open the letter and she found the following message:

Forgive the intrusion of your privacy ma dame, *but we have cause for urgency in any information you may know. While accompanying a certain composer, we heard whispers of "A new overture rising from the south" and a "maestro soon to reclaim his baton." Whether drunk on metaphor or mischief, we are unsure, but we are certain of his reference to a certain cacophonous Corsican. He still has dreams of domination and we must silence the audience before the performance can begin.*

We must have any information you have or can collect as quickly as possible. Write your list of Corsican comrades as small as possible and roll them into the hem of your gloves. Leave them at the opera house at the Rue de la Loi in Paris in box 17 within three days' time of receiving this letter. It shall be vacant during this time, so you have no need to fear being discovered. You may stay as long as you like to enjoy the show, as long as the gloves are left on one of the seats.

Your Servant,
Pierre

Putting a hand to her head, Em sank back into her chair. After her spectacle last night, she doubted she would be allowed in public. If only her headache would disappear so she could think clearly about a solution. She had managed to collect a small list of names, but none that were previously unknown. They were open supporters of Napoleon. How embarrassing to completely fail her attempts at preserving her way of life, of doing something that would make her mother proud of her.

Just then, there was a knock on the door and Anne re-entered the room with a quick bob. "Forgive me *ma dame,* but this just arrived for you as well from the solicitor's office."

The pair of girls each let out a sigh for their own varying reasons. Em's head rolled to her shoulder as she stood. She dismissed Anne, opening her letter. The first few lines were enough to shock Em into dropping the letter, covering her mouth with both hands. It was as if a bucket of cold water had been poured over her head. Stooping to pick it up, she read the letter again more slowly before running for the door, calling for Anne. There were changes to be made.

Chapter 27
SECRET PLANS

*M*A DAME,

As per your request, I have reviewed the stipulations of your father's will. He left the entirety of the estate, split evenly between you and your sister, Albertine. Should one of you pass away, the entirety will fall on the surviving sister. Your mother is to act as the trustee until the girls either become of age on their eighteenth birthday, or are married. Given these arrangements, you are the sole and complete heir of Guermantes Château *and all the fortune that comes with it.*

We do need you to sign the paperwork stating that you are legally taking over the estate. Thank you for your inquiries into the matter, we look forward to your visit and for the opportunity to serve you.

Your servant,

Maître *Duval*

EM SPENT THE DAY in the study visiting the family solicitor and signing all the necessary documents. Guermantes was fully hers. Why she had never considered asking about the legalities of the estate after Albie passed was beyond her. She couldn't help but wonder who had acted as her voice on this matter and on her behalf. She was unsure if it had been Théo; they had not ever discussed such conflicts, or just how frustrated she was with her mother. She reminded herself to ask the next time she saw him.

It took a few days for Em to gather the courage to face Maman. Not because she was afraid of the scolding. She was used to that by now. Not to mention this time she knew she was in the wrong for showing up to their last meeting like that. No, this time, Em had realized that she was legally the one in charge, and she was going to start acting like it.

For the first time in her life, Em felt a sense of freedom and a small bit of control over the things going on. She was not only going to let her mother know, but everyone. She was tired of being the pushover. She took a deep breath as she walked up to the study door and smiled as she walked in.

"Yes, Ernestine? Wait, before you answer, how are you feeling today? Are you in your right mind? I'll not put up with any of your nonsense today."

"I am indeed. I have some news for you, in fact. I've been visiting with the solicitor. He told me some very interesting things. Turns out, I'm fully in charge of the *château*."

With a slight guffaw, Maman responded, "Once you are of legal age, you will be. But for now, I am the trustee. You still have several months before you take over. I'm still your mother, child."

"Indeed, you are still my mother. However, as a married woman, I am now the one in charge–"

"Meaning—"

"Meaning I will need you to step down. You may offer advice. As my mother, you do have more years of experience running the *château*. But you are no longer the decision-maker, and I am allowed to not take your advice."

"This is absurd. You made more sense on the extra dose of laudanum—"

"In addition, I will be treated with more respect which means no more interruptions."

Eulalie opened her mouth to speak, then shut it quickly. Straightening up, Em continued.

"You may stay in the *château*. I will on occasion ask your thoughts and advice. I'm not a savage who would kick my family out. I just wanted you to know that I am finally in control and no longer prey to your frustration or whims of fancy."

With her head held high, Em turned and walked out without waiting for a reply from Maman. Walking down the hallway to the entrance of the *château*, she felt a great sense of victory knowing that she was able to tell Maman that she was now in charge. She knew there would be a lot more work to be done, but she would also be able to spend her time as she wanted. Suddenly all the work was worth it.

She started taking paperwork outside with her on nice days. Sometimes she would set it aside in favor of one hobby or another. Now that she didn't need an excuse to be outside in the gardens, she began spending more time with Théo. Sometimes it was embroidery, other times she would sketch an idea for some leatherwork. During this time, she would also learn much more about Théo and share the thoughts and ideas that seemed to constantly be in her head.

This time helped so much with her malady that she started to depend less on the laudanum. She still took it daily, or when her outbursts became particularly painful. Théo didn't mind the vocal outbursts. The servants in the house didn't dare talk back to the lady of the house. Maman no longer had any say. Things were going so much better around the *château* and Em finally felt a small measure of peace.

The only thing that really bothered Em these days was trying to figure out how to complete her mission. Em was so lost in her thoughts on this that she didn't even notice Théo had stopped talking. He was suddenly over her shoulder, looking at her current sketch. It contained roses, lilies, and freesia in a small bouquet with sprigs of baby's breath throughout. "Em, this is absolutely beautiful. This bouquet simply speaks volumes."

"I made it with you in mind. I've been thinking about the meanings behind the flowers and this says so much of what I would want to say to you, but don't always have the words. I was thinking of making this into either an embroidery pattern or working it in leather. What do you think?"

"I think either would turn out to be a complete masterpiece. You have so much talent, Em. You seem so much happier these days and I absolutely love it."

"I owe much of it to you. You have been my one constant support, and I know you are always looking out for me. In more ways than one. It was you that spoke with the family solicitor, wasn't it? It couldn't have been anyone else; no one else considers my thoughts and feelings the way you do."

Théo shook his head, clearly surprised by the statement. He started to speak up but was interrupted as Em continued, "Taking over the *château* has done so much for my happiness. I feel so free and actually have something I can control, even if it isn't my own body."

"If that is what brought you so much joy, you certainly cannot lay the credit at my feet. I am a simple man. Those things are beyond me. I didn't even realize there was trouble in the *château*."

"I wonder, though, who spoke to the solicitor? It's been too long since Albie's death to think she made inquiries in my name. She would have done it in her own name anyway. She was of age and taking over the *château*."

"I do not know. Come to think of it, there is so little I know of your life in the house. I only know you and how you are here with me. I do not know of your other friends."

"Ha, that's because there really aren't any other friends, *monsieur*. You are easily my best friend, which is why I spend so much time with you and care for you the way I do. Though now that you mention it, I don't know much about your life outside of the gardens either. We have created our own little world here, haven't we?"

"I believe you are quite right. It's our own little slice of paradise."

Their shy smiles spoke volumes as he returned to tending the flower beds and she returned to her sketch. They each worked in a comfortable silence, grateful for the companionship of the other. When Em felt the sketch complete, she removed the paper from her notebook, and gave it to Théo. "I want you to have this. I think by now I know this drawing well enough to create it from memory. I think I'll do it in leather. Since you like it so much and since it reminds me of you, I think you should have it."

"Will you sign it, *ma dame*?"

"That's my favorite part. Our names are hidden among the flower petals. It has already been signed for you and our names are now forever entwined."

"What a beautiful and clever detail. You never cease to amaze me."

They sat for a moment in silence until he began to slowly lean in closer. Em felt her stomach do a few somersaults but did not back away. She could feel his breath as he moved closer, only to back away sharply at a rustle in the bushes. The two pulled away, both tinted with an additional shade of rose in their cheeks. Em quickly collected her things and ran inside, mumbling her excuses as she ran toward the house. Théo watched her disappear over the rise.

He returned to working on the flower beds as the rustling continued. It moved closer and closer until a man's head popped out of the bushes. "Pardon me, you wouldn't happen to be named Théo, would you?"

"I'm afraid you have the advantage over me, Sir. You are correct, but I do not know your name."

Louis crawled fully out of the bushes and proceeded to brush himself off. "Splendid, I've been looking for you. Please, allow me to introduce myself. My name is Louis. I am Ernestine's husband."

Théo blanched at this announcement, suddenly feeling apprehensive.

"You and my wife are quite close, are you not?

"I am not one to lie, Sir," Théo stammered, reaching out his hand before remembering it was not his place. Pulling back his hand, he retreated a step or two, not sure if he should stay or flee. He knew Louis was a soldier and didn't relish the idea of what he would be capable of. Every bone in his body wanted to run. He placed his hand on the mighty oak next to him, knowing that escaping wasn't an option. He would have to face this, whatever was coming.

"Excellent." Stepping forward with a grin, he wrapped his arm around Théo's shoulders. "You would like to see my wife happy, wouldn't you? She trusts you, an advantage I do not have. Let us walk a bit and discuss a few things…"

Chapter 28
CHANGES

I WISH I COULD WRITE a letter to Albie. I miss her so much. So much has changed and I want to discuss everything with her. She would be so proud to know I have finally taken a little bit of control of my life. I miss her enthusiastic embrace that would knock me over when she hears exciting news like this.

I wish I could ask her advice on running the château. *She would be more kind and more understanding. Maman is NOT happy with this arrangement. Sometimes she gives very helpful advice. Other times, not so much. Once this week, she even scoffed at me and said, "If you are so smart, figure it out for yourself."*

Will we ever have a healthy relationship? Just once, I would love for her to treat me like a daughter she cared about.

A COUPLE OF DAYS later, Em managed to make it to the opera house, accompanied by Louis. *Fidelio* by a German composer named Beethoven was the night's portrayal. She had never really been to the opera, given her malady, and she was still unsure how she would react. Arriving during the Overture, she was immediately sucked in and found her box quickly. There was something soothing about the music. It was very different from the music of Paganini. They were each different, yet each contained their own sense of beauty.

She could hear other members of the *noblesse* outside the door of her box socializing, but Em was bound by the music, even if she could not understand the German tongue the opera was sung in. She knew she should go mingle to discover more names she could add to her list. She had made a small opening in the hem of her glove before leaving and had the list inside, but left it open should there be any additional information she could discover.

During the Prisoner's Chorus, however, Em found herself moved to tears. She just couldn't leave now. She would mingle during intermission, but she had no doubt that she would stay to the end of the opera. She set the gloves on the banister in front of her, just in case things didn't go according to plan.

She prayed things *would* go according to plan.

If only her body would simply behave.

As the prisoners marched back into their prison on stage, Em might as well have been among them. Her shoulders tensed, pulling them up toward her ears. She looked to her husband, who was fully engrossed in his brandy with a glassed-over look in his eye. Em could feel the "shhhhh" on the back of her teeth, itching for an escape, just as the prisoners were longing for freedom.

She slowly released the sound, hoping the hissing would be enough. The itch increased with the release of pressure. She did her best to keep her voice low as she murmured, "*Chienne d'existence!*"

She was finally allowed to take a breath in, but it only served to provide fuel for the continuous hiss. With any luck, she would run out of steam before she had to face others. At least she wouldn't have to do it alone.

Looking over at her husband, Em could only roll her eyes at his state. Alone in the box like this, he seemed rather out of sorts. She was a bit surprised he had chosen to stay with her rather than socializing during the show. Louis was actually able to hold his liquor well and was mostly bored at this point. He would perk up as soon as he had people to impress.

Finally, intermission arrived, and Em stood to attempt socializing outside of her box. She knew all of the rules she needed to follow, but she couldn't help but feel a tinge of nerves as she walked into the ornate hallway. Already, she could feel the nerves bringing her malady forward as her right shoulder began to creep toward her ear.

Em couldn't help getting sucked into a downward spiral each time her malady appeared. How many knew of her illness? Did they simply think she was incredibly rude? She didn't dare broach the subject; it was more than awkward enough as it was. Regardless of their thoughts, she wasn't chased from the room, nor did she run. She was on a mission, and she would gather as many names as she could. She would keep this under control. She hoped.

Sucking in a breath through her teeth, Em spotted the young Marquis Antoine Sévigné. She thought back to when she met him at the first party she was able to attend. How much had changed since dear Albie's birthday! Oh, how she missed her sister! The thought of her made it easier to smile as the Marquis approached. After introducing Louis and meeting the new Marquese Lucille Sévigné, there was a short lull before Louis, of all people, jumped to her rescue, taking over the conversation.

"Well, cheerful show tonight, isn't it? I much prefer the comic opera myself. I saw more than enough tragedy on the battlefield."

The Marquis gave a small chuckle. "And we continue to see it day in and day out."

Tilting her head, Em had to inquire, "How so?"

Grinning as he turned to Louis, Antoine proclaimed, "Ah, the innocence that youth affords! To be so trusting of others and their motives."

Louis simply shrugged, "If I could be as innocent and skip the days of soldiering, I certainly would." Pouring another glass of port, he continued, "Conflict is overrated. No matter who is in charge, there will be people who suffer and others who succeed. It does little to change the day to day comings and goings. As long as I am comfortable, it makes no difference to me who leads. I've seen enough tragedy to know it is fairly commonplace regardless of who is in charge."

Lucille put a delicate gloved hand to her intricate pearl and sapphire necklace. In her soft voice she whispered, "But it does, *monsieur*! Different men have different morals. There should be someone who will care for the people of France above themself. Which is what led to the Revolution. The Bourbon family have shown they are incapable of leading France to prosperity."

Louis smirked at this response. "Yet you stand there in your fine jewels and fashionable gown while under Bourbon rule. Should Napoleon return as the rumors say, you would still retain your status and standing. The lower class would still be lower class. You, my dear, are an idealist, not a realist."

Sensing the rise in emotions, Em jumped in, changing the subject, "Do you think Beethoven will compose many more operas? This one is simply divine, don't you think?"

As the conversation drifted to overtures and ornamentation, Em felt a swelling sense of pride and accomplishment in discovering a new set of names for the list and navigating a tense conversation.

As the lights began to flicker signaling Act II, Em dashed to her box to update her list while Louis stepped away for the facilities. She was even able to close the seam on the glove before he returned.

During Act II, watching Leonore's love and loyalty to her husband, Em's thoughts wandered to her own husband. Louis was very good around people, something Em seemed to struggle with. He had never been unkind or cruel, which is more than she could say for many men if the whispers and rumors were to be believed. She may not be willing to put on a disguise to rescue him from a prison, but she was fortunate in her match with Louis.

After the final curtain, Em stood, conveniently forgetting her gloves as instructed and pulling on a spare set she brought to avoid suspicion. Now she simply wished to go home for another dose of laudanum before anything happened. However, Louis had left shortly after the second act began and Em went in search of him, stopping occasionally to greet an acquaintance here and there. She was even beginning to enjoy herself. Until she ran into Charles. It had grown late and she was looking for her husband. Of course, he would be right next to his old military comrade. She turned around, not wanting to face him. She was confident, not stupid. The man was a brute and an interaction with him would not go well.

Unfortunately, he had seen her before she turned around. He raised his voice as he spoke to his friend, "Louis! Here comes your *branleur*. She must be a bit of a *casse couille* if she is trying to pull you away already, the night is young and the wine flows freely! Send her away, Louis, before her curse rubs off on you. Tell me, is it quite contagious?"

Em spoke so quietly, she could hardly hear it herself. "*Arret.*"

"What was that? Louis, she speaks like a Spanish cow."

Em stood frozen in complete shame, unable to move or speak. Unfortunately, that wasn't entirely true. The muscles in her right shoulder tensed and her head rolled to the side. She rubbed the itchiness in her hands, trying to keep the physical movements at bay. Tears threatened to squeeze out of her eyes. The entire room had their attention focused on her and she didn't know what to do.

Charles tossed his head back in laughter as Louis roughly grabbed his arm and pulled him in the opposite direction. Em bit her lip to keep back both the tears and her curse. She hadn't even done anything to this man or made any kind of outburst for such treatment. Em ran outside and ordered her carriage to take her home. Louis could walk across all of Paris for all she cared. The apartment wasn't that far away. If it wasn't so late, Em would have gone all the way back to the *château* and left him in Paris. As it stood, she would go in the morning. She needed to be back in the gardens with Théo.

Chapter 29
DAYDREAMING

Is it common to be so confused by one's own husband? He can be so unpredictable. There are moments when he can be sweet and understanding and other times when he seems to care only about the drink in his hand. Maman once told me that I must try extra hard to be there for him because he has changed so much since becoming a soldier.

I confess, there are often times when I feel like I have enough of my own struggles to worry about. How could I possibly also attempt to soothe his woes? I don't even know if that is really the issue or just Maman's observations. He doesn't seem to want to talk about it. When I try to ask, he pours another glass. At least Théo is willing to talk with me about things.

EM CONTINUED TO WORK on her projects and spent as much time as she could in the gardens with Théo. He had become her confidante in all things and she trusted him completely. Em shared the events of the opera last night and her frustrations with her husband's friend. When she finished, she felt the need to stick her hands directly in the dirt and work the flowers just as Théo did, feeling relief that the only thing she had held back from Théo was her mission from Pierre. She felt a tiny pang of guilt for keeping it hidden, but she knew even her sweet Théo could not know.

As she worked, all the anger seemed to exit her hands. There was something so satisfying about sticking her hands in the dirt and doing some gardening.

"Théo, sometimes I just wish things were different."

"How so?" he said, pausing only to give a brief look of concern before getting back to work with the lilacs.

"It's just…I'm unhappy. I wish it were not so, but it is true."

"Are you so unhappy about all of it?"

"Well, no. I'm happy I met you."

"Well said!" Théo laughed, causing Em to do the same. *He's so handsome,* she thought to herself. *If only I could grab his hand and tell him that myself,* she mused, before actually saying instead, "I'm happy for what we have. I'm happy with the gardens. I suppose… Well, I mostly wish I hadn't been so cursed with this malady. How different my life would have been! I wouldn't have married so young, I wouldn't be so shy and insecure. I would have full control of my life."

"You don't know that."

Em drew back, surprised at his bluntness.

"How can you say such a thing!"

"I don't say this out of malice, Em," Théo said. "I simply mean that one cannot predict the future or the past. Sometimes things happen just because they happen."

"Do you really believe this?" Em said, her mind churning at a new perspective.

"I do! I used to dream of being a prince, not a lowly gardener."

Théo stood up, putting a string of lilacs on his head like a crown and stiffening his back.

"I'd eat what I wanted, when I wanted, and no one would tell me what to do. 'Round up the horses, I'm off to hunt!'" he cried, brandishing his hoe like a scepter.

"You look quite regal indeed!" Em chuckled.

"I am! I am Prince Théo. In charge of my very own destiny! No more orders from anyone!"

He came back to the earth, taking off his flower crown as he did so.

"And yet, how lucky I am to not be a prince. If I were, I might not have met you, my princess."

Em blushed, saying, "That's so kind of you to say…and it's actually quite comforting to think that maybe there are some things I'm not in control of. But one thought remains."

"That I would look dashing in a top hat and starched cravat?" Théo teased.

"Indeed you would, Prince Théo. But the thought that remains has to do with my mother. If she had been a more loving one, I can't help but believe I'd fundamentally be different. More…myself."

She then threw her arm in the air and shrieked.

"I'm not sure you could be any more you than that!" Théo chuckled. As her arm flailed, he took her hand, calming her instantly. "Different doesn't always mean opposite. You may not feel like you have control over your life now, but you are aware of the choices you make. Doesn't that give a measure of control? Would you just be doing what everyone else is doing if you didn't have this condition?"

"I suppose that could be true. I don't know what I would be like."

"If you could wake up tomorrow morning and have it disappear completely, would you?"

"Oh yes, of course! I would love nothing more."

"Would you miss any part of it?"

"I don't think so. It's been nothing but trouble. Why do you ask?"

Théo took a few moments before answering. "Just like if I had been a prince, I am not sure we would have ever met if you had never had it. If we had, would I have liked you as much if you were the same as any other member of the *noblesse?*"

"As strange as this is to say, I believe you. I really do. And it–you–are so wonderful, Théo."

"As are you. I see how humble and thoughtful and considerate you are, which isn't common among the wealthy. Would you be more like the mother you struggle with so much? Anyway, it's not important. It's not like we can change the past."

"Yes, I suppose you are right." Em felt a small shift in her being. A weight, after so many years, was lifted in an instant.

"Thank you, Théo."

"Always. Any other big issues I can solve for you? War? Estate planning? Leatherwork?" he smirked. "Have you been working on the one like the drawing you gave me?"

"I have actually finished that one. I etched the flowers and vase onto a leather canvas then painted them for contrast. I did the same onto the frame as well. I have an embroidery with me today that I wanted to focus on. Something about the dirt just called to me today. Why do you ask?"

"I would love to see how it turned out. The drawing was simply stunning, but I've never seen your leatherwork in person."

"Well, then let's go see it."

Em stood and dusted off her knees. She held out her hand to Théo.

Théo took it, but his eyes were wide. "You are inviting me to the *château?*"

"It's not just 'the' *château*; it's 'my' *château*. And the answer is yes."

"I don't know. I've never been in the main house. I don't know if I should."

"Someone wise I know once told me that I could do whatever I set my mind to."

Théo followed gingerly behind Em all the way to the house. As the large double doors opened, he hesitated, crossing the threshold into the building and following through the house with his head down. Both were aware the house servants whispered as they walked past. Once they entered the library, where Em often did her leather-work, everything else melted away.

Théo's head swung in wide circles as he took in the expanse of books on every wall, broken up only by windows letting in the afternoon sun. In the center of the room was a great easel which had a thick piece of soft, light leather stretched across it. In the center of the leather was the design that Em had drawn for him, with certain flowers darkened with various shades of stain.

"*Ma dame.* Em. This is breathtaking work. You have created a masterpiece. These flowers are so beautiful; they look so closely like the real flowers themselves. The arrangement is stunning. I thought the sketch was masterful, but this has done so much more than a sketch ever could."

"You think so?"

"I really, really do. Well done."

"Thank you, Théo. And not just for your kind words. Thank you for being there for me when I felt alone, for teaching me, and for being my sanity and escape. You have become so very important to me. So…I just…Thank you."

Before Théo could say anything, they were interrupted by a voice from across the room. "What an intimate picture!" Em and Théo turned to find Eulalie standing in the door frame. "Of the leather, that is."

Em's face instantly drained of color and she instinctively ducked her head. Théo flinched at the accusation hidden in her words and turned a deep shade of red. "Ernestine, what is a gardener doing inside the house? There is a trail of muddy footprints throughout the entire *château*. Now the servants will have to clean again, and supper will be delayed."

Taking a step forward, Em scolded her mother. "Maman, be kind. I invited Théodore here and he is a guest in this house."

Gliding across the room toward Em's work, Eulalie continued, ignoring her daughter's speech. "My goodness, *ma biquette*, did you create this? How lovely! Is this your entry for the competition coming up?"

"Oh, thank you, but no. I don't think I'll enter. I'm just a novice, I'm sure there are experts with much better works than this. Besides, the competition isn't important anymore. I made this because I enjoyed it, it's nothing to make a fuss over."

"What a shame. It would do well, I'm sure. Now, you have some work to do, Ernestine! Get your muddy shoes outside so the servants don't have to clean up after you again. Then you are needed to go over the expenses of the estate."

"*Oui,* Maman. I'll be along shortly."

Em took Théo's hand, guiding him out of the room and leading him back outside into the sunshine, where they were both more at ease. Once outside, Em heaved a sigh of relief. "I apologize; it seems we will be cutting our time together a bit short today. I completely forgot about the finances meeting."

"Oh, not to worry, *ma dame*. You have responsibilities. I understand completely. We shall meet again."

With a short bow, Théo turned and headed down the pathway back to the gardens.

Chapter 30
THE AWARDS CEREMONY

Chére Marie,

How I wish I could come back to Oberhofen some days! I know you love Maman, and I do as well. It's just so hard living under her thumb sometimes. And despite running the château, she is still my mother and I feel almost subservient sometimes. How could she still hold so much power over me?

In other news, we still have no diagnosis for this malady. There are not even any treatments that really seem to work outside of the laudanum. I'm not so certain I want to have to take so much of it for the rest of my life. It's so helpful when things get extreme, but it puts me to sleep if I take enough for it to disappear completely.

It's a nice respite, but not a cure.

A FEW DAYS LATER Em received another letter in the mail. It was less of a letter and more of an announcement about a celebration to be held for the winners of this year's horticulture exhibit which would take place at the Tuileries Palace. Em had completely forgotten about it after deciding not to send a submission.

Her heart dropped when she saw that it would be presided over by none other than the nephew of Napoleon; that scoundrel, Charles.

Since she had no submission, she knew it was an optional event. It was still a chance to socialize and perhaps gather names for Pierre, so she arranged for transport to Paris with Louis and Maman. The three of them would spend the week in Paris and attend the awards ceremony during that time.

The day before departure, Em met Théo in the gardens with her embroidery as he tended to a patch of yellow blooms he called goldenrod. "I'm nervous about going, Théo. That awful Charles who thinks he is in charge of everything will be there. He has shamed me so much in the past; I just do not want to have to face him. Since he is a friend of my Louis, it is almost completely unavoidable."

"He wouldn't be able to say anything to you while presenting you with your award though, right?"

"I won't be receiving an award. I never made a submission. I knew you were so upset, so I never sent a project. I couldn't bear to hurt you like that."

"Well, say you had won…"

"But that is impossible, Théo…"

"*Ma dame.* Em. Say you had, just for imagination's sake."

"Théo, did you do something? Where is the drawing I gave you?"

"Hanging by my bedside. It is the last thing I see at night and the first thing I see in the morning. I refuse to part with it. Besides, how would I even know where to send it?"

Eyeing him suspiciously, Em conceded that was true. "You seem to know something, though. What do you know?"

"It was just a question. We can ignore it if you are uncomfortable. I just wanted to know what the worst case scenario would be. If you imagine the absolute worst, then it can only turn out better than you thought, right?"

"You could have just said that to begin with."

"Forgive me for not having a talent with words the way I do with flowers, *ma dame*."

"I am still suspicious. Something feels off, but we can absolutely move on to how much I am going to miss you and the gardens. How will I survive an entire week without this solace?"

Théo took her hand in both of his. "Paris is not so far away. I'm sure you could return sooner if you wished. You also have the solace of knowing that I will be thinking about you every day, and eagerly awaiting your return."

While Em blushed, she wondered what it would be like if she had married Théo instead of Louis. Maybe marriage wasn't the answer, but love was. She took a step closer to Théo, looking up into his eyes. Her husband may be a gentleman, but Théo was the one who had stolen her heart and had become her confidante.

With a burst of courage and trying not to think about it too much, Em leapt forward, planting her lips on his. Théo brought his hands up to caress her cheeks then gently pulled away with a smile on his face. Em squirmed under his gaze for a moment before daring to look up at him. He was the first to speak, "Forgive me; I have soiled your gown with the dirt from my clothes."

Taking a couple steps back, Em stumbled over her words, muttering something about needing to change. She gave him a small smile as he took a step toward her and said, "No matter how you change your clothing, I see who you really are. You are a passionate, beautiful woman with a kind heart and a brave soul."

Théo's words made Em weak in the knees. She could not contain the smile on her face or the butterflies in her stomach. With her hands on her heart, Em turned her head as she heard the bell ring to dress for dinner. With one small step back toward the *château*, she caught the hem of her dress and fell. Théo moved as if to help her up, but she scrambled to her feet and ran toward the safety of her room.

THE NEXT MORNING, THE party set out for Paris. Em watched the *château* fade behind her, then turned around with a sigh.

"Ernestine, *ma biquette*, did you remember to bring your medicine? We really can't have you embarrassing us in Parisian society the way you do around Guermantes. No talk of politics. Stick to the feminine topics please. Maybe then you won't be referred to in such cruel names as during the last *soirée*."

As Maman continued, Em gazed out the windows for a moment before she interjected, "Maman. I regret to inform you that I have no interest in your advice on this topic. I thank you. I know it is hard to break an old habit of lecturing me, but I do not need it anymore. I know. I do try my best." Her speech was followed by a hiccup, a bark, and a curse favorite, "*merde*."

Louis glanced over with wide eyes. "The bark is new."

"There is always something new. Did I ever tell you about the first time I started saying words at all? It was during my very first party, a birthday party for Albie in fact…"

As Em continued to share the story of that night, Louis's face changed. His eyes grew soft with understanding and a sense of awe. The muscles in his jaw, which always seemed tight, went slack. Em was surprised by Louis's reactions to her story. He asked for another. There were times he would be holding in a chuckle, times where he was concerned. All the while, Maman was unusually silent with wide eyes. It was as if Eulalie had never considered these stories from Em's point of view before, not to mention the ones that Em and Albie had kept secret from her.

Em and Louis continued to talk about the many stories Em had acquired over the years about her malady, some made them laugh at the memory. Before they knew it, they had arrived in Paris and began to settle in for the week. Em was surprised at how much she had enjoyed the ride with the two people that made her the most nervous.

Not only was it enjoyable, but she was so proud of herself for standing up to Maman in the manner that she did. If she could stand up to her mother, what else could be possible on this trip? Suddenly, the week in Paris was full of opportunities. It was more than the rare occurrence that she was found outside of her dear *château*. She had the chance to make a difference, not only in the lives of others, but maybe even make a change in her own life.

The thought made her so nervous she could feel her muscles tighten and she took a couple drops of her laudanum. When the effects of her medicine didn't arrive as they usually did, she took a few more to calm her nerves. This was how she was supposed to feel with such a revelation. She was going to be able to make a difference and things could only get better.

As the awards ceremony drew near, she frequently found herself thinking of Théo back at home and how beautiful the gardens must look. If Théo had entered the competition, she wondered what his submission would have looked like. There was no doubt in her mind that he would have won, but she wondered how well he would have liked all the fuss and celebration. No, he would have absolutely hated every bit of it. She couldn't help but smile as she thought of this. She missed his company. His quiet support, his knowledge, and his kindness.

Just then Louis walked into the room to find Em sitting at her vanity with Anne putting a few flower sprigs among Em's curls. Smiling to himself, he cleared his throat before saying, "*Ma poupée*, it is almost time to leave. Are you ready?"

"*Oui, 'bâtard.* Oh! Forgive me, I must still be a bit nervous. Maybe I should take some medicine before I leave."

Louis narrowed his eyes and paused before asking, "How much have you had thus far?"

It took Em a minute to think back on her day before she replied, "Three or four drops I believe? But all very early this morning. Maybe I'll just take the bottle with me in case of an episode rather than taking some now."

Turning to walk out the door, Louis agreed that would be for the best. With a final glance at her reflection in the mirror, Em let out a deep breath before standing to follow. Grabbing her dark blue lace wrap, she followed her husband down the stairs and out the door.

Once they arrived at the ceremony, Em's eyes grew wide. Maybe it really was all of the *noblesse* invited, but also half of Paris! The gathering was so large, the ceremony was held in the Tuileries Palace. The gardens along the street had been tended with such care that even Théo would have marveled at the beauty. People were everywhere enjoying the beauty that nature and a gentle hand could provide. The entire street was filled with the intoxicating scent of the flowers and the beauty was overwhelming.

The trio made their way into the palace where the awards ceremony was to begin. Louis seemed almost impatient to get there. "I just want a good seat. We must sit near the front; we will have the best view," he claimed. "And are you not anxious to see the displays of the winners? They must be simply spectacular!"

Only Eulalie could find something to complain about. "Really, if it is a celebration of horticulture and flowers, this is nothing compared to the beauty of Versailles! They could have at least held the awards ceremony in one of the theatres in Carre Marigny instead. I just cannot see it the same way knowing that Corsican once lived here."

"Maman, Versailles is not what it used to be. This place is lovely as well, and could certainly hold more of the *noblesse* than one of the garden theatres in town."

They entered the courtyard in front of the palace. A red carpet had been rolled out to lead guests to the entrance, and chairs assembled on either side of it. For a moment, Em wondered if this was how Cinderella had felt when she entered the grand ballroom and met her prince. Or at least something close to it. She giggled to herself at the thought of Prince Théo, flower crown and all.

Why not daydream? she told herself. She had no fairy godmother to create the most beautiful gown anyone had ever seen. No heads turned when she entered. Sometimes fantasy was better than reality. Then again, being here was beyond her wildest dreams.

Em was no Cinderella, but she was in awe of the spectacle before her. She was so overwhelmed by the gallant pageantry she uttered a soft, *"Enculer."* She wasn't even sure if it was the malady acting up or her own shock.

Whatever it was, it didn't stop a smile from creeping over her face at the excitement of it all. It was a small thrill to be allowed at such a gathering. It was by far the biggest she had ever attended. How would she ever meet all of these people to report to Pierre?

There were seats that had been reserved for them near the front, and they waited for the ceremony to begin. Em was far too curious to be sitting already, but as the seats filled, she still managed to gather information for Pierre simply based on the initial question of how they liked the venue. Em took her seat, sitting a little bit taller than she had all week.

As Charles took the stand to begin the ceremony, a hush fell over the crowd. "We would like to welcome you all here tonight to celebrate the beauty that is found all around us, as well as within us. Tonight, we honor the creativity of individuals who have the eye, the soul, and the skill to create works of art.

"Each entry was required to in some way honor the natural beauty of France. Tonight, we celebrate the beauty of the motherland through her children, the people of France. We thank you for coming this evening, dear citizens. Your attendance is valued.

"As each winner is announced, we ask that the grand prize winners come to the front to receive their reward for their hard work and dedication to their craft. All other prizes will be announced and delivered to the home of the winner. There are three winners per category. All three names will be announced in ascending order. To ensure all names are heard, please hold your applause until all three names have been announced."

Em took a breath to calm down. The energy in the room was electrifying.

Charles continued. "As the grand prize winner comes to the stand, their work will be presented to my left, and the artist will attend to my right side. After the awards ceremony, the grand prize winners and their party will be admitted entrance to the *palais* where they will answer questions from the press for tomorrow's newspaper. With this understanding, we will begin."

Em was on the edge of her seat, excited to see the magnificent works of art and their creators. She was in awe of the delicate embroidery on a large quilt that must have taken years to complete. What really gave Em a surprise was hearing about a category all on its own. There was a leather work category with only one entry worthy of a prize.

Em wished for a moment that she had submitted something. She was quite proud of the work she had done for Théo. Then again, she did not want to betray his trust in any way. She was happy with her choice. So, when she heard Charles announce that the winner was "le Comtesse Picot de Dampierre, Ernestine Émilie Prondre de Guermantes," her stomach lurched forward as she fell back against the chair.

Her legs turned to jelly, and she barely managed to stand without the help of her husband. She stared open mouthed at him as Louis encouraged her to step on to the red carpet leading to her medal. She walked slowly, hoping to understand what was happening. She paused when her work was brought out onto the stage. This was the work she had done for Théo. It was intimate and private. How could it have been entered? This was all wrong!

Still, she had to keep moving forward. Each step grew more painful as she realized that she would have to stand next to that nephew of the Corsican ogre. The man who was helping to destroy her way of life. Not to mention the man who had repeatedly embarrassed her and shamed her publicly.

Her shoulder tensed and began to twitch. She rubbed her hands and bit her lip to keep herself under control. She would not make a scene. Not with her mother present. Not in front of half of France. Then again…

Why shouldn't she? Em no longer sought the praise of her mother. Her stories had made Louis laugh. Théo still loved her.

Maybe Louis did, too. Everyone thought she was possessed anyway. Her life at home wouldn't change. There was also the possibility that her social life could improve, because could it really get any worse? After all, letting loose around a bandit brought her a form of salvation. What if…no, she didn't dare.

As she climbed the final steps and bowed to receive her medal, a grimace crossed her face. She was done with feeling like this. She was tired of wondering "what if". Em smiled to put on a nice show, straightened, and turned to face Charles. Then, she barked. He flinched and she smiled wider.

The barks were scattered in between a volley of insults. Em was having too much fun to remember most of them. She knew there were a few "*Sa mère's*" and a "*Fesses de singe enflammées.*" Charles' face turned more and more red with each bark and volley. She wasn't sure how long she continued. It was long after her malady had given way. With a smile, she stopped, feeling fully satisfied for the first time in her life, and returned to her seat.

A few laughs and claps and cheers accompanied her walk back to her open mouthed mother and her smirking husband. Em didn't pay attention to anything else the rest of the ceremony. Charles was red faced for the next five entries, at least, and was very clearly shaken. It only made Em's heart swell with pride all the more.

Em found she was quite looking forward to the meeting with the press. She was certain (and correctly so) that she would be the center of attention. There were several representatives asking questions about the artistic process with the various winners, but a few turned their questions to a more political angle. One reporter even had her outburst as the front page headline. Em was determined to keep every paper that mentioned her outburst. It was easily the most fun she had had in a long time.

On the carriage ride back to her apartment, Louis chuckled the whole way, remembering Charles' face flushed with embarrassment. "It's not often one is able to get the last word in around him. It's nice to see him be the one squirming for a change."

Eulalie was also quite pleased with how the evening turned out. Em couldn't remember a time seeing her mother so cheerful about her daughter. The smiles were contagious all around as Eulalie crowed about her daughter. Leaning back with a smile and happy sigh, Eulalie said, "I always knew you had the potential to do great things, but this was far better than I could have imagined. Not only did you win a prestigious award among artists, but you put that ogre in his place! Oh, my cheeks hurt from smiling so much; what an evening! Well done, *ma biquette*, very well done."

Em's cheeks also felt strained from smiling. She couldn't remember feeling such a sense of pride in herself. As an added bonus, Em couldn't help but think how much she was able to further the cause. This certainly put a blight on the name of the Napoleon family.

Em also made a discovery about herself that night. She had never known just how much she actually enjoyed being the center of attention. It was almost as good as a dose of laudanum. In fact, maybe it was even better.

Chapter 31
Letting Go

Chère Jeanne!

Your performance the other night was magnificent. The name of Napoleon has been the laughingstock of the hotel for days now. Charles (who is now claiming the title of Napoleon III) and by extension, Napoleon himself, are no longer so formidable. This has been shown by a huge growth in our numbers, and we have you to thank for it. I look forward to your report on this event, as well as any information you may have gathered at the event.

Your servant, Pierre

EM COULD HARDLY BELIEVE how much easier her mission had become overnight. She had received both threats and encouragement from her escapade. There wasn't even a scolding from Maman, who thoroughly enjoyed seeing the *cochon* put in his place. Em was given a very high dose of medicine for the duration of the ride home to help her relax and recover. Em didn't even remember leaving the walls of Paris before she had blacked out, only to awaken the next day at home in the *château*.

Once she had regained her senses, before she could run in search of Théo to tell him of what happened, Louis intercepted her. "*Ma poupée*, would you like to take a walk with me through the gardens? I would greatly appreciate your company and feel like we have much to talk about."

Grudgingly, Em agreed, because he was indeed right. They did have much to discuss. He was probably going to mention her mother's desire for a grandchild or how disappointed he was with her shaming his dear friend. He had been, after all, a soldier for Napoleon in the days of his youth. They walked in silence until they arrived at the *parterre*.

Em broke the silence first. "Listen, Louis, I know you are a soldier for Napoleon and that Charles is a friend of yours…"

He broke her apology with a kiss. "You have no need to apologize. I know that I am not your first choice when it comes to lovers, but I must tell you how beautiful you were up there receiving your medal. You simply glowed when you returned to your seat. Had we been in a more private setting, I would have kissed you then.

"It is magnificent to see how much you have changed in our short time together. I quite admire you, you know. You are quite clever. I know you would much rather be with the gardener right now. Go. Just know that I am here if you need anything."

"Louis…I…I had no idea you felt this way."

"To be fair, I hardly know it myself. I'm not exactly an expert on emotions and how to love. As a soldier, I do know respect, and I do know I have plenty of that toward you. I do not ask much. My aim at this stage of life is simply to be comfortable. You have easily provided me with that much. I ask nothing more. Now, if you don't mind, I have some old friends to meet up with at the local tavern. I'll not be back until late. Spend as much time as you like with Théo. I know how you two feel about each other. You'll get no repercussions from me."

Em's mind was full. She had so many thoughts that her mind went momentarily blank and was unable to process what had just happened. She couldn't quite believe that Louis was completely alright with everything that played out at the awards ceremony. "You really aren't upset with me?"

"Heavens, no! Why would I be?"

"I don't know, I embarrassed your friend and basically spat upon the regime that you fought for during your time as a soldier?"

He shrugged. "It was a job and a career. I did it for the money and to have status in the rising regime, it is true, but I have that now, regardless. That is where my loyalties lie, and you have the power to still give me the money and status I seek. So now you have my loyalty. Moreover, as I have mentioned, you have my respect, which Napoleon did not have. He was a brilliant strategist, sure. His personal manners left something to be desired.

"As for Charles, the man is a complete *ducon*. To be honest, I am right there with him on that. Birds of a feather and all. He will recover, I promise. It will be a great laugh for the next several years and I appreciate having one up on him to poke fun at. Now if you will excuse me, I have some drinking buddies to catch up with."

Em could only laugh. Of all the men she could have married, she didn't end up with someone so awful. They would have a good life together with such an easy arrangement. In a rare display of affection, she reached out to embrace this man she was to share her life with. At least, some parts. With a wink, Louis turned and left.

Em turned and ran out to the oak tree where she and Théo so often met. She saw him long before he saw her. She watched him smile as he tended to the roses with gentle ease. Wiping sweat from his forehead, she saw him leave a streak of dirt across his forehead.

His entire face seemed to be covered in such marks. She loved how passionate he was about his work.

She started to run toward him. As she closed the distance, he saw her coming and stood, removing his work gloves as he started to walk toward her. She slowed to a walk as they grew nearer. When they were right in front of each other, she embraced him. He kept his arms up, trying not to soil her gown. When she seemed to snuggle in with no sign of release, he embraced her.

"Oh, Théo, I have so much to tell you! I missed you so and you will never believe what happened! First of all, I wanted to say I'm sorry. I didn't know I had been entered into the competition. I had no idea until my name was announced as the grand prize winner. Somehow the piece that I made for you was sent in. I didn't want to betray you like that."

"Shhh, darling, I know. It's alright."

Em pulled away with a quizzical look on her face. "You knew? But how? You told me how much you hated the very idea of such competitions."

"And you told me how much this one meant to you. I had no idea how to enter it, but I may have suggested it. You have someone who cares for you a great deal."

"What? Who entered my work?"

"Your husband, of course."

"Louis did this? He never said a word!" Em's eyes grew wide as saucers.

"I do believe congratulations are in order. The grand prize?! That's wonderful!"

He caressed her cheek, softly, tenderly.

"Yes, that was good and all, but you will never believe what happened!"

As Em related the story of that evening, giving extra detail to the beautiful gardens and the talented works of art that celebrated the beauty of nature, they walked back to the oak tree and sat in the shade of its branches. Em could never remember being any happier, reliving that night in Paris while sitting in the gardens she loved so much.

"Turns out, I quite enjoy being the center of attention like that!"

She laughed with abandon, joined by bird's chirps in the tree-tops and Théo's laughter, echoing hers in perfect unison.

"Of course you do!" Théo grinned. "You were always meant to shine brightly. I've always seen your light; it's why I love you so."

Em flushed with joy at his response. She leaned into him and snuggled in; propriety be damned. "Théo, I've just never felt so much more like myself. I just wish you had been there. Then again, you would have been miserable, wouldn't you? You care for flowers the way I care for people. We are from completely different worlds, you and I."

"That may be true, but that doesn't change the way I feel about you. Your success makes me happy. Had I known, had I been invited and permitted, I would have absolutely been by your side at that moment. The way you glow when you are happy would have made it all worth it."

They sat together in contented silence, snuggled together under the shade of the oak tree, Em's head on his chest, listening to his heartbeat, while the gentle touch of his hand slid up and down her arm. After a while, Em began to twitch, and she sat up so Théo wouldn't have to share the discomfort. As she turned to apologize, he leaned in and kissed her gently. The twitching died down.

Spending that afternoon with Théo, Em realized she had never been happier, or more comfortable with her body, than in that moment. Malady or no, she was happy. She was loved. She may not have had control of every part of her life, but she did have a lot more control than she realized. Even better, she realized she didn't need to be in complete control. Sometimes things just turn out better than she could have ever dreamed.

That afternoon under the tree, after Théo had tucked her in with a blanket before running off to finish some much needed weeding, she had a dream. She was once again a little girl, throwing an ink pen. She was then a bit older, at Albie's birthday party, the first party she was allowed to attend. Then, she was a young woman with dear Marie at Oberhofen. At the end of the dream, she was exactly who she was at this moment, nestled under a blanket with her dear Théo.

And then she woke up. It was not a dream. There was Théo, the sun setting, leaning over her with those big blue eyes and tousled curls.

"You were out for hours, my love," he said. "I brought you some food from the servant's kitchen. That is, if it's…if I'm…I want it all to be good enough for you!"

Right then and there she kissed him.

Smiling up at this man who had stolen her heart, she replied, "Nothing was good enough until this moment. And now, I shall dine on this love for the rest of my life."

Suddenly, there was a whole future ahead of her. She might even be willing to consider children at this rate. Maybe this curse was only a curse because no one knew what to do with it. Em no longer felt the need to hide. She knew that she could be seen as possessed, or cursed, or even incredibly rude and brash. Attention was attention, and she loved it. She could use this, and the thought thrilled her.

Fin

Epilogue

July 1884

EM WALKED TO THE cemetery, her steps slow and unsteady. Leaning more on her cane, she walked among the headstones to the hallowed ground where her family lay. She passed stones bearing the names of family members she didn't recognize, gone long before her time. Gabriel. Adélaïde. Emmanuel. Louise Marie. So many lives come and gone. So many stories long forgotten. Would she be the same? Did she leave any kind of lasting impact?

Finally, she arrived where her mother and stepfather lay resting. Adjacent was the stone bearing her father's name. How she longed to know how he would have treated her, even still. Would he have been loving and understanding? Her life would have been so different had he lived to raise her as a father should.

Her steps slowed as she passed the stone bearing the name of her husband. She had been widowed longer than she had been married. He had treated her kindly, even if their marriage was more one of convenience and "medical necessity" than anything else. At least he was decent as best he knew how. It was more than could be said for the indifference between her mother and stepfather. Em had cared for Louis and thus saw how fortunate she really was.

Thinking of Louis always made her think of Théo. The simple gardener had completely changed her life. He continued to work in the gardens right up until he had passed, just a few years prior. He was not buried here with her family, that would have been quite unseemly. Instead, he was buried with his family in a local cemetery. Oh, how she missed that sweet man. They had remained friends to the very end despite drifting apart as lovers.

Slowly, her steps led her further. She finally came to a stop in front of the stone bearing the name of her sister. It had been sixty years, yet Em still missed her every day. She missed her mischievous ways, her giggles, the close bond they shared, and the trust between them. She had learned so much from her Albertine in the short years they spent together. She owed so much of what she had become to her sister's confidence and joviality.

Oh, to go back in time. To enjoy once more an escape to their tree. To laugh with Albie rather than having to work hard to trust her sister's words. There are so many things Em would do differently now that she had grown into herself.

Then again, that was a part of the process, wasn't it? To grow and learn and change. As many years as Em had been alive, she knew how much things could change over time. One day, there might even be a name for her...her...condition.

Yes, condition was the word. It was no longer a curse. It was no longer a malady. It was simply part of her existence. It obviously held no negative effects on her health. Otherwise, she would not have outlived so many. Eighty years was a long time. She knew she had at least that many but was unsure of the exact number. It didn't matter at that point, anyway.

Em eased herself down to sit on the cold stone bench at the edge of the cemetery. Once seated, Em pulled out her reticule. It was no longer a *faux pas* to carry them–fashion had changed so much–but she still felt a sense of pride in the *risqué* behavior. From its contents, Em withdrew two letters, delicate and yellow with age. The first, of course, was from her dear Albertine.

"My dearest Em,

Oh, how I love you. I know that you know this. But sometimes I fear you do not understand why. You are my partner in so many schemes, so willing to jump in and play and explore. You love fully and deeply. You come up with such clever ideas. Remember that time that you suggested we sneak into Maman's closet and try on all her gowns? I never felt more beautiful. You kept watch while I changed and when Maman came to dress for dinner, you distracted her while I escaped. How daring you were! I was so afraid!

You are unique, even if it were not for whatever interruptions plague you. Those bring an added layer of excitement, to be sure. But with or without them, you are my entire world. I hate to leave you, but I am afraid the time is coming soon. I'm sure it's Maman keeping you away. I need you to know that I do not blame you. I am not upset with you or hurt in any way.

I know you seek validation from many around you, but you are wonderful just the way you are. I wish Maman could see it. Even more, I wish you would show your true self to others. You are a joy and a blessing Ernestine. Just for being you, the world is a better place. You deserve love. Your wit and talent aside, you are simply good and kind and should receive such in return.

If there was any gift that I could give you before I die, it would be for you to love yourself the way that I love you. It is not selfish to love yourself. As your older sister and heir to this estate, I give you permission to step away from Maman, take breaks from those who do not give you the love and attention that you deserve, and for you to stop allowing things you cannot control to vex you.

I know there are many things that you feel are beyond your control. But you are so, so much more capable than you realize. If I do not make it through this illness, you will become the heir to the estate and family fortune. You are wise, trust yourself. You are kind and just. The family is in good hands.

I will always be with you, even if you cannot see me. I will always be your support. One day when the estate falls into the hands of your children and we can be together again, I will embrace you so tightly, you may wish to return! What fun we shall have when we are together again!

All my love,
Your Albie

Tears flowed freely onto the letter, mixing with the yellowed bloodstains of Albie's coughs in her last days. Oh, to be with her again! Em's memory flooded with each struggle this letter had seen her through. There was no doubt that this letter had been the cause of so many choices she had made. She wanted to make Albie proud, even still.

With a heavy sigh, Em pulled out the second letter.

"Ernestine,

I know we have not started off on the best foot. I honestly believed Albertine would heal, just as she always had. I'm sorry for my part in keeping you apart during her final moments. I was simply trying to appease your mother.

The more I get to know you, the more I realize your mother is wrong about you. I have so much respect for who you are and what you have to deal with from day to day. While I have failed you in the past, know that I stand with you. You are incredibly capable of running the château. *It belongs to you, and I leave it in your hands. I will not try to take it from you or influence your decisions. I'll be here.*

Chaleureusement,
Ton Mari *Louis*

This letter had surprised her the most. He was a good man, her Louis. Over the years, they had reached an amicable friendship and had their own understanding, but she doubted he ever knew just how much his support had meant. Every once in a while, Em wished she had given him children, but she never did. What was done, was done.

Looking back, she could never have become who she was today without these letters. As memories flooded her thoughts of her struggles and successes, Em simply felt grateful. Her life had been a good one.

Standing, Em gave one last look at the stones that shielded and protected her loved ones. Muttering under her breath, *"Putain de cochon,"* Em smiled. Her valet approached her and offered his hand.

"Are you ready, *ma dame*? Your carriage to Paris awaits."

"Oui, fesses de singe enflammées, I am ready for anything."

A few days later, Ernestine Émilie Prondre de Guermantes, Countess Picot de Dampierre passed away in her Paris apartment. Her family announced her death lamenting…"their sister, aunt, great aunt, great-great aunt and first cousin died in Paris, July 8, 1884, in her 84th year, equipped with the Sacraments of the Church. Pray for her."

The following year, a name for her condition arrived. Georges Gilles de la Tourette published a paper on a nervous disorder with symptoms such as sudden uncontrollable movements and shouting. He had studied Dr. Itard's notes on "Mme. Dampierre," a noblewoman who exhibited such symptoms. Finding others who exhibited similar symptoms, thus creating an official diagnosis known as "Tourette syndrome."

French Glossary (General)

Adieu: farewell

Arret: stop

Bien sûr: of course

Bon: good

Bourgeois: business owners/wealthy people

Chaleureusement: Warmly

Château: large country house or castle

Chére: dear

Cochon: pig

Comte/Comtesse: Count/Countess

Du matin: in the morning

En retard: late

Façade: false front

Faux pas: an embarrassing or tactless act or remark

Familie de Bourbon: The Bourbon family

Fleur-de-lis: lily flower, a common symbol for French nobility

Fou: mad (as in crazy, not upset)

Le médecin: doctor

Les Enfants Méchants: Naughty Children

Ma belle: my beautiful

Ma Biquette: my darling

Ma dame: my lady

Ma poupée: my doll

Maccherones: the unflavored cookie part of what we know today as macarons

Mademoiselle: young unmarried miss

Mais non: But no (exasperated no)

Maître: master
Mon Bijou: My jewel
Mon chou: my darling
Mon coeur: My heart
Mon Dieu: My Lord
Monsieur: Sir
Naïveté: Naive, simplistic
Noblesse: Noble-born class
Orgueil et Préjugés: Pride & Prejudice
Oui, Maman: Yes mother
Palais: palace
Pardonne-moi: forgive me
Parlez-vous français: Do you speak French
Parterre: Garden Maze
Risqué: risky/scandalous
Singe: monkey
Soirée: evening party
Spécialité: specialty
Stagiaire: intern
Trés magnifique: very magnificent or very beautiful
Ton Mari: Your husband
Voyage sécurisé: Safe travels

FRENCH GLOSSARY (COPRALIA)

*This glossary is specifically for the coprolalia outbursts (swearing/ inappropriate words) Em or other characters use throughout the book

-Bâtard: Bastard

-Branleur: Wanker

-Casse couiller: ball crusher

-Chienne d'existence: bitch of a life

-Ducon: Asshole, dickhead

-Enculer: fuck, cocksucker, piece of shit

-Fesses de singe enflammées: inflamed monkey buttocks

-Merde: Shit

-Poufiasse: Slut

-Putain: Used as shit, fuck, literally translates to prostitute

-Putain de cochon: fucking pig

-Pute: Bitch, whore

-Sa Mère: Motherfucker

-Salaud: Bastard

-Une rate: literally translates to a "miss" as in hit or miss, missed the mark. This equates to calling someone a loser.

Author's Note

THANK YOU SO MUCH for reading *Madamn*! I hope you enjoyed it! And thank you for wanting more information and reading a bit of the behind the scenes I want to share. There are several things I want to address here.

First and foremost, I put a LOT of research into this book. If you see any inaccuracies, I'm sure there are bound to be a few, but some of them just might surprise you.

For example, I know during this time period in England (which we know a lot about thanks to the likes of Jane Austen and many other writers during this time period), women were not allowed to inherit money or property. However, in France, things were a bit different. Ok, a LOT different, thanks to the French Revolution. Women were able to inherit, as Em did.

I know there are inaccuracies in the timeline. Em lived to be eighty four years old and she lived through SEVEN forms of government, so I wanted to reflect that, even if Napoleon's Hundred Days would have begun and ended before Em even went to Switzerland (called the Swiss Confederation at the time). Most of the book takes place during the reign of the Bourbon family.

Also, Em's husband, Louis, really did serve under Napoleon, though he showed no fervor in the political arena after Napoleon's exile. I had a hard time deciding which Bonaparte would have been connected to these instances. Lucien or Louis Bonaparte would have been closer in age to Em's husband, but I didn't want two characters named Louis. It was Charles who became Napoleon III and who Em actually did receive an award from. She also did have a tic attack in his face during that instance. Which is why I opted for Charles, even though he was younger than Em.

The last note that needs to be made is about the use of laudanum. I only lightly touched on the concept of addiction. I did want to show that it is a very real possibility and I wanted Em to have some kind of reprieve like modern medicines are able to provide. I feel like it helped make the storyline a bit richer.

However, that being said, both alcohol and opiates (which are the primary ingredients in laudanum) commonly aggravate tics, more than help. Opiates are a sedative (as is alcohol) and so there are some people that might relax enough to placate the tics temporarily; or if the dose was strong enough to put them to sleep would receive a reprieve. However, coming down off of opiates a common side effect is twitching and tremors. These can be short or long term increases.

As Em finds greater joy and purpose throughout the book, she gradually comes down off her need for her medicine. Since it was a gradual reduction, I did not show many of the terrible side effects that come from withdrawals and addiction. There are very real and severe withdrawal symptoms, but the story did not continue long enough for a full resolution as it would if that were the main theme.

Other than that, I've tried to keep things as historically accurate as possible. My first priority was to Em and making sure her story was told and incorporating all the big events of her eighty-four years of life. Then my priority was to you, the reader, to make sure it was engaging and that pacing wasn't too slow while covering all of that history. After that came the accuracy of history. So forgive me if it isn't perfect, but please know I did a TON of research and included as many fun tidbits as I could.

Moonlit Manor *Madamn* Regency Wrap
Amanda Woodbury - The Mindful Hook Designs
For the Book *Madamn* By J.S. Baehr

MATERIALS

- Yarn Option 1: Lace Weight 0 - KnitPicks - Gloss Lace (70% Merino Wool, 30% Silk, 440yds/50g) approx 3 hanks(skeins)
- Yarn Option 2: Weight 3 (DK) natural fiber blends or Acrylic (LB mandala) approx 1 large cake
- Hook: 4.0 mm (G)
- Needle, scissors, stitch markers (2), tassel maker

SKILL LEVEL:

- Lace weight: Intermediate - Projects may include involved stitch patterns, color work, and/or shaping.
- DK weight: Easy - Projects may include simple stitch patterns, color work, and/or shaping.

SIZES

- Length: Should be wrist to wrist armspan (my length in inches __")
- Width: Approx. 18 inches for average wrap size, you can make your own adjustments. (my width in inches __")

GAUGE

- Not blocked, stitches counted individually and not v-stitches.
- Lace Weight: 24 stitches = 4" X 14 rows = 4"
- DK (3) Weight: 21 stitches = 4" X 9 rows = 4"

PATTERN KEY

- Ch: Chain, Sc: Single crochet, Dc: Double crochet, Sl st: Slip stitch

SPECIAL STITCHES & TECHNIQUES

- v-stitch: (Dc, Ch 1, Dc) in the same stitch
- Shell: 5 Dc in the same stitch

NOTES

- This is a "choose your adventure" style pattern. You've been given basic stitch patterns and what to measure, but you get to decide the actual size, and stitch counts! At the end of each row, there is a space for you to note your stitch-counts so you can keep track!
- Foundation chain is a multiple of 5 for desired length (wrist to wrist arm span).
- Pattern worked in Rows.
- Lace Edging is worked in Rounds.

INSTRUCTIONS:

Foundation Row:
Multiple of 5 chains. My Chain count ____

Row 1: skip 4 Chs (counts as 1 Dc + 1 Ch), [1 Dc, Ch 2, skip 2 Ch] until last 2 sts, Ch 1, skip 1, 1 Dc in last st, turn (my stitch count ____)

Row 2: Ch 4 (counts as Dc + Ch 1) v-st in next Dc across row, Ch 1, Dc in last st (turning Ch), turn (my stitch count ____)

Row 3: Ch 4, v-st into ch-1 space of each v-st across, Ch 1, Dc in last st, turn (my stitch count ____)

Rows 4 to desired width: Repeat Row 3 until desired width is reached, ending on an even number of rows. (my row count ____).

Last Row: Ch 4, 1 Dc in ch-1 space of v-st, [Ch 2, 1 Dc into ch-1 space of v- st] across row, Ch 1, skip 1 st, 1 Dc in last st, turn (my stitch count____)

Fasten off and sew ends OR do not fasten off and continue to Lace Border

Lace Border (optional):

This adds a Regency-like delicacy to the edges.

Round 1: Ch 3(counts as 1st Dc), 2 Dc in 1st ch-2 space, *[Sc in next ch-2 space, Shell in next ch-2 space, Sc in next ch-2 space, across row, at corner (3 Dc, Ch 3, 3 Dc in turning ch space), rotate to work across end rows, Sc in next Ch space, Shell in next Ch space, across to corner]*, repeat * to * one more time, in same space as 1st corner, 3 Dc, Ch 3, Sl st into top of 1st Dc,

Round 2: Ch 1(not a st), Sc in the first Dc, Sc in next Dc, Picot, Sc in next Dc, *[Sc in next 3 Dc, Picot, Sc in next 2 Dc] across each Shell, corner, (Sc in next 2 Dc, Picot, Sc in next Dc, Sl st into next 3 chs (not the gap) ,Sc in next 2 Dc, Picot, Sc in next Dc,) [Sc in next 3 dc, Picot, Sc in next 2 Dc] across each Shell*, repeat * to * one more time, last corner Sc in next 2 Dc, Picot, Sc in next Dc, Sl st into next 3 Ch (not the gap), Sl st into 1st Sc, fasten off.

Blocking:

Since this wrap has a lacy stitch pattern, blocking it will help it lay flat and open up the lace. Lightly wet (or steam) the wrap and pin it to desired dimensions, then allow it to dry completely.

Tassels (Optional):

Make 4, tie into each corner
Using a tassel maker or a 5"x5" cardboard piece, wrap the yarn around about 45 times, cut one end of the bundle and lay flat over a 6" piece of yarn, tie that around the center of the bundle, fold one end of bundle over the tie (make sure straps are on the outside to tie onto the wrap) and using a second 6" piece of yarn, tie that around entire bundle about an inch from center tie. This should create the head of the tassel. Blend in the strands into the tassel. Tie each tassel to the corners of the wrap.

Join our Facebook Community, Group: The Mindful Hook for Crochet conversations, Tips, CALs, support and more!

J.S. Baehr

CONTACT - Email amandawoodbury@themindfulhook.com

Facebook - www.facebook.com/themindfulhookdesigns
Instagram - www.instagram.com/themindfulhook.designs/

Acknowledgements

I can't begin to tell you how many people have made this book possible. This has been five years in the making and as a result, there have been a lot of people involved. First and foremost, credit should absolutely go to Ernestine Émilie Prondre de Guermantes. Not only for the life she lived, but because there have been so many moments where it simply felt like she was whispering the story to me.

Next, I absolutely have to thank my endlessly patient husband who was supportive not only as I went from full time employment to part time employment so we could sustain our household as I constantly worked on this project. Not only that, he was invaluable when I couldn't find the right word or needed to flush out characters or talk through scenes.

Then Andrea Frazer Paventi must be mentioned. She not only came up with the clever title and allowed me to use it, but led numerous writing circles with wonderful women who gave awesome feedback; as well as did a strong "punch up" to give the novel much more color and life.

No writer can publish a decent novel without exceptional editing, which was done by Maddison Race and Peggy Arsenault. I asked a lot of them and they were able to do so much for this book.

All of the artwork was done by Jared Salmond. The style I had in mind was new and a stretch from his normal style, so I'm grateful for him to step up and help complete my vision with his talents and patience through several changes and revisions.

I also want to thank my amazing beta readers who were willing to plow through it on such short notice and caught a lot of little things that somehow had managed to slip through. There always seems to be something, so I'm grateful for their sharp eyes and contributions as well.

I also need to thank the wonderful people on Kickstarter who supported and funded my campaign. Specifically: Felicia Black, Camy Tang, DL Fowler, Katie, Beka, and Cara Wade. Running a Kickstarter campaign was incredibly helpful in being able to provide additional artwork scenes and improving the overall quality of the book, so I can't share enough how grateful I am for their support!

About the Author

Masquerading by day as a cashier and cleaning lady, J.S. Baehr spends her free time stepping back in time with her fancy quill and fountain pens, oil lamp, and historical novels.

Growing up on a steady diet of *Little House on the Prairie, American Girl,* and *Dear America* books, J. S. Baehr was grounded from reading in middle school for living so much in the past (Who needs sleep?).

To understand reality better, she studied sociology in college. There, she met the love of her life, but didn't convince him to marry her for another decade. Instead, she developed an "alter ego," her Tourette syndrome, that she calls Paula.

Letting Paula lead (as a pen name), she published four nonfiction works. J. S. Baehr finally decided to let her love of history take the lead and now writes biographical fiction.